Dangling
By a Thread

Center Point
Large Print

Also by Lea Wait and available from
Center Point Large Print:

The Mainely Needlepoint Mysteries
Twisted Threads
Threads of Evidence
Thread and Gone

**This Large Print Book carries the
Seal of Approval of N.A.V.H.**

Dangling By a Thread

A Mainely Needlepoint Mystery

Lea Wait

CENTER POINT LARGE PRINT
THORNDIKE, MAINE

This Center Point Large Print edition
is published in the year 2017 by arrangement with
Kensington Publishing Corp.

The text of this Large Print edition is unabridged.
In other aspects, this book may vary
from the original edition.
Printed in the United States of America
on permanent paper.
Set in 16-point Times New Roman type.

ISBN: 978-1-68324-620-6

Library of Congress Cataloging-in-Publication Data

Names: Wait, Lea, author.
Title: Dangling by a thread : a mainely needlepoint mystery / Lea Wait.
Description: Center Point large print edition. | Thorndike, Maine :
    Center Point Large Print, 2017. | Series: Mainely needlepoint
    mystery series
Identifiers: LCCN 2017044902 | ISBN 9781683246206
    (hardcover : alk. paper)
Subjects: LCSH: Murder—Fiction. | Large type books. |
    GSAFD: Mystery fiction.
Classification: LCC PS3623.A42 D36 2017 | DDC 813/.6—dc23
LC record available at https://lccn.loc.gov/2017044902

Dangling
By a Thread

Chapter 1

"Time has wings and swiftly flies
Youth and Beauty Fade away
Virtue is the only Prize
Whose Joys never will decay."
—Sampler stitched by Chloe Trask in
Middlesex County, Massachusetts, about
1800. Originally dated with four digits,
in later years someone (probably Chloe
herself) removed the stitching on the
final two numbers to conceal her age.

The August fog felt damp and soft on my face as I sat on a bench on Wharf Street, sipped my coffee, and watched anchored boats in Haven Harbor appear and disappear. The early morning fog hid the Three Sisters, the islands that protect our small Maine harbor from the ocean's strength.

In the distance I heard the motor of a lobster boat making early morning stops to check traps.

A figure in a small gray skiff, almost seeming part of the fog, was rowing smoothly toward shore, out of the mists. Whoever he was, he knew the waters. I watched as he tied his skiff to the town pier and pulled himself onto the dock. That's when I noticed he was limping.

I knew Haven Harbor's boats and their owners.

I didn't remember ever seeing that skiff or its occupant.

I'd been back in Haven Harbor over three months now and was beginning to feel comfortable again in the house that had seen the joys and pains of my growing up. I'd agreed to stay six months: settle in, manage Mainely Needlepoint, the business Gram had started, and come to terms with the past.

The house seemed empty since Gram had married and moved out. I didn't blame the house. I'd been lonely before, in other times, other places.

I'd battle through it. I was already thinking six months in Haven Harbor wasn't long enough. I might stay longer.

Still, some mornings, like today, I was restless, and nothing but the sights and sounds of the sea would soothe me. Those ten years I'd spent in Arizona, far from the consistent tides I'd depended on to bring order to my life, had left a hole only closeness to the ocean could fill.

Too often in the past weeks, like today, I'd woken early to the motors of lobster boats leaving the docks and the screeching of the gulls following them.

I'd filled a travel mug with coffee and headed for the wharves, where I'd be close to the sea and smell the salt air and dried rockweed and mudflats. Where I could forget Mama and my past. Forget what brought me back to Haven Harbor.

The man on the dock was tall and thin, his skin almost the color of his straggly gray beard. He might have been forty, or sixty. His faded flannel shirt hung on him as though intended for someone heavier, someone stronger. His jeans were belted with rope.

He picked up two canvas bags from inside the skiff and walked up the ramp, limping, but not hesitating, toward where I was sitting. He didn't look at me or at Arvin Fraser, who'd finished hoisting his bait barrels on board the *Little Lady* and was preparing to leave for the day's work with Rob Trask, his sternman.

Whoever the strange man was, he was focused on whatever had brought him to Haven Harbor. He didn't look around, greet anyone, or seem to notice one of his worn sneakers was untied.

Curious, I watched him head south on Wharf Street until he was lost in the fog.

I walked down the ramp to where Arvin and Rob were about to cast off.

"Morning, Angie," said Rob. "You're out early again."

"Who was that man?" I asked. I pointed to his skiff, gray as the morning. "The man who rowed in."

Arvin grinned. "Guess you ain't never seen him before. He's a character, but he don't bother no one. Lives out on one of the islands beyond the Three Sisters."

"I didn't know anyone lived out there," I said. "Those islands are just outcroppings of ledges with a few trees on them. No houses that I remember. No water, no electricity. Just birds."

"Right," said Rob. "He don't seem to mind, though. Been out there a couple of years now."

"What's his name?" I asked.

Arvin and Rob looked at each other. Arvin shrugged. "Don't rightly know. Never asked. Folks in town call him The Solitary."

Chapter 2

"Let spotlefs innocence and truth
My ev'ry action guide
And guard my inexperienc'd youth
My vanity and pride."

> —From sampler stitched by Dorothy
> Lancaster (1781–1806) near Portland,
> Maine, in 1785. Dorothy used the old
> *f* form for one *s* in her verse, perhaps
> copying it from an old book. By the
> beginning of the nineteenth century most
> printers had dropped this letter form.

I shivered in the damp fog. The Solitary.

Solitary. Alone. That's the way I felt this morning. It wasn't a good feeling.

Who was he? How would it feel to live by yourself on an island? Islands beyond the Three Sisters were three or four miles offshore. Far enough out so waters could be dangerously rough, especially in winter. Too far out, in choppy deep waters, for a comfortable or safe row to the mainland.

I looked down Wharf Street after the strange man. Where was he heading on this early morning?

For no reason other than curiosity, I followed him.

My years working for a private investigator in Arizona automatically kicked in. I stayed far enough behind him so the fog enveloped both of us.

He walked easily, his slight limp almost unnoticeable. Too able for any crippling disease I could think of. Maybe he'd slipped getting into his skiff and badly bruised his leg, or cut his foot on barnacle-covered rocks.

I invented stories as I walked, following the uneven sound of his sneakers hitting the pavement, knowing I should turn around and mind my own business.

The Solitary didn't notice he had company. At the end of Wharf Street he turned inland, up the hill toward the west side of town.

I followed, staying close to the storefronts. The fog here, away from the harbor, wasn't as dense. If he turned around, he'd see me: a stranger who, like him, was wandering the streets of Haven Harbor just after dawn.

I could smell fresh bread baking at the Thibodeaus' patisserie two blocks away. I should end my foolishness, leave the mysterious man alone, buy a scone or croissant, and head for home.

But as he walked farther, my curiosity grew.

He turned right, past the hardware store. I paused, letting him get far enough away so he wouldn't see me. The sun was rapidly burning the fog off. A truck turned into the parking lot in back of the hardware store. Gulls cried over the harbor.

During most August days these streets were busy. This early in the morning they were eerily still. I stood, listening. A door slammed. A car engine started. A crow in the distance called and was answered by a crow closer by.

I walked to the corner.

The Solitary was sitting on the steps of the post office. I glanced at my phone to check the time. Pax Henry, the postmaster, wouldn't open for another hour.

The man stretched his legs, rubbing the one that bothered him and noticing his errant shoelace. He tied it, as the door of the post office opened. Pax stood in the doorway, his bushy red hair and beard shining in the sun. He gestured, and the man waiting outside followed him in.

I checked my phone again. No, the post office shouldn't open for another hour.

But this morning it had.

I'd spent too much time working for a private investigator. I had too many dark fantasies.

There were no secrets here. The mysterious man was in town to pick up his mail.

What was strange about that? What was strange was my stalking him.

I changed direction and headed for the

patisserie. Henri and Nicole always unlocked their door as soon as their first baked goods of the day were out of the oven. It was time for breakfast.

Chapter 3

"O resignation heavenly power
Our warmest thoughts engage
Thou art the safest guide of youth
The sole support of age.
Teach of the hand of love divine
In evils to discern
'Tis the first lesson which we need
The latest which we learn."

—Stitched by Eliza Tukey in Portland, Maine, 1817. Eliza was the sixth of nine children born to George and Betsey Snow Tukey. The sampler lists the genealogy of her family, and Eliza's birthdate as September 2, 1803. Two of her sisters, Sophia and Margaret Ann, died as infants.

The bell on the patisserie door sounded loud in the morning quiet, but the warm smells and footsteps coming from the kitchen said the Thibodeaus had already been at work for hours.

Nicole came to the counter, wiping her hands on her full apron. "Morning, Angie! Out early today."

"And couldn't resist the smells."

"Nothing smells better than bread baking," Nicole agreed. "It's almost as good an advertisement as how it tastes. What can I get for you?"

I'd planned to visit Dave Percy, one of the Mainely Needlepointers, this morning. "Who can resist your croissants? Four, please."

She selected the pastries and put them in a white bakery box. "They're still warm. Couldn't be fresher."

I handed her money. "You know everyone in town."

"If they eat bread or sweet things, I do," Nicole agreed, handing me the bakery box and my change.

"Do you know a tall, thin man with a gray beard? He might walk with a limp."

She hesitated. "A few of those around. Does the man you're asking about dress a bit oddly?"

"That'd be him," I agreed. "Arvin said he lived out on one of the islands."

"I've seen him walking past our windows in the early morning. Never in the light of day. I don't know what he does for money, but he doesn't spend any here, I can tell you." She shivered. "Strange fellow. Keeps to himself. I've heard folks say he's a little not right in the head, you know. Never bothered me, I'll say. But you never know."

I nodded. "True enough. I just wondered about him. Saw him at the wharf this morning."

"Chances are he'll keep his distance. That's his way."

"How's Henri's mom?"

"About the same. She's still getting used to living with us here instead of in her home in Quebec. Luckily we've found a lovely French-speaking home health aide to be with her when we're not home. But transitions are hard for her. Alzheimer's is hard on all of us."

"Transitions aren't easy," I agreed. *Even if you don't have Alzheimer's.*

It was still too early to stop at Dave's house, so I headed up the hill toward the white house that had been home to my family for generations. A little of the cheese Gram had brought back from her honeymoon was still in the refrigerator. Cheese and a croissant would make an excellent breakfast.

Gram had married Reverend McCully and moved to the rectory six weeks ago. She was only two blocks away, and I should have gotten used to living alone by now. After all, I'd lived alone, most of the time anyway, for ten years in Arizona. But there I'd lived in small apartments, cozy and temporary.

This house was large, permanent, and held indelible memories.

Sometimes I looked at the porch and saw myself jumping rope there, twenty years ago. "Step on a crack, break your mother's back." Gram had left the door to Mama's room closed for years, part of her hoping Mama might come home. I'd emptied Mama's closet and bureau in May. It was time to accept the past.

But in my heart that room at the top of the stairs would always be Mama's, and Gram's now-deserted room would be Gram's. I missed them both, more than I'd expected to, or would admit to anyone.

Gram had left most of her furniture and kitchen necessities for me; Reverend Tom's rectory was already furnished. Without what she'd left, the house would be empty. But along with her clothes she'd taken her favorite paintings and china and photographs.

Wallpaper had faded around the bright spots where pictures had hung, and now there were empty spaces on shelves in the living and dining rooms instead of the Victorian glass she'd inherited and the plaster of Paris handprint I'd given her when I was in kindergarten.

I was twenty-seven, old enough to take home ownership seriously. But my bedroom was still decorated with ocean-smoothed stones and sea glass I'd found on Pocket Cove beach in my teens. Shelves there mocked me, too. I'd never been a reader. The only books in my room were the Bible I'd been given when I was confirmed, worn paperbacks of *Peyton Place* and *The Hobbit*, and a few old Nancy Drews. To make my bedroom more welcoming, two weeks ago I'd moved a shelf of books on the history of needlepoint from the bookcases in the living room, which now doubled as the office of Mainely Needlepoint, to my room. I still had a lot to learn about embroidery.

I'd only brought home two souvenirs from my years in Arizona: my Glock, which I left in the sideboard in our front hall where I could get it quickly when I left the house, and a painting of a desert sunset. After Gram had taken her pictures, I'd hung the Arizona painting over the living-room fireplace.

I loved that painting. Maine sunsets were explosions of red and orange and purple, too, but they weren't as showy.

New England constraint, no doubt.

My painting didn't quite fit in Haven Harbor.

Did I?

Of course I did. This was my family home.

I'd let my mind get lost in the morning fog again.

I poured another cup of coffee and settled myself at the computer. I had bills to send to gift shops closing after the tourist season, and I needed to check on the progress of the needlework projects I'd assigned to the five Mainely Needlepointers.

I was most worried about Dave Percy. He'd taken on a large project—two seat covers and a matching wall hanging—for a woman from Iowa who wanted to take the work home with her at the beginning of September.

Labor Day was only three weeks away.

An hour later I stood and stretched.

It was a beautiful day, as beautiful as I remembered August days had always been in Maine.

I picked up the box holding the (now two) croissants and headed for Dave's house.

Then I detoured to the post office.

"Morning, Angie." Pax Henry was tall and thin, and had been the Haven Harbor postmaster since before his red beard was tinged with white. "What can I do for you this morning?"

"One book of stamps, please," I said, taking money out of my pocket.

"I've got birds or flags today," said Pax, showing me. "You like birds, as I recall."

"I do," I agreed. I slid the book into my pocket. "Say, Pax, I was by here early this morning and saw a man waiting for you to open."

"Ayah," he answered. "That'd be Jesse Lockhart, I imagine."

"He the one who lives out on one of the islands?" I asked. The Solitary had a name.

"Does. King's Island. Don't have a post office out there, so he picks his mail up here."

"Get much mail?"

"Now, you know mail's private, Angie. Between the US government and the one getting it." He leaned forward. "Gets the usual junk mail and what look like government checks, regular. Guess they're disability, 'cause of his leg, you know. And letters from a Chicago bank, sometimes. That's about it." Pax shook his head. "Fellow don't talk much. Stops in every week or ten days or such to get his mail. I hold it for him. That's all I know."

"He ever send any mail?"

Pax shook his head slowly. "Not that I remember. 'Course, he could be like you, buying stamps and mailing from anywhere."

"Not from an island," I pointed out.

"True enough," agreed Pax. "I don't know what he might send out. I only take care of what's coming in."

"Thanks, Pax," I said, heading for the door. "I was just being nosy."

"You and all of Haven Harbor," Pax said. "You ain't the first to be asking."

"Morning, Angie. You're out and about today." Jed Fitch, a heavyset man who'd been a football star at Haven Harbor High years before, passed me on his way in to see Pax. "Say—I've been trying to reach Reverend Tom. If you see him or your grandmother, tell them Carole and I'll be happy to be greeters at the church next Sunday. Tom doesn't need to call me back. He can count on us."

"I'll tell her," I said. In a small town, people

knew each other. Jed and his wife had grown up in town, married, had kids, and he was now a part-time Realtor and part-time handy man. Two of the windows in my house were cracked. Maybe Jed could fix them. I turned to ask him, but he'd disappeared inside the post office.

My windows weren't an emergency. Winter winds wouldn't hit for three months or so. I'd see Jed again before then.

I headed for Dave's house. Checking on the needlepoint Dave had committed to was partially an excuse to get out of the house, I admitted to myself, but I hadn't seen him recently, and talking to Pax hadn't filled my need for friendship. Dave was usually glad to see me.

July and August were busy months for everyone in Maine. I'd hardly seen anyone but Gram in the past weeks. As Reverend Tom's new wife, many of her days had quickly been absorbed by the Ladies' Guild and Summer Bible Camp at the church. She wasn't known for her singing voice, but she'd even been talked into joining the choir.

Fellow needlepointer Sarah Byrne and I had seen a lot of each other earlier in the summer, but recently Sarah'd seemed tied to her antique shop seven days a week. Most times I suggested we get together in the evening she'd already made other plans.

Ob Winslow was out on his charter boat, and his wife, Anna, had been focusing on her garden and putting up vegetables for the winter. Katie Titicomb was still visiting her daughter Cindy in Blue Hill, and even Ruth Hopkins had been busy, finishing two of her manuscripts.

I was the only Mainely Needlepointer who seemed to feel at sixes and sevens.

Life would slow down after the leaves fell. But that wouldn't be until mid-October.

Chapter 4

"Jesus permit thy gracious name to stand,
As the first effort of an infant hand,
And while her fingers on the canvas move,
Engage my tender heart to seek thy love."
　　　　　—English sampler, worked in wool
　　　　　　by Susanna Ebins, age nine, 1839.

School would open in three weeks. Dave was probably already planning for this year's crop of biology students at the high school.

I raised my hand to drop his brass lobster door knocker, when the door opened in front of me.

"Excuse me," said a deep, startled voice. The tall man I'd seen at the town dock brushed by me, limping toward the street. Jesse Lockhart's canvas bags were now full. On top of one I saw cans of vegetables, a large canister of oatmeal, and a box of matches. The other was full of bottled water.

I watched for a minute as he headed down the street. Then I called through the open door, "Dave? It's Angie. Have a minute?"

"Come on in," Dave answered. "I'm brewing more coffee. Want a mug?"

"Sure." Dave made great dark coffee, the way I liked it. "You've already had company this

24

morning," I commented as I joined him in the kitchen. "That man practically knocked me over getting out of here."

"He's shy," said Dave. "I'm sure he was as surprised to see someone as you were." Two empty mugs were on the counter. He and his friend must have finished the pot he'd brewed earlier.

"Who is he?" I asked. "I saw him rowing down at the pier this morning. I thought I knew most people in town." I didn't want to admit I'd been questioning people about him all morning.

Dave poured two mugs of coffee. "He doesn't live in town. And he doesn't want to know most people."

"Arvin Fraser said folks call him The Solitary."

"Could be." Dave pointed at a kitchen chair and sat in the other one.

"So who is he?"

"An old friend," said Dave. "Now, what can I do for you this morning?"

"Everyone needs friends. I'm glad he has you."

"I'm not going to tell you anything more about him, Angie. He's had troubles in his life, but now he's comfortable the way he's living."

"Alone? On an island?"

"That's right." Dave smiled, closing the subject. "I'm guessing you came to check on my needlepoint project."

"I did." I handed him the bakery box I'd been carrying. "And to bring you breakfast."

He opened the box and offered me one of the croissants.

"No, thanks. I already had two this morning," I admitted. "Those are yours."

"Thank you. And you can relax. The seat covers are finished, and the wall hanging is close to done. I haven't forgotten the client wanted the work done by Labor Day."

"Great. I just wanted to check."

"I promise I'll have finished the order before I take attendance."

My turn to change the subject. "I've hardly seen you this past month. What've you been doing?"

"Needlepoint. Tending my garden. Freezing sauces and vegetables."

I hesitated. "Food? From your garden?"

"Not exactly," Dave said, smiling. "I'm a regular at the farmer's market. My poison garden is one hobby. Cooking is another—separate—interest. Which I probably should emphasize after the couple of murders you were involved with this summer."

"Which you helped me with," I acknowledged. "I'm hoping that sort of excitement has died down."

Dave winced.

"I mean, I hope I'm not pulled into any more investigations. They were my Arizona life. Maine is the way life should be. Right?"

"That's what the bumper stickers say," he agreed.

"And the way life should be should not include murders," I declared. "Have you seen Sarah in the past month?"

"You're asking me? You and Sarah are close."

"I thought so," I admitted. "We helped Skye West clean out her estate in June, and Sarah helped identify that old needlepoint Mary Clough found in July. But she's hardly answered my calls since then."

"It's tourist time. If she's lucky, her shop has been filled with antique buyers and collectors, and she's had to add to her inventory. She's open seven days a week, now, right?"

"From nine until six, like most Haven Harbor shops this time of year. And late Thursday nights during the art walk."

"I've heard keeping all the shops open Thursday night has brought more customers to town," said Dave. "The Harbor Haunts Café is packed then, too. I'll be glad when the tourists go home and we get our town back. No wonder Sarah's busy."

"I hope that's why she hasn't been back in touch," I agreed. "Still, I may stop in to check on her today."

"Is she behind on the needlepoint you've assigned her?"

"No," I admitted. "She even left several extra

pillow covers on my porch the other day. I just miss seeing her. We used to do things together."

"I live alone, and Ruth does, and we don't talk to each other every day," Dave said, logically. "I'm fine. Enjoying the warm weather and being outside. It's tourist time. Sarah's busy."

"And Ruth's been editing a book. I've called her several times a week, to check on her. The rest of us who live alone are young. I'm always afraid Ruth might fall, or need help."

"I try to keep in touch, too," agreed Dave. "And how's Charlotte doing? I'm not a regular churchgoer, and I've only seen your grandmother once, at the post office, since her wedding."

"She's taking to married life at the rectory wholeheartedly," I admitted. "Her new life is filling most of her time. I don't see her as often as I used to."

"So you've felt alone for the past month."

Dave had nailed it. "I guess so."

"Go check on Sarah, then. It'll make you feel better. And if you don't have other plans, why don't you have dinner with me tomorrow night?"

Was Dave feeling sorry for me? Was this a date? He was smart and patient, and not bad-looking. We always found things to talk about. But he was also a Mainely Needlepoint colleague. Seeing him socially might be confusing.

Which he picked up on immediately. "I didn't mean to put you on the spot. But I've had dinner at your house with Sarah and Ruth. I've been thinking it's about time for me to reciprocate. Besides, I have a new recipe for lasagna I've been wanting to test. Tomatoes and peppers and spinach are fresh this time of year. And it's almost impossible to make lasagna for one."

Dinner with Dave. Who knew what it might lead to? "You're on," I agreed. "I love lasagna. It's one of the many things I've never made."

"What do you think? Shall I invite Sarah and Ruth, too? All the single needlepointers."

My dinner with Dave had changed to a group meeting. Part of me was relieved. A surprising part was disappointed. "Great idea. We could get caught up with one another before you're back teaching and the leaf peepers arrive to distract Sarah. And Ruth should be almost finished with her book by now."

"And you'll be calling us with Christmas needlepoint orders for the shops soon. So we're on. I'll call Ruth and Sarah." Dave smiled. He touched my hand, briefly. How long had it been since a man touched any part of me? I didn't want to think. "It's okay to feel alone, you know. But Haven Harbor's a small place. There's also safety in numbers. Friends need to hang together."

I was smiling as I left his house. Friends. I was lucky to have found several of them since I'd come back to town.

And I *was* a little concerned about Sarah.

As I headed to Main Street my cell rang.

"Anna! How are you?" Anna Winslow wasn't a close friend, but I liked her. Like me, she was taking needlepoint lessons from Gram. Her husband, Ob, was one of the Mainely Needlepointers when he wasn't out on his charter fishing boat.

"Been a rough summer, as you know. But Ob and I are coping. Life's coming together."

"Glad to hear that. I've been thinking about you both." *And should have called,* I added to myself. My being alone was at least partially my own fault.

"Not to worry. Everyone's running hither and thither in July and August. I called to ask if you'd been in touch with Skye and Patrick West recently."

"The last I heard Skye was studying a script for a movie she's making this fall, and Patrick was still in Boston, having therapy for his burns. Why?"

"Because I'm looking out my living-room window right now. The men rebuilding their house have been there for the past couple of months, but the place looks close to finished, and right now there's a limo over there. I don't want to run over and ask, but I looked with my birding binoculars, and I'm pretty sure I saw Patrick. Skye, too."

"I haven't heard anything," I admitted. "But

I'm on my way to see Sarah. She might have heard. I'll ask her and let you know."

"Thanks, Angie. I don't want to look like a nosy neighbor, but if they're back, I'd like to take over a casserole or something. Welcome them back to town."

"Of course. I'll let you know as soon as I talk to Sarah."

Skye and her son back in Haven Harbor? That could add some excitement to town. At least for Sarah.

I'd felt chemistry with Patrick West back in June, when he and his famous mother had bought Aurora, an old crumbling estate in Haven Harbor, but Sarah'd seen him first, and after he'd been burned in the fire that destroyed the carriage house he'd planned to live in, she was the one he'd kept in touch with.

Now I had another reason to see Sarah. I'd find out what she knew about Anna's gossip.

Nothing like a small-towner to have her birding glasses at the ready when something interesting happened across the street.

Chapter 5

"Life is uncertain, death is sure;
Sin is the wound and Christ is the cure."
——Verse stitched (with an alphabet) by
Susan M. Brooks, age thirteen, born
July 14, 1824, in Searsmount, Maine.

Sarah's From Here and There antiques shop door was open. She nodded at me in greeting while she continued wrapping two flowered blue china teacups and saucers for a young woman.

"They're fabulous," the blue-jeaned woman was saying. "I'm collecting different patterns of blue cups to display on a shelf that goes all around my kitchen. I heard Martha Stewart collects cups, too. Did you know that?"

"Martha Stewart has a home in Maine farther down the coast, but I've never met her," Sarah said, taking the woman's credit card. "I'm glad you found these, then. Not many cups are blue and white. They're special."

"What a lovely accent you have! Are you from England?"

"Australia," replied Sarah.

How many times on a typical day did she answer that question? Sarah did stand out in a crowd. If her accent wasn't memorable enough, her short white hair streaked with pink and blue was.

I'd asked her several times how she'd ended up here, an antiques dealer in Maine. She'd never answered me directly.

Everyone had secrets. Like The Solitary. Now I knew his name was Jesse Lockhart, and he had ties to Chicago, but neither of those facts explained why he lived alone on an isolated Maine island.

On the other hand, privacy was hard to maintain in a town where neighbors had binoculars.

I wandered around Sarah's shop until she finished with her customer. I didn't know much about antiques, but each time I visited From Here and There I learned a little more. I loved hearing her stories about what intriguing-looking items were, where they came from, and what they'd been used for.

Today an unusual doll under a glass globe caught my eye. The doll wasn't a baby or child; it was a wrinkled old woman, dressed in a tattered brown dress, wearing a long red cloak and large straw hat, and carrying baskets and bags full of tiny toys, kitchenware, and sewing supplies.

I stared, trying to see all the small items in the doll's basket.

Her customer's purchase completed, Sarah came and stood next to me. "She's a peddler doll."

"Peddler doll?"

"They weren't for children. In eighteenth- and early-nineteenth-century England they were popular decorations for women's workrooms. See? She's carrying all sorts of goods to sell or trade."

I shook my head. "Today we just go to a store."

"Exactly. But in those days, if you lived outside of a town, peddlers brought what you might need. Plus, they carried gossip, news from other homes and towns they'd visited. Their arrival was a good excuse to stop work and have a good chat. 'Can human nature not survive Without a listener?'"

Knowing Sarah, that last line was probably one of Emily Dickinson's. Sarah quoted them at off moments. "Speaking of gossip," I put in before she recited the entire poem, "Anna Winslow called me. There's a limo over at Aurora. She thinks Skye and Patrick may be back."

Sarah walked back to her counter. "Patrick texted me a week or so ago that they hoped to be here soon. His therapy must be over, or can be continued here in Maine."

"You didn't tell me!" I said. "We could have prepared food, or filled their refrigerator, or brought flowers, to welcome them back."

Sarah shrugged. "I'm sure Skye hired someone to get the houses set for them. Patrick picked out furniture for the carriage house from catalogs and ordered it from Boston. He hired a decorator from Portland to set it all up for him."

I hadn't known any of that. "So, when are you going to see him?"

"I'm pretty busy right now."

"I thought he was the man you were looking for! And you've been the one he's kept in touch with!" *The one I'd resisted because you'd claimed him.*

"I was being overly romantic a couple of months ago. Sure, he's an attractive guy. But right now I have other things to think about."

"Your business?" I looked around. It didn't look as though Sarah was going to run out of inventory anytime soon. And Patrick had left Haven Harbor in a helicopter, heading for the burn center at Mass General. Surely he deserved a welcome back.

"Business. And other things," said Sarah vaguely.

"Sarah Byrne, is there a new man in your life you haven't told me about?"

"Not the kind you're thinking of. Oh, and Dave called. He invited me to have dinner with you guys tomorrow night. I told him I had another commitment. Make sure he knows I really do. I felt bad having to say 'no' when he's never invited us all before."

"So are you going to tell me about this new

35

person in your life?" I asked. "I'm curious, of course!"

"Not yet. It's kind of personal."

"Personal?" I asked.

"Don't look that way. It's not bad. It's just something I'm not ready to talk about."

"Even to me?"

"Even to you, Angie. But don't worry. It's nothing dreadful." Sarah picked up a stack of business cards on her desk and began sorting them.

Today seemed a day for secrets.

"So, how would you feel if I stopped in to see Patrick and his mother?"

"Go ahead. You and he got along in June. I feel bad that I've been ignoring him, but right now I have too many things to think about. Please, be Patrick's friend. After all he's been through, I think he needs one."

Chapter 6

"Make much of precious time while in your
    power,
Be careful to husband every hour."
            —Verse stitched in silk on fine linen
    by Mary Batchelor in 1817. Mary was nine
                years old and lived in Hampton,
                    New Hampshire. She also stitched
            two alphabets, flower baskets, a deer,
                    a self-portrait, and initials of
                        members of her family.

"Gram, what do you think? Sarah's acting odd.
She has a secret she won't tell me, and she said
she didn't mind if I spent time with Patrick
West. She even encouraged me to stop in and
welcome him back!"

Gram's large yellow coon cat, Juno, filled my
lap as I sat in the rectory kitchen while Gram
made tomato and cheese sandwiches on oatmeal
bread for lunch.

"You're not in sixth grade anymore, Angel.
Why are you asking me? Sarah's your friend. You
both liked Patrick. Before you do anything you'll
be sorry for, be sure she wanted you to pursue
him. You know what you should do if your friend
has her eye on a man."

"I've never done anything to mess up Sarah's relationship with Patrick," I declared.

"You had dinner with him that night of the fire."

"It was only one time. And it wasn't planned. Sarah said she understood."

"You and he had a good time. I could tell, when you told me about it."

Gram was heating the sandwiches to melt the cheese. Despite the two croissants I'd had for breakfast, I could hardly wait for my sandwich. Gram's cooking always tasted better than mine, even when I tried to follow her instructions. "You're right," I agreed. "We had a lovely evening. Until we got back to Aurora and found the carriage house on fire, and Patrick went in to try to save his mother." That whole night was one I wanted to forget, despite how it had begun.

"On the other hand, if you're sure Sarah's stepping aside, for whatever reasons of her own, and you like the man, do something about it."

"You make it sound so simple."

"It is simple." Gram put our sandwiches on the table and handed me a napkin. "Tea?"

I nodded. "What if Patrick isn't interested?"

"Then it won't go anywhere. But if he's going to be living in town you'll be seeing him around anyway. Give the relationship a chance. If it's meant to be, it'll work out. If not . . . no harm done. You have plenty of years ahead of you to find the right man. Keep your mind open."

She was right. But I wasn't comfortable with the whole situation. "I was at Dave's house this morning, to check on a needlepoint project he's doing," I said, changing the subject.

"Speaking of good men who aren't attached," Gram said pointedly, putting our two mugs of tea on the table.

"I like Dave. But he's a friend," I said, taking a bite of my sandwich. "He's invited Sarah and Ruth and me for dinner at his house tomorrow night." Juno raised her head and nudged the edge of my plate. She smelled the cheese. I put her on the floor. This was my lunch.

"That should be fun. You haven't gotten out much recently."

"I told him I'd come. But Sarah's busy. I hope Ruth will be there."

"Angel, you're twenty-seven years old. All grown up. You don't need a chaperone."

Gram knew me too well. "No," I admitted. "But maybe I'm not ready for a serious relationship. I need to figure out what I want to do with my life first, before anyone else is a part of it. I don't want to date someone just so I'm not by myself."

"That makes sense," Gram agreed. "You've made a lot of changes in your life in the past few months. You need time to settle in a little." She sipped her tea. "But you don't know what Patrick or Dave might be looking for. Could be they're looking for casual companionship, too. Having dinner doesn't commit you to a lifetime."

Juno stopping rubbing against my legs and headed for her dish of dry food.

"You're right. And—before I forget! I ran into Jed Fitch at the post office this morning. He said to tell you and Tom he and Carole would be greeters at the church this Sunday."

"I'll pass that on to Tom. Sounds like good news. Carole's been having a hard time lately."

"Oh?" I'd met Jed's wife, Carole, earlier in the summer, but hadn't seen her since then. Not even at church.

"She's been to Portland several times for biopsies," Gram continued. "Last I heard, they'd diagnosed breast cancer and she'd started chemo. Jed's been taking care of her. I suspect they're having money problems, too. When he's with Carole, he isn't working."

"Sounds rough. I'm glad you told me. Next time I run into him I'll ask about Carole."

"Tom's visited them a couple of times, and I've sent over bread and homemade soup. Their sons are both home this summer, too, although I don't know how much help they are. And Carole's said she doesn't want any visitors yet. So it's a good sign she's feeling well enough to be a greeter this weekend."

Gram and I were lucky. So far we were both healthy. I looked over at Juno, who was chomping on a mouthful of food. "I miss Juno being there when I get home."

"You're telling me you miss my cat, not me?"

"Now, Gram."

"Don't you 'now, Gram' me, Angela Curtis. You're not sure what you want; that's clear. Do you want to be an old lady living in that house with a cat or two, the way I was?"

I laughed. "I'm not an old lady yet, Gram. And you weren't alone very long. Mom and I were with you after Grampa died, and I stayed after Mama left. And after I went to Arizona you found Reverend Tom."

"True enough. But when you were young, after you were in bed at night, that house was mighty quiet. I missed having someone to talk with. After you left for Arizona, Juno was good company, and a few years later I was lucky to find Tom. But I was a widow in my fifties. You're young and single. Don't pattern your life on mine!"

"Okay, Gram. Message received. By the way—when I got to Dave's house he had a friend there. Or, his friend was leaving. A tall guy, long beard, looked a bit strange. I saw him at the wharf this morning."

"Rowed in, did he?"

"You know who he is?"

"He arrived in town about two years back and moved out to King's Island. Comes into town once a week or so for mail and supplies. Don't know much more than that. Speaking of people who're alone!"

"Arvin and Rob, down at the wharf, called him The Solitary."

"I've heard folks call him that," Gram said. "Could be worse names. Seems to want to be left alone, and we Mainers are good about accepting boundaries. If he doesn't want folks to know anything about him, then, my guess is we won't. If he was at Dave's house, then he has one friend. I'm glad. That man's worried people in town, living out there with only cormorants and gulls to keep him company. Especially in winter storms. Seems I remember the coast guard going to check on him in a nor'easter last winter, but he wouldn't be rescued." Gram shook her head. "Each to his own. He's hurting nobody but maybe himself. And he has the right to do that. There are worse choices in life than preferring your own company to others'."

If only I could decide whose company I preferred.

"Did you see the yacht in the harbor yesterday?" Gram asked. "Moored outside of Second Sister Island. Too big to anchor inside the harbor."

I shook my head. "I was by the town wharf this morning, but the fog was heavy. Couldn't see much. Who'd it belong to?"

"I heard it was Gerry Bentley's."

"Who?" I didn't keep up with the news, and sometimes, I admitted to myself, it showed.

"I can't explain exactly. I don't understand all this new technology. But he designed special software for video games, back a while. Made millions. Maybe billions. I read about him in *People* magazine."

"Nice," I allowed. His yacht might make him stand out, but he didn't have anything to do with my world.

"Ladies at the church said Bentley and his wife anchored their launch at the Yacht Club yesterday and had lunch there. They're cruising Down East and wanted to take a look at Haven Harbor."

"Not much to see here," I said, finishing the last of my sandwich. "It's not Portland or Camden or Bar Harbor. Just a small harbor town."

"They stopped at Ted Lawrence's art gallery, too." Gram took our empty plates off the table. "Don't know if they bought anything, though."

Not that anyone in town paid attention to anyone else.

Ted Lawrence's gallery was by far the highest-end gallery in town. I'd never ventured inside. Art galleries were beyond my means. I'd found the painting I'd bought in Arizona at a sidewalk art show.

"Lawrence's customers are almost all people from away," I guessed.

"His artists are out of my price range, for sure. Maybe the Bentleys were tired of cruising. Or they were curious about the town, or the gallery. They're West Coast folks, I assume. Supposed to be pretty out there, but it's not Maine. Good to see folks from there visiting, though. Especially when they spend money in town."

"Unless they order a lot of needlepoint, I don't care where they visit. But you're right. Anyone's welcome to come to Haven Harbor and spend a little time. And money."

"A-men," said a deep voice from the doorway.

"Hi, Reverend Tom," I said.

"Good to see you, Angie." He bent over Gram and kissed her lightly. "I think it's time you dropped the 'Reverend.' Now we're family. I'm Tom. Any chance of a man breaking into this party and getting some lunch?"

"No problem," said Gram. "It'll just take a minute. I didn't know how long your Chamber of Commerce meeting would be so when Angie stopped in we went ahead and ate." She got up and sliced cheese for another sandwich.

"Meetings are always too long," said Tom, sitting. "So who's coming to Haven Harbor to spend money?"

"Rumor is Gerry Bentley and his wife were in town yesterday," I explained.

"I heard about the Bentleys," said Reverend Tom. "Jed Fitch was at my meeting. He said they stopped at his real estate office yesterday." Gram handed a cup of tea to Tom. "I can tell you that really got Ed Campbell excited."

"Ed Campbell?"

"Maybe you haven't run into him yet, Angel. He owns the big used car lot outside town. He's also president of the Chamber."

"The Bentleys are looking to buy a place in Haven Harbor?" asked Gram, putting Tom's sandwich on the table.

"Jed wouldn't exactly say. Whatever they're thinking, it's private right now. But why else visit a real estate office?" Tom bit into his sandwich. "Thanks for this. I was starving."

"Looking at real estate is fine. But I'm not sure I like the idea of someone that well-known living in town," said Gram. "I can't imagine what house around here would be suitable for people with his money."

"Skye West bought Aurora," I pointed out. "She's a movie star."

"And made a generous donation to the church earlier this summer, too," Tom said. "I wouldn't mind having a few parishioners who could write checks for a new roof or an addition to the education building. The Bentleys would be welcome. Ed Campbell was imagining they'd invite their friends to visit, too. Friends with money."

"As long as they don't change the town. I like it the way it is. No expensive restaurants we can't afford to eat in or stores full of designer clothing or folks who think they're better than locals." I was thinking of Scottsdale, Arizona, full of home decorating stores and art galleries and high-end jewelry stores. None I'd ever visited, except when I'd been on the job. Surveillance could take you anywhere.

"Hard to guess what the Bentleys would have in mind," Tom said. "But no harm if they look around. Haven Harbor's welcomed all sorts of people in the past. Seems to me we could welcome a couple more if they should decide to buy here."

"Likely they're checking out places all along the coast," said Gram. "Nothing for anyone to get excited about. Some folks window-shop for houses."

"Probably right, dear," said Tom. "But I wouldn't mind if someone that wealthy decided to share a little bit of it with Haven Harbor."

"No need to think about it. Most likely they'll head to Southwest Harbor or Dark Harbor where homes are more to the liking of multimillionaires than those around here." I stood. "Thanks for lunch, Gram. Thinking of newcomers to town, I think I'll take your advice and stop in at Aurora and welcome Skye and Patrick back to town." I winked at Gram. "Neighbors should be friendly, right?"

Chapter 7

"Religion should our thoughts to engage
Amidst our youthful bloom.
'Twill fit us for declining age
And for the awful tomb."
　　　—Sampler stitched in 1832 by Abigail
　　　Bragdon (1820–1893) in Wells, Maine.
　　　Abigail also stitched four alphabets in
　　　different stitches, the names of the first
　　　twenty-four states, and when they were first
　　　settled. (Maine is first on her list, settled in
　　　1630.) She married ship's carpenter Benjamin
　　　Bonin in 1841 and they had nine children.

Until recently Aurora had been a large, deserted
Victorian house, the sort people called a "white
elephant" and suggested should be torn down.
Instead, actress Skye West had bought it, and
construction crews had been working on it all
summer. Skye's artist son, Patrick, planned to
refurbish the estate's carriage house and turn it
into living quarters and a studio.

I hadn't seen him or his mother since June.

I hadn't even driven by to see how the
construction was coming along.

Maybe I should have.

At least on the outside, Aurora now looked like

a different house than the one Sarah and I had helped clean out two months ago.

Its white clapboards had been scraped and repainted. New shutters replaced those that had been broken or missing. The driveway had been repaved. Where the foundation of a statue had once stood was now more space for parking. Today a dozen people were busy planting white pines along the stone wall that marked the street-side edge of the property.

Tall, straight white pines were the reason Maine was called The Pine Tree State. In colonial times representatives of the British Crown went through Maine's forests, marking the tallest and best white pines with broad arrows to claim them for the British Crown, destined to be masts and spars for the Royal Navy. Anyone felling them for other purposes was severely punished.

Maine history books add that residents of the District of Maine, as the area was known then, pruned young white pines so they wouldn't grow tall and straight, and so wouldn't be claimed by the king.

Mainers were independent from the beginning.

I didn't see the limo Anna'd mentioned, or any other vehicles but landscapers' trucks, in front of Aurora, so I followed the drive to where the old carriage house had stood.

The new building's exterior had been designed to look the way the carriage house must have when it was first built, over a hundred years ago. But now its front included large doors that I assumed concealed a garage . . . essential for Maine winters if you didn't want to spend hours shoveling . . . and living quarters. In back of those areas was a modern two-story addition that included a glass roof and two glass walls.

Patrick's dream studio?

The limo Anna had seen, and a smaller car, were there. In June Skye and Patrick hadn't used a limo.

Haven Harbor had accepted the presence of a celebrity in town and not bothered Skye. She'd been approachable, but busy, and although television told us regular folks that celebrities' lives were different from ours, Skye hadn't brought an entourage of drivers and personal assistants and bodyguards with her to Maine. Had that changed?

I took a deep breath and rang the doorbell. I hadn't let myself imagine what Patrick looked like after the fire.

Sure, Patrick and Skye had been friendly in June, when they were new in town and needed help with Aurora. But this was late August. Patrick had spent the summer in the hospital and rehab.

Maybe I shouldn't have dropped in.

In Maine, people did that.

But Skye and Patrick weren't from Maine.

I should have called first.

I'd turned around and was about to leave when the door opened.

Patrick's broad smile told me I'd been right to come unannounced.

Chapter 8

"In vain we mourn those transitory days
Consumed in riot and licentious ways
'Tis temperance alone preserves our strength
And mind and body to life's full length."
　　　—Stitched by fourteen-year-old Hadassah
　　　　　Thompson (1806–1832) in the school
　　　　　　　of Catherine Swain Lyman in
　　　　　Norridgewock, Maine. Although the
　temperance movement was gaining ground
　　　in 1820, it was unusual to stitch a verse
　　like this on a sampler. Hadassah married
　　　James Wilder, a chair maker, and gave
　　birth to a son, Francis, in 1831. She was
　　　twenty-six when she died in 1832.

Patrick's deep brown eyes took me back to that evening in June. The evening we'd been high on wine and happiness and an elegant dinner together. The part of the evening before the fire.

I smiled back. Then I glanced at his hands.

Scarred and swollen. Skin grafts.

His eyes followed mine. He held out his hands. "They're not beautiful, but they're still mine. I'm teaching them to work again."

"Can you paint?"

He flinched. "That's a work in progress. Come in. We're having drinks. Champagne? Something stronger?"

"Champagne sounds wonderful." I followed him into the redesigned carriage house. The exterior had reflected the Victorian building it had been, but the furniture and fixtures inside were modern. "You did all this from Boston?" I asked, turning around to look. An oriental rug covered part of the polished pine floor, and the comfortable furniture and modern lighting fixtures fit perfectly together.

"On-line catalogs. The first thing I learned to do with my fingers was 'search,'" he explained. "Planning the house gave me something to think about."

"You have great taste." I walked over to a large painting swirling with red and blue and yellow colors, like the flames that had consumed the old carriage house. "Yours?" I'd never seen any of Patrick's work.

He nodded. "I had it sent from my studio in California."

"It's beautiful," I said. "I don't know anything about art, but I love it."

"Then you have good taste." The words weren't Patrick's.

I turned from the painting. An older man, gray hair, dressed elegantly in trim jeans and a silk shirt, had entered the room. He was holding a flute of champagne. Patrick waved and walked into another room.

"I don't think I've had the pleasure. I'm Ted Lawrence."

"You own the art gallery downtown," I said.

"Guilty as charged," he agreed. "And a larger gallery in the barn out at my home. And you are?"

"Angie Curtis," I said, holding out my hand.

"You're right. We've never met. I would have remembered," he said. "But you're Sarah Byrne's friend. You run the needlepoint business."

"Yes." How did he know Sarah, or Mainely Needlepoint? But the Lawrence Gallery wasn't far from Sarah's shop. Maybe he'd met her there.

He looked at the painting again. "I'm hoping I can get Patrick to show at my gallery when he has new work."

"That would be wonderful," I agreed.

Patrick reappeared, carefully holding out a glass of champagne. "For you," he said. Had he been able to pour the champagne into the delicate flute? He wasn't holding a glass himself.

I raised the flute to him. "Welcome home." The champagne was tingly and delicious. Being wealthy must be nice.

"I see you've met Ted. I didn't know whether you two knew each other. Now, come and see Mom and Uncle Gerry." Patrick led the way into the second room.

Skye was dressed elegantly, in gray slacks, a loose gray tunic, and pearls. Her gray hair streaked with white looked perfectly coiffed. In June she'd worn dirty blue jeans and T-shirts.

Suddenly I felt self-conscious. I was wearing my usual worn jeans and a rumpled long-sleeved shirt. I hadn't realized I'd be drinking champagne with my elegant neighbors.

Skye got up from the gray couch and came over and hugged me. "I'm so glad you stopped in, Angie. We're celebrating being back in Haven Harbor. I've flown in and out a few times this summer to check on the work here, but this is the first time Patrick's seen his plans come to life."

"Your home looks terrific," I agreed, taking another sip of champagne. "I stopped to welcome you both back to town. I didn't know you had company."

"You're always welcome, Angie," Skye said, putting her arm around me. "I see you've already met Ted, who's a new friend. Here are Gerry and June Bentley, who're visiting."

Gerry Bentley. Uncle Gerry? The same Gerry Bentley whose yacht was off Haven Harbor? Skye indicated a couple comfortably sitting on chairs near the entrance to what I assumed was Patrick's studio. The man was in his fifties although his wife looked considerably younger. And considerably pregnant. He wore tan slacks and a red shirt. She was wearing a long blue maternity dress embroidered in white.

"So pleased to meet you," I said. What did you say to multimillionaires? Hi? How's your money?

"Angie's one of our first Haven Harbor friends," Skye was saying. "She helped us out when we were cleaning Aurora in June, and her company did the restoration work on the large needlepoint panels you were admiring earlier."

I felt out of my depth. Where had Patrick disappeared to?

"I'm going to show Angie my studio," he said, coming back into the room and rescuing me. "If you'll excuse us."

"Of course," said Mr. Bentley.

Patrick guided me around the furniture and through the wide doors leading into his two-story studio. How would he heat this place in winter? But, then, fuel costs weren't a problem for him. As I'd suspected from the outside, the roof was one giant skylight, and two of the walls, those facing south and west, were glass. The wall on the street side of the building was solid, but included windows, and a door leading to a courtyard where sea stones were set in swirling patterns that reminded me of Patrick's painting. Redwood chairs and lounges surrounded a large table.

"Like it?" he asked.

"I love it. It's spectacular," I said, walking over to the glass wall that overlooked the field between the estate and Haven Harbor. Then I turned back. "But where are your paints and easels?"

"They'll come," he said. "I didn't want anyone else to arrange them. I'm having some supplies shipped from my studio in California and buying others here. That's one reason Uncle Gerry brought Ted Lawrence to see me today. Ted knows the best Maine sources, the ones local artists use."

"Uncle Gerry?"

"My father's younger brother. He and his wife were boating up the coast, and when he heard Mom and I were coming home, he decided to stop in, see the house, and see me. He's always been supportive of my art. And he wanted me to meet Ted."

"Ted Lawrence really liked your painting."

"I hope he meant it. I'd love to show in a Haven Harbor gallery. Especially one as prestigious as Ted Lawrence's. But I won't know if he's serious until I'm ready to paint again." He glanced down at his hands. "My therapist in Boston was encouraging, though."

"You've been working hard."

"I have. But it's time to prove I can manage outside of a rehab center. Mom and I arrived yesterday. We planned to have some quiet time so I could settle in and find new therapists. And Mom needs time to study her script for the movie she's doing this fall. The rest of August will be a test for me. She'll be living in the big house. I'm hoping to prove I'll be all right after she leaves."

"So she isn't staying long."

"No. But assuming all goes well, I'm here for the winter. Mom plans to come back for the holidays, but I'm looking forward to having the place to myself for a while. In the hospital, I was never alone. I dreamed of being here, in my own house, with the beauty of Maine around me. Of painting again." He stepped slightly closer to me and looked into my eyes. "Of seeing the friends I made here and getting to know them better."

I tried not to look at his hands. His arms were covered by his shirt.

"Are you sure you're ready to do that? Live alone and paint?" I asked bluntly.

"I'll need help for a while. Mom insists I have a housekeeper come in once a week to clean, and she's arranging for local restaurants to deliver meals once a day." He looked at his hands. "I can make toast and coffee, but I'm not ready to chop vegetables or carve a turkey."

"Sounds like a fancy version of Meals on Wheels."

He laughed. " 'If it's Tuesday, it must be Italian,' more likely."

No restaurant in Haven Harbor delivered food.

At least not on a regular basis. But, then, Skye and Patrick had the money to make things happen other people didn't. I'd seen that in June. I'd even been the beneficiary of two of their generous checks.

"I've often thought of you. Of that evening, before everything fell apart," he said.

"I've thought about you, too." He hadn't called or texted. Was this a line? "But I've been busy, with Mainely Needlepoint and my grandmother's wedding."

"I remember your planning that," Patrick agreed. "So you're living by yourself now?"

"I am. If you need any help—shopping, or driving or doing anything here—I'd be happy to do whatever I can." Why did I say that? He could afford all the help he needed. Would he think I was being presumptuous? I moved a little away from him.

"I can't drive yet," he said. "Mom's arranged for me to have a driver. I hate that, but it should only be for a little while. And I'll have help with the basics. But I could use a friend. Maybe you could join me for dinner? Here? Tomorrow night?"

I shook my head. "I have plans for tomorrow night."

"Another time, then?"

"After you have a chance to get settled."

"I'll call you," he promised.

We both stood, silent. Awkwardly.

"Your glass needs to be refilled," said Patrick. "Why don't we go back with the others?"

I would have loved more champagne. But I felt like an intruder. "No, thanks. I have work to do; I can't stay," I assured him. "But I'm glad to see you back here. Your home is lovely."

"I hope you'll be a frequent guest," Patrick said. "And I could use needlepoint cushions for the couches and chairs."

Was he trying to buy my time?

"But now I have to leave."

He opened the sliding door onto the patio, and I fled to the front of the house where I'd left my car.

Everyone had been welcoming, especially Patrick.

But Patrick's world wasn't mine.

I headed my little red Honda back into the village, passing shops that advertised MAINE T-SHIRTS, DISCOUNTED! And LOCALLY MADE ICE CREAM and BEST LOBSTER AND CRABMEAT ROLLS! HERE! They were part of my world. They were my comfort zone.

And I hated to admit it, but his scarred, swollen hands made me uncomfortable.

Uncomfortable enough not to want to see him again? No, I told myself. I could get used to the way his hands were now.

Could he?

If he couldn't paint as he had before the fire, how would he cope?

Was I strong and patient enough to be his friend as he fought his way back to normalcy?

I hardly noticed the rest of the drive home. I parked in my driveway, unlocked my door, and went straight to the refrigerator. White wine. It might not be champagne, but it was what I needed right now.

Chapter 9

"How pleasant 'tis to see kindred and friends
  agree
Each in their proper station move,
And each fulfill their part with sympathizing
  heart,
In all the cases of life and love."
              —In 1812 Sarah Moody (1786–1865)
              worked this sampler in Saco, Maine.
              She was twenty-six, and the head of a
              school where she taught embroidery
              as well as reading and writing.

I paid more attention than usual to my appearance before leaving for Dave's dinner party. Dave would be dressed casually, and Ruth would wear slacks and a cotton sweater. But I was still self-conscious about what I'd been wearing at the Wests' the day before.

When I was four or five I'd loved trying out Mama's lipsticks and high heels. But when I was old enough to wear my own, she was gone, and makeup and heels reminded me too much of her. Women in Haven Harbor didn't dress up much and rarely wore makeup.

I was afraid of trying too hard, the way Mama had. So, instead, I didn't wear dresses or skirts.

I never tried to look elegant. I told myself I was comfortable with who I was.

Most of the time I was.

But yesterday I'd felt out of place at Aurora.

I replaced my usual jeans with a pair of tan slacks, a pale blue T-shirt, and a tan sweater, promising myself I'd be careful not to drop or spill anything. Dave had said "lasagna," so I chose a bottle of Italian red from the wine rack Gram had left in the dining room. (She and Tom had been given a much larger rack as a wedding gift, so they'd given me their old one.)

Tomato sauce and red wine. I almost changed back to jeans.

But I didn't. I even put on lipstick and a little beige eye shadow.

I looked at myself critically and then wiped most of the eye shadow off.

I didn't want Dave or Ruth to think I was trying too hard.

Sandals completed my outfit. I could walk to Dave's.

His yellow Cape with green shutters and a white picket fence would have been too cute for a lot of men, but it suited Dave.

"Angie! So glad you came."

I handed him the wine I'd brought.

"Valpolicella. Perfect. Come on in!"

I sniffed. "Yum! Garlic and tomato sauce."

"And my apple pie," said Ruth. She was already

settled in the highest armchair in Dave's living room, her wheeling pink walker next to her.

"You brought a pie?" I asked.

"I did. It's a little early for apples, but I couldn't resist Granny Smiths at the grocery yesterday."

"I have a green salad and garlic bread to go with the lasagna," said Dave. "When Ruth said she'd bring a pie I decided we could give up cheeses and crackers in favor of vanilla ice cream on top of the pie for dessert."

I held my stomach. "Carb city. Dinner sounds—and smells—wicked good!"

"Ruth and I were about to have wine. You too?"

"Absolutely," I agreed. "Need help?"

"No, I'm fine. Go on in and keep Ruth company."

I sat on a cozy corner of the couch, surrounded by needlepointed cushions. The cushions made for a comfortable and decorative room. Had Patrick been serious yesterday when he'd said his new house could use some? Tan and white living room furniture was elegant, but his living room could use color. A pillow reflecting the colors and design of his painting? I made a mental note to ask him if he was serious about the cushions.

"Good to see you, Angie. I'm glad Dave invited us. I've been tied to that computer of mine most of the summer, and I could use a break from sex," Ruth confided.

"Good thing we know what you're writing, or people would talk, Ruth!" Dave said as he handed each of us a glass of red wine. "To us! Needlepointers and friends!"

I raised my glass. I felt comfortable with Ruth and Dave. "Will you make your deadline?" I asked Ruth.

"I set my own deadlines now. One book's already finished. That one's with the fellow who does my formatting and cover. The second manuscript's almost done. Working without a publisher makes my schedule easier, but I have to edit tightly or my readers complain."

"So you're still self-publishing?" I asked as Dave put the wine bottle on his glass-topped coffee table.

"After years and years of traditional erotica publishing I've found most people today prefer e-books, for privacy. So why bother with the print version, or give most of the profits to a publishing company? My readers know what to expect in my books, and I deliver."

"I finally read one of your Chastity Falls books," I said. "It was . . . creative." I was no innocent, but I blushed as I remembered.

Ruth laughed. "Well said, Angie. Some Sundays I sit in church and wonder what all those praying folks would think if they knew the little widow woman with the walker wrote books they only read in the privacy of their bedrooms.

I'd love to know which of those sedate ladies and gentlemen in their Sunday best read Chastity's latest the night before."

"Sounds like I should check out your work, too," said Dave. "My reading matter this summer has been limited to botanical journals and forensics articles about detecting poisons. Not exactly light reading on a Saturday or any other night."

"I can't believe school starts again in three weeks," I said. "Summer has gone all too fast."

"As always," Ruth agreed. "But September and October are two of my favorite months in Maine. No humidity, cooler temperatures, fewer tourists, and brilliant colors. A grand finale before winter."

"Tourists are still around," Dave pointed out. "I heard a pretty spectacular yacht was anchored out beyond the harbor yesterday."

"Wonder who was visiting?" said Ruth.

"Gerald Bentley and his wife," I answered. "They're friends of Skye and Patrick West."

"You have a good grapevine," said Dave. "I hadn't even heard the Wests were back in town."

"Anna Winslow called to tell me," I admitted. "So I stopped in to welcome them back. The Bentleys were there. The guy who runs the art gallery downtown was there, too."

"Ted Lawrence?" asked Ruth. "I haven't seen Ted in a while now. This arthritis of mine keeps me too close to home. I used to go to all his openings. Never could afford to buy anything, but I'm a good looker. I loved his dad's oils. Sea scenes, mostly."

"His father was Robert Lawrence, right?" asked Dave. "I've seen his work in museums. Very impressive. And Ted Lawrence is the one Sarah's spending so much time with now."

I looked at him. "Sarah? And Ted Lawrence?"

"She hasn't told you? When I invited her to join us tonight she told me she was busy, so I kidded her a little—told her I felt insulted that she's always busy these days. She said she was sorry, but she was spending a lot of time out at Ted Lawrence's."

"He's a bit old for her, I'd say," said Ruth drily. "Younger than I am by some, but in his seventies. He could be Sarah's father, for that matter. Or grandfather. That place of his out on the point is spectacular, though. Oceanfront view and its own private beach. His father bought the place years ago."

Dave shrugged. "I don't know what their relationship is. And I didn't know Ted Lawrence was that old. I've never been to his gallery. But Sarah seems happy. That's what's important."

"Earlier this summer she seemed besotted with that Patrick West," said Ruth. "Guess I'm out of date."

I felt out of date, too. I'd known Sarah had a new interest in her life. And Ted Lawrence was good-looking, for his age. But a romantic interest for Sarah? It didn't make sense. And she'd specifically told me she didn't have a new man in her life. Why hadn't she told me about Ted Lawrence? She'd told Dave. I sipped my wine as Ruth and Dave talked about Robert Lawrence's work.

I'd lived in town most of my life and Dave was a newcomer, but he knew more than I did about the Lawrences. Ruth did, too. My family had been more interested in paying grocery bills than visiting art galleries.

Was Ted Lawrence the reason Sarah wasn't interested in Patrick anymore?

Patrick hadn't asked about her, either. Had they had a long-distance falling-out? Why wouldn't Sarah have told me?

I could have been having dinner with Patrick tonight. Rich, handsome, early thirties, and, according to Ted Lawrence, a talented artist.

Dave and Ruth had changed topics. Now they were comparing tomato sauce recipes.

Dave was graying, in his forties, and had never expressed any romantic interest in me. He was a friend. He taught biology at the high school. He was a good cook, and he had the only poison garden I'd heard of.

Gram had implied he could be more.

I wasn't sure. But I had to admit I was more comfortable sitting in his living room, chatting with Ruth and Dave, than I had been visiting Patrick's carriage house.

Gram always told me to keep my options open. But she'd also reminded me I didn't know whether Patrick or Dave were even looking for a relationship.

"Angie, where are you?" Dave asked. "I've asked you twice whether you wanted another glass of wine. I'm about to open a second bottle."

"Sorry. I was daydreaming. Another glass of wine would be great. And when are we going to eat? Those tantalizing scents from your kitchen are driving me crazy."

"A little hungry?" Dave asked. "You're smelling the garlic bread. Dinner should be ready in a few minutes. I've even cleaned my needlepoint stash off the dining-room table so we can eat in style."

"I'm impressed," said Ruth. "This is such fun. I should get out of my house more often. Some days I think arthritis has given me an excuse to be lazy."

"I noticed you walked here," he said. "That's a long four blocks. After wine and dinner, when you're ready to go home, I'm going to drive you. Independence is well and good, but I wouldn't want you falling, or wearing yourself out."

"We'll see," said Ruth.

As she spoke the door burst open. Dave jumped up as The Solitary limped into his living room.

"Sorry. Didn't know you'd have company tonight," Jesse Lockhart said. He turned away as if to leave.

"Jesse, it's all right. These are my friends, Ruth and Angie. Fellow needlepointers."

"Never understood you doing all that sewing," said Jesse. He nodded at Ruth and me. "But I should go. I'll come back tomorrow."

"You will not. You'll stay for dinner," said Dave, taking Jesse's arm and moving him over to one of the chairs. "Let me get you a glass of wine."

"Haven't had wine in"—he looked around the living room—"a long time. Guess I could do with some."

Dave went to the kitchen for a glass. Jesse sat uncomfortably and didn't look directly at Ruth or me. "I'm Angie Curtis," I said, "and this is Ruth Hopkins. Like Dave said, we're all Mainely Needlepointers."

He squirmed in his chair. "I'm Jesse Lockhart."

"I saw you here yesterday," I said. "Dave told me you live out on King's Island."

Dave handed him a glass of wine and sat down. "What brings you to town so soon, and at this time of day?"

"I'm in trouble," said Jesse, looking at all of us. "I didn't know what to do, so I came here."

Chapter 10

"And while her fingers over this canvas move
Engage her tender heart to seek thy love."
—Hannah Marcia Tucker (1816–1886)
of Saco, Maine, stitched this when
she was about ten years old.
When she was nineteen she married
Daniel Cleves, a successful ship owner,
banker, and merchant. Of her seven
children, four died in infancy.

"Of course, if you have trouble, you should have come here," said Dave reassuringly as Jesse gulped his wine. "You're always welcome. What's happened?" He refilled Jesse's glass.

"Someone wants to buy my island," said Jesse. "He's trying to push my birds and me off."

"Now you take it easy. Jesse, is that your name? Good old-fashioned name," Ruth interrupted. "I don't know you, but I know the law. No one can buy your island if you won't sell it to them. Calm down. Just tell them it's not for sale."

"I did," said Jesse. "This afternoon, when that man came to the island. He came ashore without permission. He yelled and scared my birds. Nesting season's about over, but my island's posted. He told me it wasn't my decision to sell.

He's going to call Simon. And I don't know what Simon will say."

"Who's Simon?" I asked, confused. "Why should anyone else have a say in what you do with your island?"

"Simon's my cousin," said Jesse, rolling the stem of his again-empty wineglass between his fingers. "He and I inherited the island from our grandfather."

"So you own half the island," I said.

"We own it together. Simon lives in Chicago. He never comes to Maine. I live here. I take care of it. I take care of the birds. I pay the taxes. It's my island." Jesse's eyes were dark and scared. "No one can buy my island."

"Who came to see you?" asked Dave.

"A fat man who talked too much," said Jesse. "He gave me his card. Said I should call him when I decided on a price. As if I had a telephone! I told him King's Island wasn't for sale. It didn't have a price."

"Do you still have his card?" asked Dave quietly.

Jesse searched in one of his torn pockets. He handed Dave a folded business card.

"Jed Fitch," Dave read. "Jed's a local Realtor. He helps people buy and sell homes."

"And islands. That's what he said. He said someone wants to buy my island and he's going to make it happen."

"Sounds like Jed's trying to browbeat you," said Ruth.

"He didn't beat me," said Jesse. "He yelled at me. And scared my birds. I won't let anyone on my island again."

"Jesse's island is one of only a dozen nesting sites in Maine for great cormorants. They're a threatened species," Dave explained.

"Threatened species?" I asked.

Ruth nodded. "I used to be active in the Audubon Society. Anna Winslow's president of the local chapter now. An endangered species is in danger of becoming extinct. A threatened species isn't endangered now, but might be in the near future."

"If they're close to endangered, then why would anyone be allowed to build there?" I said. Then I caught myself. Jesse lived on the island already.

"I didn't build. I live quietly. I don't bother the birds," Jesse explained. "They build nests on high ledges and trees. I don't go near them."

"Do you have electricity on the island? Or fresh water?"

"When it rains, I have water," Jesse explained. "Dave lets me fill bottles here for drinking."

"Then why would anyone want to buy your island? It would cost a fortune to build the sort of house most people would want today. They'd have to have a propane generator and some way to get fresh water."

"The fat man—Jed—he said the people who want to buy my island are rich. He said I could buy another island, a better island. But I don't want another island. I want my island!"

"Did Jed say who this man was? The one who wants to buy your island?" I asked.

Jesse shook his head. "He said it's the man on the big white boat anchored near the harbor," he said. "I don't care who he is. I won't sell to anyone."

The big white boat.

Only one yacht had been anchored near Haven Harbor recently.

Gerald Bentley must want Jesse's island. Rich people thought they could buy anything.

"We'll help you," I said without thinking it through. "Somehow we'll find a way for you and the birds to stay on your island."

"I can start by recommending a good lawyer," Dave added.

Chapter 11

"Great minds conquer difficulties by daring to attempt them."
—Cross-stitched in 1823 by Elizabeth Helen
     Hutton, ten years old, in New York City.

The rest of the evening went by quickly.

Jesse seemed more relaxed after I'd told him we'd help him (and after his third glass of wine), but as we ate our way through Dave's lasagna, salad, and homemade garlic bread, and savored Ruth's apple pie, I kept wondering what we could do for him. No one else volunteered any ideas.

Instead, we talked about weather and the town and Jesse told us about the great cormorants on his island (seven nesting pairs; together they'd had twenty-six chicks this summer, but an eagle had stolen two of them. Jesse was very angry at that eagle.)

Dave convinced Jesse to stay the night instead of rowing home in the dark. While Dave was driving Ruth home, I stayed to talk with his guest.

"How well do you know your cousin Simon?" I asked.

"When we were kids we vacationed together at my grandparents' house near here. Grandpa would take us out to the island to camp for a night or two. After high school Simon went to college and became a banker. I joined the army. We hardly saw each other after that."

"Where did you meet Dave?"

"We were in the same VA hospital in Massachusetts. I'd gotten shot up in the Middle East. Dave had an accident when he was on leave. We were in PT together. My head had problems, and we'd both messed up our left legs." Jesse didn't look directly at me; he seemed to look into the past. "We talked a lot."

"What about?" I asked, curious.

"Neither of us wanted to go back into the service. I didn't want any more fighting. No guns. No IEDs. No loud noises." He hesitated. "A lot of guys felt that way. At night, in the wards, they'd have nightmares. I started thinking about the island when I was in the hospital. I told Dave about camping there when I was a kid. Dave liked to hear about Maine, but he wasn't a camper. He was in the navy. He wanted to settle down. He was figuring how to go back to school. Did it, too. He's a teacher now, you know."

"And what did you want to do?"

"I just wanted to get away from everyone. I wanted to live in a place like the island I remembered. Or in the woods. Maybe have a little farm. Quiet. No one to tell me what to do. I had to stay in the hospital longer than Dave. He went to school nearby and visited me. Neither of us had families to go home to. We kept in touch. And then my grandfather died, and left Simon and me King's Island and his house on the mainland."

"And you decided to move to Maine."

"Grampa's house was down the coast. Simon and I sold it. That's what Simon wanted, and I didn't care. I didn't want a house in town. Simon said King's Island was a joke. He wasn't interested in a rock out in the ocean. I said I was. He said I could have it if I paid the taxes and didn't bother him about it. When I got out of the VA Dave and I drove up to Haven Harbor. I borrowed a skiff and rowed out to the island. I wanted to see if it was the way I remembered. The great cormorants were nesting there. They hadn't done that years ago. Cormorants are special."

"They are," I agreed. "No other seabird I know doesn't have oil on their feathers and has to dry their wings in the sun after diving."

"People used to think that—about the oil. But it's because of the shape of their feathers that they don't dry easily. A marine patrol officer told me that. Cormorants are like statues, standing with their wings spread out. I rowed around the island and kept looking at them. King's Island was special. It was their place."

"Is that when you decided to move out there?"

"Not then. King's Island was a place for birds. I didn't want to disturb them. Dave liked Haven Harbor, though. When he heard the high school was looking for a biology teacher, he bought this house. I stayed with him for a while. Dave wanted me to meet people, get to know the town. But I wasn't looking for friends. I had Dave. I was looking for peace." Jesse took another drink of wine. "I've talked more tonight than I have in weeks. Maybe months. Feels strange."

"What did you do, then?"

"Bought a skiff and rowed around a lot, thinking. One day I rowed out to the island. Teenagers were there, throwing stones at the birds and laughing." Jesse's face hardened. "I chased them away, told them I'd tell the marine patrol. That's when I knew what I had to do."

"And that was?"

"Move to King's Island and protect the great cormorants."

How could anyone object to someone who wanted to protect birds? I wasn't a birder, but I'd always enjoyed the local birds. Gram had bird feeders all year long, and I used to watch over the cardinals and chickadees and goldfinches. One summer Gram told me cowbirds laid their eggs in other birds' nests. I was so angry I chased them away from the feeder whenever I saw them.

Gram had just smiled and said birds were like people; there were all kinds.

Sea- and shorebirds had always been a part of my life.

Herring gulls, great black-backed gulls, and laughing gulls hung around the wharf where I'd worked summers, steaming lobsters, in my teens. We'd posted signs saying to BEWARE OF GULLS! WATCH YOUR FOOD! and were amused whenever anyone ignored the warnings and a gull dove down and made away with a beak full of French fries . . . or even a lobster. Funny to see. Not fun to explain we didn't give refunds for stolen dinners.

Cormorants, or shags, as some people called them, never competed with the gulls on the wharves. They did their fishing in the harbor and at sea, not at restaurants or dumps. When I was little I'd called them "dinosaur birds." I thought they looked like the pterodactyls I'd seen in books.

Actually, they still did.

I left after Dave returned from taking Ruth home, my head full of birds and a strange man who'd found his purpose in life.

At home I looked up great cormorants and King's Island on my computer.

Great cormorants were larger than the more common double-crested cormorants and lived in Maine all year. (Double-crested cormorants wintered in southeastern states.) Only about a hundred pairs of great cormorants were left in Maine. They nested on one of seven islands. They were almost extinct because during the eighteenth and early nineteenth centuries people had eaten their eggs and killed them for food or fish bait.

King's Island qualified to have an official SEABIRD NESTING ISLAND sign posted saying it was closed to the public from April 1 until August 31 to protect nesting birds.

I assumed Jesse wasn't the public. But Jed Fitch was.

Those who owned such islands were supposed to "protect seabird nesting islands and adjacent waters from further development." But I couldn't find anything that said the owners *had* to do that.

What if Jesse's cousin Simon wanted to sell King's Island?

I hoped Dave connected Jesse to a good lawyer.

Selling half a small island didn't make sense. King's Island was only about eight acres.

The great cormorants needed a quiet place with trees and high ledges where they could build their large nests.

Not places with mansions or docks.

I turned off my computer and, instead of thinking about how quiet my house was tonight, I thought of large seabirds whose survival depended on people who didn't even know they existed.

Jesse, or someone else, had to convince his

cousin Simon that birds were more important than money.

I didn't know Simon, but I suspected that wouldn't be easy.

Chapter 12

"This needle work of mine can tell
When I was young I learned well
And by my elders I was taught
Not to spend my time for naught."
—Stitched by twelve-year-old Lydia
Archer in Salem, Massachusetts, in
1807. Lydia's sampler also included
three alphabets and an elaborate border
of strawberry vines and violets.

Ruth's call woke me the next morning.

"Angie? In the excitement of hearing Jesse's problems, I forgot to tell you I'd stitched up several Christmas tree balsam pillows."

"Your hands are better, then!" I said.

"Not as good as I'd like, but yes. Warm days are easier on arthritis than cold ones.

I stitched a little every time I took a break from writing. Shall I drop the pillows off with you?"

"Don't worry about that, Ruth. I'll stop by to get them later today."

"Good. I'll see you then."

I hadn't finished my morning coffee when my cell rang again.

"Angie, it's Patrick."

"Good morning!"

"I'm following up on our talk the other day. Any chance you'd be free to come for dinner tonight? Mom's going out with Uncle Gerry and his wife, and I hate to eat alone."

Uncle Gerry. The man who was trying to buy Simon's island. But without Skye and the Bentleys, seeing Patrick would be more relaxed. And I could find out more about why the Bentleys chose King's Island. "That would be great, Patrick. What time?"

"How does seven sound? I'll order enough for two."

"See you then." I finished my coffee while I made toast for breakfast. Dinner out two nights in a row. Who was I to complain about my social life?

I almost laughed when my telephone rang again. Was it a conspiracy? This time it was Sarah.

"Hi! I'm sorry I was a little rushed when you stopped in the other day. I couldn't sleep last night, so I stayed up needlepointing and finished the sampler for the Owens family. Should I bring it by tonight?"

"You've finished it already?" Barbara Owens had commissioned an old-fashioned sampler with an alphabet, their family tree going back two generations, and a simple picture of their home. It was to be a Christmas gift for their first granddaughter, Brittany. Sarah had worked it based on an early-nineteenth-century sampler done in Saco, Maine, and added a border of daisies and lupine. I'd seen it partially stitched several weeks before. It looked spectacular. "I'm dying to see your finished work. Why don't I come to the shop?"

"Great. I'll be here, per usual, all day," said Sarah.

"Can I bring you anything?" I asked. "I have to stop at the grocery this morning."

"A loaf of whole wheat bread and a dozen eggs would be great," said Sarah. "Oh, and a quart of skim milk. And a brownie mix. I've been dying for something chocolate."

"You've got it. I'll add your stuff to my shopping list."

The grocery aisles were full of people buying hamburgers and hot dogs for barbecues, marshmallows and chocolate for s'mores, and beer and chips. I picked up Sarah's items and the few things on my list. I almost bought a bottle of wine to take to Patrick's. But he was probably equipped with far fancier wine than I could afford. Instead, I bought a tart covered with fruit for our dessert.

"Thank you!" said Sarah, as I handed her the bag of her groceries. "This saves me from racing out right after I close tonight. How was Dave's dinner?"

"Fun," I said. "And we had an unexpected

guest." I filled her in on Jesse and his situation.

"That poor man," said Sarah. "It sounds as though all he has are those birds. It would be cruel to take them away from him."

"Not to speak of what might happen to the cormorants," I agreed. "I'm hoping his cousin won't want to sell. That would solve the whole problem. King's Island can't be as valuable as properties nearer shore where there are pipelines for fresh water and electricity. It would be hard for someone to make it livable. Maybe the Bentleys will find another island."

"They have so much money they may be able to offer a lot more than the island would normally be worth," Sarah cautioned.

"True. But I can't figure why they want that particular island. Did you know Gerry Bentley was Patrick's uncle?"

"No! How did you find that out?"

"I stopped in to see Patrick and Skye the other day. He was there; I met him. He's Patrick's father's younger brother."

"Interesting. Could be that explains why he wants the island. He has relatives in Haven Harbor."

"His yacht is almost as big as King's Island," I said drily. "Anyway, I came to see your sampler."

Sarah pulled a tissue paper–wrapped package from under her counter. "Here it is," she said. "I've been working on it in between customers for the past month. Several people commented on it. We might get other orders as a result." She held up crossed fingers.

"You did a beautiful job," I said, examining her even stitches and the script she used for the family tree. "I love the border."

"Me too," she admitted. "I found a book of flower patterns, and the yellows and purples went well with the other colors Mrs. Owens wanted. 'So build the hillocks gaily Thou little spade of mine Leaving nooks for Daisy And for Columbine.' "

"Emily?" I asked.

She nodded.

"Mrs. Owens wanted the sampler to look like an old one, though," I said, hating to criticize. "Your colors are so beautiful and bright. Most of the old samplers I've seen are much duller."

"True," said Sarah, "But they weren't dull when they were stitched. The colors have faded over the years. Families framed samplers, but that was before archival backing and glass that screens out strong sunlight. Mrs. Owens decided I should use the colors her daughter featured in her granddaughter's nursery. I can't wait to show it to her."

"She'll love it. How could she not?" I said, admiring it again. "But first I'd like to borrow and photograph it. I'm adding a section to our Web site that shows off the custom work we've done recently, and this is a first for Mainely Needlepoint."

"Bring it back soon, please! And you said you'd seen Patrick and Skye. How is he?"

"His hands are swollen and deformed," I admitted. "I didn't see his arms; he was wearing a long-sleeved shirt. He's still having occupational therapy."

Sarah shook her head. "Sad. Especially for an artist."

"But he seems pleased with the way the carriage house turned out."

"How does it look?"

"Gorgeous and modern, very different from the way it looked in June. You were right . . . he designed it and ordered furniture on-line, and had a Portland decorator set it up for him. The only part that isn't finished is his studio. He wants to do that himself."

"Can he paint yet?"

"I don't think so. But he's optimistic. Ted Lawrence was there, too. I'd never met him." Dave had said Sarah and Ted Lawrence had been spending a lot of time together. I waited to see what she'd say about him.

"He owns the gallery down the street" was all she replied. "He can help Patrick find sources for the art supplies he'll need."

"That's why he was there," I agreed. I was about to push a little further, to see if I could find out what the relationship was between Sarah and Ted, when the bell on her shop door jingled.

"Here," she said, wrapping the sampler again and handing it to me. "Take it and photograph it. I'll put the food you brought away in my kitchen before more customers arrive."

She headed to her second-floor apartment with her groceries, adding, "Keep me informed about your friend and his island. I'd like to know how it all turns out."

"I will," I said.

Her customer was examining a pile of kid gloves on one of the tables. I walked to the door slowly, so the customer wouldn't be alone in the shop. Sarah was back quickly. She waved as I turned and left.

I'd drop my own groceries off at home and then visit Ruth.

Chapter 13

"While I my needle ply with skill
With mimic flowers my canvas fill
O may I often raise
My thoughts to Him who made the flowers
And gave us all that we call ours
And render youthful prais." [sic]
—Elizabeth Grimes, age ten, created this
in cross-stitch, surrounding it with a man
shooting birds, a dog at his side, a tree,
sprays of colored flowers, and an African-
American man. In 1803 she sent the
sampler to her grandmother in England.

Ruth handed me the bag of pillow covers she'd stitched. I peeked in. "You added beads to the pine trees," I said. "We've never done that before. I love it."

"I was in a 'Christmas in July' mood."

"One of the Christmas shops put in an order for small cushion covers with trees and reindeer and holly last week," I said. "These will be perfect for them."

"I was looking at patterns the other day," said Ruth. "What about stitching mistletoe for the holidays? Maybe a small framed sign?"

"I like that idea," I agreed. "Why don't you

make one up? I'll add it to the list of our products on the Mainely Needlepoint website. I'm hoping people will order on-line. I'm going to include the chair covers and panel Dave's been working on, and the sampler Sarah finished."

Ruth smiled. "Good. I'm hoping I'll be able to do more stitching this fall. I'll be ready for a break from writing. If I sit at home without anything to do I'll go crazy. I have my Red Sox to watch if they make the play-offs, and I can do needlepoint at the same time. Can't do that with writing!"

"Sounds good. I can use all you can produce," I assured her.

"I've been thinking of that friend of Dave's we met last night . . . Jesse."

"Me too," I said. "I hope he can stay on his island."

"If there's a chance those great cormorants would be displaced, the Audubon Society or the Nature Conservancy would be interested. They don't have a lot of money to buy protected areas, but they might get involved if Jesse agreed to leave his rights to the island to them."

"I wonder who'd know about things like that."

"Check with Anna Winslow," said Ruth. "She'd know. I used to go with her to do the Christmas Bird Count. I'm pretty sure she still does it."

"The Christmas Bird Count?"

"Members of the Audubon Society all over the

country go out on Christmas Day and count the number of each species of birds in their area. Because it's on the same day every year, they get records of how many birds are where, and what species are moving because of global warming or other environmental changes."

"I don't know enough about birds to be able to count them!"

"Talk to Anna," Ruth said. "If you're interested, she could connect you, I'm sure."

"Have they been doing that a long time?"

"Since about 1900. And make sure you tell Anna about Jesse's situation. The Audubon Society would want to know if any threatened species was involved in an area real estate transaction."

"Got it," I said. I texted Anna and asked her to call me for details.

The afternoon went quickly. I spent more time than usual dressing for my dinner with Patrick.

Looking decent without looking as though I was trying was harder than I'd hoped.

I'd always told myself looks didn't matter. But I had my pride.

And maybe while I was having a delicious dinner with a charming man, I'd also be able to find out more about why Gerry Bentley wanted to buy King's Island.

Chapter 14

"Gold and silver braiding is much used for ornamental articles, for slippers, smoking caps, and cushions. The French braid is the best, wearing longer without tarnishing than any other. It should be sewed in with silk the exact color of the braid."

—from *The Ladies Guide to Needle Work, Embroidery, etc., Being a Complete Guide to All Kinds of Ladies' Fancy Work*, by S. Annie Frost. New York: Adams and Bishop, Publishers, 1877.

Patrick must have been watching for me; he opened the door to his carriage house before I'd had a chance to knock.

I held out the fruit tart.

"Thanks," he said, "that looks delicious." But he was looking at me, not at our dessert. His long-sleeved tan shirt was dressier than most men in Maine wore (they were addicted to T-shirts) and he looked relaxed and elegant. I hoped my carefully chosen outfit passed muster.

"I wanted to contribute to our meal," I said, sliding past him into the house. I'm not a blusher, but I could feel my cheeks reddening. I didn't want him to see I was flummoxed by him.

This time I knew it was Patrick who made me self-conscious, not his house or his mother.

"Dinner's here. I put it in the oven on 'warm' so we could sit and talk first," he said, following me into his living room.

A bouquet of daisies (florist-arranged-and-delivered daisies, not Maine wildflowers) brightened the decorator-arranged sideboard, and a selection of olives, cheeses, and sliced Italian salamis and sausages was arranged on his coffee table, next to Italian bread and shallow dipping bowls of olive oil.

"Hope you like Italian," he said. "This was the best I could pull together. Wine?"

"Wine would be lovely." Dave had served Italian lasagna the night before. It had been delicious. But I could easily spend the evening nibbling what Patrick had displayed here.

Moments later he handed me a balloon glass half full of white wine and returned to the kitchen for his. That was when I was certain one of his damaged hands worked better than the other.

"To Haven Harbor," he toasted, touching my glass with his.

"Haven Harbor," I agreed. "And your return."

"I'm sorry we didn't have time to chat more when you stopped in the other day," he said, dipping a piece of bread in the olive oil, adding a small piece of prosciutto and handing it to me. "We didn't expect to have company so soon after we'd arrived. But Uncle Gerry insisted on stopping in, since he was in the area."

I managed to avoid dribbling the olive oil over my clothes. "So he just happened to be here?"

"So he said. Although he hasn't sailed Down East in a while. I suspect he wanted to check on Mom and me. See the town and house we'd found here, and make sure I was doing all right. He sent flowers every few days when I was in the hospital, and called Mom a lot."

"What about your father?" I asked.

Patrick shook his head. "He and Mom were divorced when I was three. He died in a surfing accident a couple of years after that. I never really knew him. Uncle Gerry's the closest thing I have to a father."

"He's important to you, then."

Patrick winced. "I forgot. You didn't have a father, either."

"No. But I had Mama, at least for ten years, and I had Gram. I did all right. Having a father was probably more important for a boy."

"Maybe," he acknowledged. "I went to boarding school when Mom couldn't arrange her film schedule around my classes. Uncle Gerry used to call and invite me to stay with him on weekends and vacations if Mom was busy. He never had children of his own. He pretty much adopted me."

I nibbled on a couple of olives. Whatever wine we were sipping was spectacular.

"Small towns are full of gossip. I heard your uncle was looking at real estate in or near Haven Harbor."

"I'm surprised you heard, but yes. He is. He's been thinking of building a family retreat. He likes Haven Harbor, and I suspect he likes that I'm planning to stay here a good part of the year."

"Has he seen any land or buildings he likes?" I asked, hoping I looked innocent.

"One place, actually. He passed an island on his way here that attracted him. It looked deserted and large enough to build a small house—of course Uncle Gerry's definition of 'small' isn't most people's. And there'd be space for a helipad as well as a dock, which he liked."

"A helipad?" I tried not to choke.

"An easy way on and off the island. For business purposes, and, as you probably noticed, his new wife is pregnant. She wants all their homes to be close to hospitals, now and in the future." Patrick took another sip of his wine. "A helipad isn't so hard to build. I know several people who have them. And a helicopter could take anyone to town or even to Portland in minutes."

A helipad? "So has he inquired about the island?"

"He talked to Jed Fitch, the Realtor we used

to buy our place," Patrick went on. "Seems a crazy hermit lives there, but that shouldn't be a problem. The island's owned by that guy and one of his relatives in the Midwest."

No problem? Despite Jesse's insisting he wouldn't sell? Despite the nesting area? I was tempted to interrupt, to tell Jesse's side of the story. But maybe Patrick knew something that would help save King's Island. Instead of talking, I listened.

"Gerry's flying in the relative from the Midwest—Chicago, I think he said. Figures he'll make him a good offer and let that guy deal with the crazy relative. Have him declared incompetent. He's not thinking straight, living by himself on an island so far out."

Jesse, incompetent? He might be a little . . . individualistic. But no way was he incompetent! "So this Chicago guy is coming here, to Haven Harbor?"

"Tomorrow, I think. Mom said he could stay with us. Uncle Gerry thought that way we could keep track of him. Plus, there aren't many places to stay in the Harbor."

Not counting the bed-and-breakfast and the inn. Maybe neither of them was up to Uncle Gerry's standards.

Jesse needed to know Simon was going to arrive, all set to convince him to leave King's Island and his great cormorants. Or have him declared crazy. I needed to tell Dave. He'd know how to get in touch with Jesse.

"Excuse me? I'd like to use your bathroom," I said.

"Off the kitchen, to your right," Patrick said. "And why don't you bring the bottle of wine back with you? It's in the cooler on the counter."

The bathroom was as fresh and spotless as the rest of the house. I texted Dave. Gerry Bentley flying Jesse's cousin in tomorrow to convince him to sell. May try to declare Jesse incompetent. Warn Jesse? How? Talk when I get home later tonight. I flushed and ran the faucet.

Bathrooms were convenient places for privacy.

I didn't learn anything else about Gerry Bentley or King's Island. Patrick and I finished the bottle of wine. Our main course turned out to be a fabulous linguini with a cream sauce of wild mushrooms and sherry. My supermarket tart looked plebian after that, but Patrick said it was good.

I made a mental note: Buy an Italian cookbook.

I could boil a lobster and pull together a pretty darn good haddock chowder. I'd even made Gram's anadama bread recipe, and I was on target with blueberry muffins. But Patrick was used to more gourmet menus.

If Dave could cook, I could cook.

I pled exhaustion and headed for home, driving carefully after the wine.

As soon as I could I called Dave. He answered immediately.

"Got your text. Where did you learn that?"

"At the Wests' house. I had dinner there." I didn't mention Skye wasn't with us. It probably wouldn't make a difference to Dave, but still . . . "Simon's going to stay at Aurora. Bentley thinks Simon will agree to sell, and then 'take care of' his crazy relative who lives on King's Island."

Dave was silent. "You're right. We need to warn Jesse. Want to go with me in the morning? I can borrow a boat from one of my neighbors. I'll call him now."

"What time?"

"I have a school conference call at eight o'clock. How about nine thirty? Meet you down at the wharf."

"See you then."

Chapter 15

"Crochet work, a species of knitting originally practiced by the peasants in Scotland with a small hooked needle called a shepherd's hook, has, aided by taste and fashion, obtained a popularity second to no other kind of fancy work. It derives its present name from the French. The needle with which it is worked being, by them, from its crooked shape, termed 'crochet' . . . it is applied to almost every article that can be produced in knitting or embroidery."

—From *Ladies' Guide to Needle Work, Embroidery, Etc., Being a Complete Guide to All Kinds of Ladies' Fancy Work* by S. Annie Frost, New York: Adams & Bishop, Publishers, 1877.

Maybe it was the wine. I slept later than usual the next morning.

Anna Winslow's call roused me at seven thirty.

"Angie? I got your text yesterday, but before I talked with you I wanted to check with the Maine Audubon headquarters. They're concerned that King's Island might be sold and the nesting area disturbed. Have you heard anything more?"

Quickly I filled her in on what I'd learned last

night. "Dave and I are going out to the island this morning to warn Jesse that Simon's on his way here," I explained.

"The Audubon folks don't have the money to compete with Bentley for the island," Anna explained. "But if Jesse's being forced to sell, they're ready to mount a publicity campaign. Lots of people in Maine love cormorants."

"That's a great idea, Anna," I agreed. "How can I help?"

"When you get back from seeing Jesse, call me. In the meantime let me think about what we can do."

"Ruth's the one who suggested I contact you. And, of course, Dave's upset about the birds, and about his friend."

"Hmm. Most of the Mainely Needlepointers. As I remember you have a friend at Channel Seven in Portland, right?"

"I went to high school with Clem Walker."

"Would she be willing to help, too?" Anna asked.

"I don't think Jesse will want a lot of publicity," I cautioned. "He's a very quiet man. That's why he lives on King's Island."

"But he cares about those birds, and he wants to stay on the island, right?"

"Sure."

"Then he may have to cope with a little attention. But don't promise him too much," she advised. "I'm not sure exactly what we can do. But birders and environmentalists can be a strong lobby. I don't know how Gerry Bentley feels about the environment, but I wouldn't think he'd want a lot of negative publicity."

I had no idea Captain Ob's wife was so media savvy. "You're right. But the first thing to do is let Jesse know his cousin is coming to town and see if he has any ideas." I suspected Jesse's idea would be to reject any help that would disturb his current way of life. But Anna was right. I didn't know. Jesse cared a lot about those birds. "I'll call you when Dave and I get back from the island," I promised. "Probably early this afternoon."

I dressed in heavier clothing than usual. A few miles off the coast winds could be strong and temperatures colder. I pulled a sweatshirt over my T-shirt and picked up a windbreaker to wear on the boat.

We couldn't waste time.

Jed Fitch might be drafting papers for the sale of King's Island right now, thinking of his share of the purchase price. I suspected Gerry Bentley was used to getting his own way.

Not everyone in town would be thinking of the fate of the cormorants.

Reverend Tom—Tom, I corrected myself—had said it would be good for the town if the Bentleys had a home here. He'd also said Ed Campbell from the Chamber of Commerce felt the same way. Between the two of them, they could rally as many people as the environmentalists could. Plus, Ted Lawrence seemed to be a friend of Gerry Bentley, and, of course, Patrick and Skye would be on his side. They all had money.

Saving King's Island for Jesse and his great cormorants wasn't going to be easy.

I got a couple of life jackets from our barn and headed to the town wharf.

Chapter 16

"Were innocence our garb alone,
And natures blooms our only pride.
The needle still had been unknown
And worth the want of art supplied.
Virtue wit with science join'd
Refine the manners, form the mind.
And when with industry they meet,
The female character is complete."
—Stitched in 1813 by Esther G. Cobb,
eleven years old, in Springfield, Vermont.
Her sampler also included three alphabets,
a border of strawberry vines, an urn,
flowers, two trees, a woman, two dogs,
and two cats, probably family pets.

When I got to the dock Dave was standing in a bright red eighteen-foot boat, pouring gasoline into the outboard engine.

"The *Sweet Life*?" I asked, reading the boat's name.

"Owner's retired. If I'm in the mood for a turn around the Three Sisters or the harbor, he trusts me to borrow his."

"You were in the navy, and you don't have a boat?"

"I was on a submarine," he pointed out. "I

don't have anything against boats, but I figure I've done my time on the water. You don't have a boat, either."

"True enough. But I wasn't in the navy. And I've only been back in Maine since May. Owning one's on my bucket list." After he put down the red gasoline tank I handed him the life jackets. "Figured we should have these on board."

"Good catch. Coast guard wouldn't approve our going out without them."

"We can just have them in the boat, right?" A life jacket would be hard to fasten over my sweatshirts.

"Legally, yup. Besides—you can swim, right?"

"In a pool or near a beach or in a lake, sure. But several miles out on a rough sea?"

"Agreed." Dave reached out a hand to help me into the *Sweet Life*. "Me too."

Neither of us put on the life jackets.

"Anna Winslow called this morning," I shared. "She talked to the Maine Audubon folks. They're on Jesse's side. Or, really, they're on the side of the great cormorants. She suggested a publicity program to embarrass Bentley so he wouldn't want to buy King's Island."

"I like that idea. Let's see what Jesse has to say about it when we tell him his cousin Simon's heading this way."

I nodded and cast off as Dave pulled the choke.

I hadn't been in a small outboard for years.

104

I pulled on my windbreaker as we expertly threaded among the moored boats in the harbor and headed between two of the Sister Islands, out to sea.

The ocean wasn't rough, but the tide was coming in. We headed into the waves. Between the noise of the motor and the thumping of the hull hitting the waves we couldn't hear each other, so we didn't talk.

I sat in the bow, taking deep breaths of sea air and making mental notes. I should move my dream purchase of a small wooden boat up on my bucket list. A used one wouldn't be too expensive after the season was over. I could caulk and paint this winter.

We passed two lobstermen working their traps. Farther offshore a small boat with orange sails was taking advantage of the morning's stiff breeze.

Sunlight sparkled on the waves and salt spray dampened my hands and face.

No wonder Jesse had decided to live out beyond the harbor, beyond having to cope with other people. Whatever made him decide to live, as the townspeople called him, solitary, at this moment I could understand it. He didn't have to think about what people thought of him. He never had to worry about what he wore. Or whether he cooked as well as others, or was as attractive.

There was enviable freedom in that.

For now, I focused on the ocean. The dark waters of the North Atlantic had ruled these seas since before fishermen and mariners challenged them. And despite all of today's technology, it was still exciting to tempt the elements. Men (and some women) had been doing it since before anyone remembered.

Monuments to those claimed by the waters stood in many Maine harbor towns, including Haven Harbor. Most old families in town, including mine, counted names on those monuments as their own. Every spring people gathered for a blessing of the fleet and the reading of names of those lost at sea since 1676, when Haven Harbor was founded. Townspeople stood silently as the names were read out and bells rang in their memory.

I'd missed the ceremony this year. Would I still be in Haven Harbor next April?

My life here was full. I was getting used to living alone in my big house. What would it be like to live alone on an island, with only birds to keep you company? I shivered. Jesse's lifestyle sounded good at first, but it wasn't for me.

What if he had an accident on the island? Or ran out of food in a storm?

To my left a cormorant stood on a buoy, his drying wings outstretched as though welcoming the winds and tides.

His ancestors had been here generations before mine.

But if his nesting grounds were destroyed, his species could end, a victim of people who valued themselves above other creatures of nature.

We passed a few small islands and headed southeast, toward a dark narrow ridge barely visible on the horizon. Jesse's home. The nesting ground of the great cormorants. King's Island.

I didn't want our journey to end.

But it did.

King's Island was starkly beautiful, like the black-and-white engravings of nineteenth-century Maine hanging in the Haven Harbor Library. Tall skeletal pines bent by repeated winter winds and ice stood above forbidding granite cliffs on the sparsely wooded island. Above us, in the tops of those trees, were the large bulky cormorant nests Jesse was protecting. As we approached we could see the twigs and driftwood, grass and seaweed they were built with, and the white bird droppings covering the tree trunks and branches.

Where could we moor and land on this island of granite?

I looked over at Dave, who anticipated my question and pointed at one end of the island.

Would I have to wade ashore? I glanced at my sneakers. But Dave hadn't taken his off yet, and he seemed to know where he was going.

I focused back on the trees, where several

cormorants, their dark wings and thin bodies almost hidden in the branches, perched. Gulls were also on and above the island, and as we neared shore three curious harbor seals looked up at us from a ledge half covered by the tide. We were close enough to see their large, dark eyes. One slipped off the ledge and followed us for a few yards before disappearing beneath the water.

Around the end of the island the cliffs dropped off dramatically and became sharp ledges leading from the island into the sea. Anyone looking to land here would need to know exactly how to thread their way through the ledges to the shore. Dave was doing just that, heading around a barren point.

King's Island was beautiful. No wonder Jesse loved it.

But what made Gerry Bentley think of it as a place for a family house? A home for wildlife, yes. But these ledges and cliffs were forbidding. I hadn't seen a welcoming harbor yet, as we rounded the point and approached the seaward side.

That's where we passed a two-by-three-foot sign rising out of the water, picturing the silhouette of a large bird in flight. We were close enough so I could read the words: FRIENDS OF MAINE'S SEABIRD ISLANDS. AREA CLOSED TO PUBLIC USE TO PROTECT SENSITIVE NESTING BIRDS.

Not far from the sign the rocks divided to reveal a small beach. Not a sandy beach, like the ones at Reid State Park or Popham or even Pemaquid. It was more like Haven Harbor's Pocket Cove Beach: a clearing between the cliffs where a boat could pull into a small open area covered with sea stones.

Dave headed us in.

Jesse's gray skiff, at first almost invisible, was pulled into the sea grasses above the small beach. I looked for a buoy that would hold a pulley line and, sure enough, a black buoy, almost hidden in the waves, bobbed in front of us.

Dave steered around it, heading, instead, directly for the beach.

I looked up at the cliffs surrounding us, hoping to see more great cormorants. Instead, I saw a shadow in the woods above.

As I squinted to see what it was, sunlight caught a streak heading directly toward us.

Dave saw it, too, and dodged. The arrow hit the water next to the boat. "Jesse! It's me!" he yelled at the cliff, but as the second arrow hit his calf his hand slipped from the tiller and he fell backward onto the deck, slamming his head on the side of the *Sweet Life*.

Chapter 17

"Beneath our feet and o'er our head,
Is equal warning given;
Beneath us lie the countless dead,
Above us is the heaven.
Their names are graven on the stone,
Their bones are in the clay,
And ere another day is done
Ourselves may be as they."
　　　—First lines of an Anglican funeral hymn
　　stitched in silk on linen by twelve-year-old
Alletha Frances Findley below five alphabets
and a row of numbers. Dated May 20, 1839,
　　in Washington City (Washington, DC).

"Dave!"

He lay, stunned and bleeding heavily, on the floorboards.

His hand had hit the tiller when he fell. Instead of heading for shore we were now rolling with the waves, heading toward the ledge on the sea side of the beach. We were going to capsize or hit rocks if we didn't change direction. Fast.

I scrambled to the prow, crawling over Dave to get to the tiller, and turned us again toward shore.

I focused on the ledges beneath us as we headed for shallow waters near the shore. I didn't have time to look for the figure I'd seen in the woods, but no other arrows headed our way.

As soon as I'd straightened us out I pushed one of the life jackets under Dave's head.

The arrowhead had pierced his jeans, pushing denim with it into the wound. Blood seeped through his pants and dripped onto the deck, mixing with salt water that had washed over the side of the boat.

I'd always heard salt water was an antiseptic.

At least Dave's head was out of the water.

If the person who shot at us was Jesse, maybe he *was* crazy. Dave was his friend.

His only friend, as far as I could tell. Why would he shoot Dave?

And if it hadn't been Jesse, who else was on King's Island? Jesse's skiff was the only other boat I'd seen.

I slowed the engine. I didn't want the boat's hull to scrape the stony beach, but I didn't see another way to tie the boat. Dave couldn't help.

When we were within feet of the shore I turned off the motor and pulled it up so the propeller wouldn't hit the rocks.

Jesse, disheveled and wearing only torn cutoffs, ran out of the woods toward us.

"Jesse! How do I tie the boat?"

He ran into the frigid water and gestured that I should throw him our line.

He pulled the boat closer to the dry stones on

111

the upper beach and tied the end of the line to a tree, leaving a little slack. The tide had better be coming in. If it was going out, we'd be stranded here—me, a wounded man, and a crazy.

"Get out of the boat," he said. I slipped off my sneakers and stepped into the few inches of frigid water at the prow.

"Dave's hurt," I said unnecessarily.

Dave tried to get up, holding his hand around the arrow, pressing to stanch the blood.

"Sorry, friend," said Jesse. Jesse was a lot stronger than I'd given him credit for. He reached down, picked Dave up, and carried him onto the beach. Jesse was trying to be gentle, but Dave was clearly in pain. "You always come alone. I saw two people in the boat."

"So you shot me," said Dave, wincing. "Had a few close experiences in life, and in the navy, but never thought I'd be shot by an arrow. Why, Jesse? Why?"

"Protection," Jesse explained. "And to scare anyone off who tries to land."

"Not a gun?" I asked.

"Not after Iraq," said Jesse, quietly. "No guns. Never. And no explosions. No fireworks. Don't want to disturb the birds. Arrows are silent."

"So they are," Dave said. "And accurate. That was some shooting—to hit a man in a rocking boat at that distance."

"It's a compound bow. And I've practiced."

"So I see. But why you'd have to hit my bad leg?"

The two friends managed to grin at each other.

"Have you any bandages? Dave's bleeding," I pointed out, obviously. "And the arrow's still sticking in his leg."

"Don't touch the arrow!" said Dave, quickly, although his voice was fading.

"No bandages. Take off his shirt," Jesse said.

"Looks worse than it is," Jesse pronounced, although I was pretty sure the wound was serious. Dave was bleeding too much for it to be a minor injury. Jesse handed me Dave's shirt. "Soak it in the water."

Gram must have been right. Or Jesse's grandfather had given him the same instructions. I soaked the shirt in the cleanest water I could find—this far from land the waves didn't carry in much rubbish—and wrung it out.

For the next few minutes Jesse and I took turns pressing the wet shirt against the wound. I rinsed the shirt out a couple of times. Gradually Dave's bleeding slowed and then stopped.

"I'll feel better after we get you to an emergency room and you've had a tetanus shot and stitches," I said. "Plus, you hit your head hard."

"My head hurts," Dave admitted, softly. "But don't worry, Angie. My tetanus shots are up-to-date."

"Why are you here?" asked Jesse. "I saw you yesterday."

Dave forced himself to talk. "I'd stay around and make polite conversation, but I suspect Angie's right. I should have someone look at this leg. We came out here because we needed to talk to you. Did you go to see that lawyer like I told you to?"

"After I left you yesterday. Aaron Irving. I made a new will. The way it was set up before, if either of us died the other one inherited the whole place."

A new will wouldn't solve Jesse's current problem. "Simon's coming to Haven Harbor," I put in. "Today."

"What?" said Jesse, turning toward me. "He hasn't been here for years. Since we were kids."

"He's coming now. Bentley's paying for his airfare, and he'll be staying at Aurora, the Wests' estate. They're friends of the Bentleys." I didn't take the time to explain they were relatives. "He'll be close to people trying to convince him to sell."

"He can't sell my island without me," said Jesse.

"The Bentleys have a lot of money. I don't know what pressures they could put on him. Or you." I was tempted to tell him about the possibility of Simon getting him declared incompetent, but he looked upset enough now.

Jesse shrugged. "That Realtor guy, he said I couldn't say 'no.' He said he had alternatives. I don't know what he was hinting. My lawyer said the papers looked in order. The will was simple. I signed it. Might make a difference someday. But I feel pretty healthy right now."

"I felt pretty healthy until a few minutes ago," Dave put in.

"I didn't mean to hurt you." Jesse's eyes filled. "Buddy, believe me. I didn't."

Dave's skin was getting more ashen. We were a long way from the Haven Harbor Hospital emergency room.

I decided to add one more piece of information before we got Dave back in the *Sweet Life*. "You met Ruth Hopkins the other night," I said.

Jesse turned from Dave to focus on me. "The old lady who talked a lot?"

"Right. Well, she called another friend of ours, who's a birder, and *she* called the state Audubon Society. They'd like to get involved. Publicize your situation. They want to save the great cormorants, too."

"I don't need more people," said Jesse, pacing as I held the compress on Dave's calf. He was bleeding again. "I'm settled now. I have to say 'no.' That's all. I don't need old ladies involved." He shook his head. "Me and the birds just want to be left alone."

"No one's going to bother you," said Dave.

"At least I hope not. But that Bentley guy has me worried. If money can change anyone's mind, he can do it."

"I don't need money," said Jesse. "My disability checks and the interest from my share of selling my grandfather's house take care of me fine. Got enough to pay the taxes and feed myself. What more do I need?"

"Taxes," I said, thinking. "Haven Harbor taxes?"

"Five hundred dollars a year, due every November first."

Five hundred dollars a year wasn't much. How hard would it be for the town to raise those taxes? This wasn't the moment to find out.

"I have to get Dave back to Haven Harbor," I said. "He needs to see a doctor. Help me get him back into the boat."

Jesse nodded. "Sorry, man. This is going to hurt." He got on one side of Dave and I got on the other, and we lifted Dave back toward, and into, the *Sweet Life*. We stretched him out on the floorboards as best we could. I tried to bail, but it was taking too long. Instead, I put both life jackets under Dave's head.

As I started the motor Jesse cocked his head. "Listen," he said.

The sound of another, louder, motor was clear over the water.

"Who else would be out here?" Dave asked.

"No one's supposed to be here during nesting season," Jesse said bitterly. "But they are."

We looked out past the *Sweet Life*. The boat we'd heard was a lobster boat. We watched as it headed around the island. Four people were on board. None of them looked as though they were lobstering. A fishing boat was silhouetted on the horizon beyond it.

"Do many lobster boats come out this way?" I asked Jesse.

He shook his head. "In winter, after lobsters move to colder waters, a few people drop traps nearby. Waters are getting warmer. Every year there are a few more traps. But not in August."

"Does anyone ever come ashore?" I asked.

"Coast guard and marine patrol check on me every so often, especially when storms are heavy. They bring food and water and try to convince me to come into town for the winter. I do fine here."

The wind was picking up. We'd had a stiff breeze coming over. I'd been glad of my two sweatshirts, but now I pulled one off and tried to cover Dave's leg.

King's Island would be frigid in winter.

"Go. Take care of Dave. I can take care of my island. Know how to use the outboard?" asked Jesse.

"Sure. Been a few years, but it works the way it always did."

"Sorry, friend," he said, as he and I pushed the boat toward the water. I hoped Dave's weight wouldn't force the hull onto the sharper small stones on the beach. "I never meant to hurt you."

Dave nodded. "I know."

"Fair winds," Jesse added.

Dave needed to get to the hospital. And we had a bumpy ride ahead of us.

It wouldn't be a pleasant journey.

Chapter 18

"May I govern my passions with absolute
  sway,
And grow wiser and better as strength wears
  away,
Without gout or stone, by a gentle decay."
  —Verse taken from an old English poem
  and stitched on a sampler by thirteen-year-
  old Ann Tottington Rudd in Alexandria,
  Virginia, in 1817. Ann was a patriot. She
  also stitched, "George Washington was
  born February 11th A.D. 1732 appointed
General of the American Armies A.D. 1775.
  Resigned A.D. 1783. Elected President of
the United States A.D. 1789. Resigned A.D.
  1796. Appointed General of the American
  Armies A.D. 1798 and died universally
  lamented December 14th A.D. 1799."

The trip back to Haven Harbor seemed to take
forever. Dave pushed the life jackets aside and sat
up a little, pressing his hand on his calf to keep
the blood from flowing. But after a few minutes
he passed out, falling back on the jackets.

I couldn't help. The *Sweet Life* was a little
boat, and the deep water currents tossed it from
one side to another. I had to keep my hand on the

tiller, directing our helm into the swells. Dave groaned as we hit each wave.

Would he bleed out? Had he passed out because he'd lost so much blood, or because he'd hit his head on the boat as he fell?

I kept focusing on that arrow. I hadn't used a gun before I moved to Arizona, but most of my friends in Maine had hunted. A few dads had used crossbows. I'd never heard of what Jesse called a compound bow, but it had done the job.

Hunting accidents were covered in Maine school first aid courses. We were taught never to remove a bullet or arrow. You didn't know what you might damage in the process. Some students argued about that. After all, in movies the hero or heroine pulled the arrow out, or dug out the bullet, and went on to save the day.

That was fiction, we were told. *Get the victim to a hospital as quickly as possible* had been drilled into us.

I remembered that. But I hadn't counted on being in a small boat three miles out with a badly wounded man.

The sea water under the floorboards was now crimson.

We only had a sixty-five horsepower motor. We were going as fast as we could.

How long did it take Jesse to row to land? If he ever injured himself on the island, how could he get help?

But that wasn't my problem today.

Two dark double-crested cormorants flew past us, low above the water.

A week ago I hadn't even noticed there were different kinds of cormorants.

Right now I cussed all of them.

If it weren't for the damn cormorants Jesse might not be living on an isolated island, afraid for their, and his, future.

And I wouldn't be bumping through waves with Dave unconscious on the floor of this boat.

About halfway back to the harbor I started trying to get my cell phone to work. Every couple of minutes I dialed 911.

Finally, with the Three Sisters islands in clear sight, I reached an operator.

Quickly I explained where I was, where I was headed, and why I needed help.

The dispatcher promised an ambulance would meet us at the town wharf.

That was all I could do.

I hoped Dave hadn't lost too much blood.

Chapter 19

"I have no Mother for she died
When I was very young.
But still her memory round my heart
Like morning mists has hung.
I know she is in heaven now
That holy place of rest
For she was always good to me
The good alone are blest.
Oh, mother, mother in my heart
Thy image still shall be
That I may hope in heaven at last
That I may meet with thee."

—From unusual, anonymous sampler
stitched in red and blue threads on white
linen, including simple flowers, trees, and
a house and fenced-in yard. Colors and
simplicity typical of Pennsylvania German
samplers; probably stitched about 1820.

True to the dispatcher's promise, Haven Harbor's ambulance was parked near the dock.

Summer guests and year-round residents were milling about on Water Street, watching. Expecting excitement. Ambulances don't usually park and wait for those who need them.

Memories of past marine skills came back

to me. I managed to bring the *Sweet Life* in smoothly, with only a small shudder as we docked. Four EMTs were waiting for us with a stretcher. I tossed the rope to another man who'd docked his outboard. He tied us up as two of the medical teams climbed into the boat.

"When was he shot? How long ago?" asked a young woman not much older than me.

I glanced at my phone. "About forty-five minutes."

"Do you have another arrow?" she asked, as two of her companions carefully slid a board down into the boat and strapped Dave onto it.

"Another arrow?" I asked, confused. "He was only shot once."

"Another arrow of the same kind. So the doctors can see what the tip is like," she explained.

I shook my head. I hadn't thought about asking Jesse for another arrow. "Dave was in the boat when he was shot," I added. "He hit his head when he fell."

"How long has he been unconscious?"

"Maybe twenty minutes." It had seemed forever.

"Okay," she said, holding out a hand to help me onto the dock. "We're going to take him to Haven Harbor Emergency. What's his name again?"

"Dave—David—Percy."

"I know Mr. Percy," called down the youngest of the team carrying Dave's body up the ramp and toward the ambulance. "He was my high school biology teacher."

The woman in charge made a note and followed the others.

I stood, not sure what to do next. My mind pulsed with relief and fragmented thoughts. The boat needed swabbing. Dave was in good hands. I should go to the hospital. I'd left my car at home.

The ambulance took off. The hospital was several miles away. I'd have to go home to get my car.

"Can I help, Angie?" Haven Harbor Police Sergeant Pete Lambert was at the top of the ramp. He and I had become, if not friends, then at least close acquaintances, in the past months.

"Dave Percy was shot. With an arrow. They're taking him to the hospital."

"Shot? Where?"

"King's Island," I said, without thinking. "We were pulling into the beach there."

"Did you see who shot him?"

"Jesse Lockhart." Pete was taking notes. "It was an accident! He's a friend of Dave's."

Pete ran his hand through his thin brown hair. "Need a ride to the hospital?"

"Please," I said.

The crowd at the dock was dispersing. Pete herded me through the few curious people who were left.

"What happened, Pete?"

"Was he really shot with a bow and arrow?"

Pete ignored their questions and opened the door of his police car.

He saved his questions for the ride to the hospital. "Dave Percy's one of your needle-pointers, right?"

"Yes."

"And you two were just out for a pleasant boat trip this morning?"

"We were going to see Jesse."

I noted that Pete hadn't questioned who Jesse was, or called him The Solitary. He knew who he was.

"Angie, I'm going into the hospital with you to see how Dave is. See if he can talk to me."

"He was unconscious when the ambulance took him."

"Let's hope he'll be all right. But I'll have to put together a report."

"A report?"

"Shootings, accidental or otherwise, need to be written up." Pete didn't look at me directly. "I'll admit I've never had a situation like this one. We don't have a lot of shootings in Haven Harbor. But when we do, they involve guns, not bows and arrows."

"It was an accident," I repeated again as we pulled into the emergency room parking lot. "Dave and Jesse are friends."

Pete put his hand on my arm. "I don't know if

Jesse Lockhart had a license for a crossbow. But it's not hunting season. And he sure shouldn't have been shooting at anyone."

"I think he said it was a compound bow." Did that make a difference? I knew a little about guns. All I knew about bows or arrows was what I'd seen in movies.

Pete made a note. "I'll check regulations. But no matter what he used, he shot someone. I'm going to have to call in Ethan Trask."

"Ethan?" That wasn't good. Ethan was a Maine state homicide detective.

"We're going to have to question Jesse Lockhart, Angie."

"Question him?"

"I hope Dave'll recover. But even if he does, right now it sounds like attempted murder to me."

Chapter 20

"He shall defend and guide thy course,
Through life's uncertain sea,
Till thou art landed on the shore
Of blefs'd Eternity."
             —Words stitched (along with birds,
butterflies, flowers, and a bowl of fruit) by
Mary Ann Coppen "in the thirteenth year
of her age, 1826." Mary Ann lived in Nova
Scotia. Sampler-stitching was not as common
in Canada as it was in the United States,
so Mary Ann may have been a descendant
of one of the Tory families who moved to
Canada after the American Revolution.

Attempted murder?

All the way back to Haven Harbor I'd been
hoping—praying—Dave would be all right. I'd
been angry at Jesse for shooting him.

It was an accident. It had to be. But legally . . .

Jesse'd said he hadn't meant to hurt Dave. But
he'd aimed and shot him. "Will you or Ethan
have to go to King's Island to talk with Jesse?" I
asked.

"Unless he comes to us," Dave said. "Under the
circumstances, it would be smart of him to come
in for questioning."

Jesse would never turn himself in. He chose to live on King's Island so he could be apart from the rest of the world.

He knew local coast guard people, and the marine patrol. But state troopers? Jesse had already proved what he'd do if someone he didn't know came out to King's Island. He'd shot his best friend because he was confused; because I was in the boat, too. What would he do if police showed up?

Pete and I went into the emergency room together.

Luckily, hospitals in small towns weren't as picky as those in cities about sharing information. Especially if you were accompanied by a local police sergeant.

"You're the one who brought Mr. Percy in, on a boat," said Dr. Karen Mercer after Pete and I had convinced the receptionist we had a legitimate interest in Dave's well-being. "Does he have any close relatives?"

"I don't know," I answered. "He's never mentioned anyone." I knew less than I thought about my friend. "He teaches at the high school."

"I recognized him."

"How is he? Is he conscious? Will he be all right?"

"He's still unconscious, receiving blood and antibiotics. We're preparing him for surgery, to remove that arrow. We'll know more after the surgery."

"He hit his head on the side of the boat, too."

She made a note. "We'll schedule a CAT scan. He may have a concussion."

"How long before he wakes up? Or you know his condition?" Pete asked.

"At least two hours. Maybe four. Maybe longer. We won't know anything before he's out of surgery."

I was wet with salt water and blood, and hungry and thirsty.

"There's nothing you can do now, and he won't know you're here. He might later," Dr. Mercer added.

I got it. I turned to Pete. "I'll go home and change. Then I'll come back."

"Nothing I can do now either. I've seen injured hunters before. Dave won't be able to tell us much until tomorrow. But I will have to bring Jesse in."

Injured hunters. But Dave wasn't an injured hunter. He'd been hunted.

We walked outside together.

"Jesse lives alone out there. He only has a skiff. He won't disappear. What if I can get him to turn himself in?" I asked. "He knows me. Not as well as he knows Dave, but maybe he'll listen to me." Especially since he wouldn't be able to protect his island and his birds if he were in jail.

Pete looked at me. "You were out there. You saw what happened. You could be hurt."

"I don't think he'd hurt me," I said, I hoped convincingly. "Give me a chance. But first I need to know if Dave's going to be all right. Jesse will want to know." Plus, if Dave didn't survive, Pete wouldn't be talking about *attempted* murder. If that happened, I wouldn't be able to help Jesse.

"Lockhart's been out on that island a couple of years now," Pete said. "You're right. Chances are he won't go anywhere today. And he's been a nuisance before this, but never violent. I'll give you until sunset tomorrow to bring him in so I can talk with him. I'll try to get Ethan here, too."

I gave Pete an unprofessional hug. "Thank you. I'll do everything I can to get him to town."

"Anything I can do for you now?"

"Drive me home?" I asked. I was exhausted. And I'd promised to go back to the hospital tonight and to King's Island tomorrow.

"Climb in," he said, opening the door of his police car.

I didn't live far from the hospital, normally a five- or six-minute drive. But this was August. Out-of-state cars filled the streets, and we crept back downtown. I felt as though I'd left home months ago.

I didn't care if anyone saw me being escorted by the police. I just wanted to get home.

How would I get to King's Island? I didn't even

have a boat. Would Dave's friend let me borrow the *Sweet Life*? I'd need to bail it out and wipe up the blood. And get more gasoline.

I didn't even know who owned the *Sweet Life*.

Getting to King's Island seemed impossible.

I desperately needed to rest.

Pete pulled into my driveway. "Keep in touch, Angie," said Pete. "You have my number, right? Even if I'm off-duty. Let me know if you change your mind about talking to Jesse. Plus—I want to know how Dave is, too. He has a good rep around town. Kids at the high school love his poison classes."

Dave was probably the only high school biology teacher in the state of Maine who brought poison plants into his classroom to teach his students what they should look out for when they were camping or hiking. Or hunting. Dave's poison garden, where he grew dangerous plants, was well-known in town.

"I'll keep in touch with the hospital and talk with Ethan, see if he has any advice. One piece of good news for your friend on the island: While you were talking to the doctor I made a fast call. Anyone using a crossbow has to have a license. A compound bow doesn't require one."

"Good," I said. One thing in Jesse's favor.

"But no hunting's allowed on King's Island no matter the month. So whatever happened out there was illegal."

I looked at him.

"I know. You said it was an accident. But you have to understand what the law says."

"Thanks, Pete."

"Take care of yourself, Angie. Today wasn't easy, and tomorrow won't be either."

"I know."

I walked up the slate path from the driveway to my wide front porch.

A white package was in front of my door.

Chapter 21

"Jesus permit thy gracious Name to stand
As the first efforts of an Infant's Hand,
And while her fingers o'er this canvas move,
Engage her tender ears to seek thy Love."
    —Sampler inscribed "Mary Christeen
    Bohlayer age 13 years, Washington City,
    1842." Mary's sampler also pictures a
    brick house with closed shutters and vases
    of flowers. The daughter of a butcher
    who'd emigrated from Germany, Mary
    married in 1852 and gave birth to six
    children before her death in 1867.

I hadn't been expecting any packages. Then I saw the small sticker on the side. COASTAL FLORIST. Someone sent me flowers? Dave was the one in the hospital.

For a moment I wondered who'd died. I'd only gotten flowers once before: My boss in Arizona had sent them after I told him Mama was dead and I wouldn't be returning to Mesa. At least not right away.

I opened the box and took a step back. These were serious flowers. Quickly I counted. Three dozen long-stemmed red and pink and white roses.

The card was tucked in a corner. "With hope we'll have many evenings as lovely as last night's. Patrick."

Patrick. I hadn't thought of him once today.

I scrounged through the kitchen cabinets and found a vase. The roses looked out of place on the pine kitchen table, but they were lovely.

Maybe Patrick sent roses to everyone he had dinner with.

I should call him.

Catching a glimpse of myself in the front hall mirror, I decided first I needed to get cleaned up. And eat. And calm down.

Time was important. I looked longingly at the claw-footed tub in the bathroom, but opted for a fast shower instead.

Then I filled the tub with cold water and threw my bloodstained clothes in.

The shower, a clean pair of jeans, and a bright red T-shirt (almost as red as the roses) revived me.

I gulped a tuna sandwich and a few carrot sticks (vegetables were healthy, right?) as I sipped a little wine. Only half a glass; I had to drive back to the hospital. I'd have another, or something stronger, when I got back from the hospital. To celebrate, when I knew Dave was going to be all right.

I should tell the Mainely Needlepointers about Dave. But where to start? Who to call?

And what to say? I didn't even know what condition he was in.

When in doubt . . . I called Gram. She answered immediately. "Thank goodness! Are you all right, Angel? Carole Fitch told me she saw you down at the wharf covered with blood. I've been trying to reach you for hours. I was about to call the hospital."

I should remember to check for messages. After I'd called 911 I'd turned off my phone so I could focus on Dave. "Sorry, Gram. I'm fine. And home. Dave's in surgery. I'm going back to the hospital in half an hour or so."

"What happened?"

I'd only said a few words when Gram interrupted. "Stay right there, Angel. I'm coming over. I'll go back to the hospital with you. Dave's been my friend since he came to Haven Harbor." She clicked off before I could say anything more.

I quickly called Ruth and Anna, filling them in on what had happened. "What's going to happen to the island now? And the cormorants?" Anna asked.

"Right now I'm more worried about Dave," I said. *And Jesse,* I added to myself. I was worried Jesse would be arrested.

I called Patrick to thank him for the flowers, but he didn't answer. I was relieved. I didn't feel like making small talk. He didn't know Dave or Jesse, and right now I didn't want to go through the whole story again.

Before I'd put my cell down Gram walked in the front door and gave me a hug.

Then she stared. "Where did all those roses come from?"

"Patrick West sent them. We had dinner together last night."

"Just dinner?"

"*Yes*, Gram."

"That Patrick's always seemed like an old-style gentleman." She sniffed the roses. "Hothouse roses. They don't smell."

"I could take some to Dave."

"If he's in surgery or recovery or intensive care they won't let him have flowers. Roses will wait a day." Gram took one more hopeful sniff and then shook her head. "So. Let's get over to the hospital. You can tell me the details about Dave on our way. You sounded exhausted on the phone, so we'll go in my car. It's out front."

On the drive I filled her in on everything that had happened. Well, almost everything. I didn't mention I'd promised to go back to King's Island to convince Jesse to be questioned in Haven Harbor. I still had no idea how I was going to do that.

"So The Solitary—sorry, Angie, but that's how I think of him—shot Dave?"

"When Dave goes out to King's Island he's usually alone. Jesse's not good with a lot of people." Although he'd been all right meeting

Ruth and me at Dave's home the other night. "He shot down at us from a cliff. He couldn't see exactly who was in the boat."

"I didn't know Dave had a boat."

"He borrowed one from a neighbor."

"So the boat should have been familiar to Jesse. And if he hit Dave with an arrow when Dave was in a moving boat he must have incredible aim and control."

"He said he'd practiced a lot."

"Hmmm. Doesn't sound very hospitable to me," said Gram, pulling into the parking lot at the hospital. "Let's go see how Dave is."

It took a while to find Dr. Mercer. "Glad to see you were able to clean up." She nodded approvingly at me. "I'll check with the surgeon. Last I heard your friend was still in the operating room."

She returned in a few minutes. "He's in recovery. You can't see him now, but you can go to the family waiting room. Dr. White's his surgeon. He'll find you there."

The family waiting room was full. An anxious family from New York was waiting to hear about their nine-year-old son, who'd had a skateboard accident in town, and a woman in the corner was sobbing quietly. Gram and I stood, hoping Dr. White would find us soon.

He did. "It looks as though Mr. Percy will be all right. He was lucky: The arrow missed the bone. But it was a penetrating injury; going to take a while to heal." He paused. "An arrow can be more dangerous than a bullet. We had to cut it, and cloth from his pants, out. He'd bled a lot before he got to us, so we're giving him blood. And, of course, he's on antibiotics. We're hoping the fact that he bled so much at first helps keep down the possibility of infection." Dr. White paused. "He was lucky the arrow hit his leg. If it had punctured his abdomen or chest it would be a very different story."

I winced, imagining it. "What about his head?" I asked. "He hit his head when he fell."

"He has a concussion," said Dr. White. "We think it's minor, but we're keeping a close watch on him. Right now he's still in recovery, and he's going to be pretty much out of it even after we move him to a private room. If you saw him now he wouldn't remember you'd been here. Tomorrow would be a better time to visit."

"When can we see him in the morning?" asked Gram.

"Visiting hours start at eight o'clock."

I wanted to stay, but Gram put her arm around me. "He's going to be all right. Tomorrow is soon enough. You've had a rough day, Angel. You need sleep." We walked slowly out of the hospital and toward Gram's car.

"Will you go to see him first thing tomorrow?" I asked.

"We can both go," she said, heading back to my house.

"I can't," I admitted. "I have to go back to King's Island. I have to convince Jesse to come to Haven Harbor for questioning."

"Questioning?" Gram asked.

"Pete Lambert said Jesse might be accused of attempted murder."

Gram pulled into my driveway. "So, why are you involved? If Pete needs to question that man he should go out to King's Island himself. Or get the coast guard or marine patrol to do it. No way you're going back to talk to a man who shot his friend."

"I don't think he'll shoot me, Gram."

"You don't think? That's not good enough, Angel. You tell Pete Lambert you're not going out there again."

"I promised I would."

"Then un-promise! You're not a policeman. You could be hurt. Pete shouldn't have asked you to do his job for him."

"He didn't, really. I volunteered."

"He shouldn't have accepted your offer." Gram shook her head. "I know you're tough, Angel. But going out there tomorrow is plain stupid. Not to speak of your not even having a boat!"

"I could call Ob Winslow. Maybe he could take me."

"This is Ob's busiest charter fishing season.

Blues and stripers are running. Don't you be bothering him," Gram said.

"All right. I give in. I'll call Pete," I told her. "I promise." I was exhausted. Dave was going to be all right. "I don't want to talk about it anymore."

She looked at me askance. "I know you, Angel. You need to take care of yourself. You can't take on everyone's jobs."

"I hear you, Gram. I don't want to argue."

She patted me on the hand. "You go get some sleep. I'll be by to pick you up tomorrow morning about eight. No shenanigans, you hear?"

I'd gotten her message. But as I unlocked my door and headed inside, I still wasn't sure what to do. How would Dave feel if he knew the police had questioned Jesse? How would Jesse react when he heard the police wanted to talk to him?

And how would I feel if I broke my promise to Pete?

Chapter 22

"And what is Friendship but a name
A charm that lulls to sleep
A shade that Follows wealth or Fame,
But leaves the wretch to weep."
        —From a poem by Oliver Goldsmith,
        stitched on her sampler by Margaret C.
        Simmons of Washington City, age nine,
        dated January 7, 1828. Margaret's father
                was a cooper; a maker of barrels.

I'd hardly gotten inside when my phone rang. I almost didn't look at it. I didn't want to talk with anyone. But what if it was the hospital?

"Where have you been all day?" Patrick said. "I've been worried about you!"

"I left you a message," I said. "I've been busy. And the roses are beautiful. Thank you."

"Glad they arrived. But Uncle Gerry was downtown this afternoon to have lunch with Jed Fitch. He said a woman covered with blood brought a man from King's Island into town. That her name was Angie."

"Yes?" I said. Sounded like half the town had been near the wharf this afternoon. Gram had heard about me from Carole Fitch. Maybe she'd been with her husband and Gerry Bentley.

"The woman sounded like you."

I hesitated. Most of the year-rounders knew me and knew The Solitary, even if they didn't know his name. I couldn't hide what had happened, even if I wanted to. But I hadn't anticipated that everyone in town, even Patrick, would find out so quickly.

"It was me."

Patrick's voice lowered. "What happened? Are you hurt? Who was the man?"

"I'm fine. Tired. It's been a long day. I was out boating with Dave Percy, one of the Mainely Needlepointers, and there was an accident. The blood was his. I just came from the hospital. He's had surgery, and the doctor says he'll be all right."

"But what were you doing on King's Island? That's where Simon Lockhart's crazy cousin lives. Uncle Gerry spent the day with Lockhart."

"Simon's in town now? I thought he wasn't due until tonight!"

"He arrived earlier than we'd expected. Got in late last night. Uncle Gerry had a car meet him up at the airport. I only saw him for a few minutes. He's staying at Aurora."

Of course. He'd told me Simon would be staying with Skye. "What's he like?"

"What does that matter? He's a normal person. I'm not interested in him. What I want to know is what happened to you today. You're sure you weren't hurt?"

"I'm sure."

"Uncle Gerry said he'd heard a weird rumor: that the man in the boat had been shot with an arrow."

"He heard that?"

"Angie, talk to me. What's happening? What are you involved with?"

I suspected none of Patrick's Hollywood friends had days like mine. Would he understand? Not only was Haven Harbor not his world, but Gerry Bentley was his uncle. I liked Patrick. But I didn't know him well enough to count on his support. "Patrick, I have to go. I'm exhausted. I need to sleep."

"Call me first thing tomorrow morning?"

"Probably not. Gram and I'll be going back to the hospital to check on Dave. And then I have a couple of errands to do."

"Errands? Nothing dangerous?"

Dangerous? On King's Island? "I can take care of myself, Patrick. Thank you again for the roses. They're lovely. I'll be in touch, I promise." I ended the call.

Should I have explained that I was trying to keep his uncle Gerry from buying King's Island and taking away the sanctuary great cormorants—and Jesse—had found there?

Someday he'd have to know.

But not tonight.

Tonight I was focused on Dave, and on Jesse.

Despite that, I was glad Patrick had called. In all yesterday's excitement, I'd forgotten Simon was now in town.

Would he try to go out to King's Island to see Jesse?

Me. Pete. Simon. Maybe Gerry Bentley. Too many people wanted to talk to a man who wanted to be alone.

What if someone else got hurt?

Jesse deserved a chance to quietly tell his side of the story to the police. He needed to prove he was competent.

After what happened today, could he do that?

As I called the Haven Harbor Police Department, I crossed my fingers that Pete would still be there. "Pete? It's Angie. You were right. I don't think it's a smart idea for me to go out to King's Island alone tomorrow."

Pete was silent for a moment. "I'm glad. I checked with the hospital. Sounds like Dave Percy is out of danger, although he won't be in great shape for a while. I've been worrying about your going out to the island. I shouldn't have agreed you could do that. You're right, I don't want you to be in danger. The police department has a boat, and I know the marine patrol officers. I'll take one of the other guys and go myself."

"But I'd like to go with you," I put in quickly. "I just don't think I should go alone. I still think Jesse might talk with me. My being there could keep him from being nervous. I'm going to see Dave first thing in the morning, but I'll be ready to leave after that."

"You don't need to come with me, Angie. In fact, my boss wouldn't be enthused to find out you were going to."

"Jesse's under a lot of stress right now. I can explain it while we're on our way to the island."

"Maybe," Pete said reluctantly. "Could you also explain why people were asking about him at the police station this morning? I assumed it was a coincidence. Now I'd like to know as much as possible about whatever Jesse's involved with. But first I want to hear Dave's side of the story. Let me think about it. I'll see you at the hospital in the morning."

"See you then."

Chapter 23

"Remark my soul thy Narrow Bounds
Of the Revolving Year
How swift the weeks Complete Their rounds
How short the Months Appear."
        —"Sarah Ann Chamberlain performed
this work in the 10 year of her age." Sarah
worked this sampler in Bristol, Maine,
in 1818 using cross, Algerian eye, satin,
padded satin, stem, and chair stitches.

Some people say they can ask their subconscious a question before they go to sleep and wake up with the answer.

I had no such luck. I had no clue what I could do that would make a difference to Dave, to Jesse, or even to the cormorants.

Gram walked in my door at seven thirty the next morning. So far I hadn't seen a need to change the lock. I didn't have secrets from Gram.

At least, no major secrets.

I'd already been awake for a couple of hours. I'd had two cups of coffee. But I didn't have any answers.

"Pete Lambert's going to meet us at the hospital. He has to talk to Dave, if Dave's well enough."

"Dave's doing better, but he has a lot of healing to do."

"Is that new information?" I asked.

"From about an hour ago. Tom added Dave to the list of people he visits at Haven Harbor Hospital. He went over there early this morning. Ministers don't have to keep to visiting hours. Dave's still pretty drugged up. But he's also upset about what happened, and about what might happen to the island." Gram stopped. "A nurse said they were going to give him another sedative. We ought to get there before he's so relaxed he can't talk with us."

"Is he in a regular room?"

"I think so."

I pulled half of Patrick's roses out of their vase and wrapped their wet ends in wax paper. "Then let's go. Does he know how much trouble Jesse's in for shooting him?"

"Tom didn't mention that. He said Dave was worried Jesse would be pressured to leave the island."

"I want us to get there before Pete questions him. I don't want Dave to lie, but he may not understand how much trouble Jesse's in. He needs to be careful about exactly what he says on the record."

Dave had a private room on the surgical floor. As Gram and I walked in he tried to sit, but then groaned and fell back onto his pillows. His window looked out at the heavy clouds over Haven Harbor and at a line of gulls perched on the roof of the clinic next to the hospital.

"Beautiful women bearing gifts," he managed to say as I put the roses on the windowsill. "Vase?" His words were blurred. He was still on those heavy meds.

"I'll find a vase before I leave," I promised.

"I'll do that now," said Gram, picking up the roses. "At my age I've visited enough people in this hospital to know where the staff stores extra containers." She headed out, giving me a look that said, *I'm giving you two some privacy.*

I liked Dave, and we certainly were adding shared experiences to our relationship. Gram might like there to be more between us, but right now I was overwhelmed by the responsibilities of friendship alone.

I spoke quickly, before Gram returned. "Pete Lambert is on his way here. He's going to ask you questions about Jesse and what happened yesterday. The police are considering charging Jesse with attempted murder."

"No!" said Dave. That word was clear. "Damn! Jesse didn't mean to hurt me!"

"I know. But he did shoot you. They want to bring him to Haven Harbor for questioning. I'm going with them to King's Island. Jesse'll listen to me."

Dave shook his head. "Not safe."

"I know he shot you," I said. "But he wouldn't shoot at a marine patrol boat. Would he?"

Dave hesitated. "Jesse doesn't like company. And he's feeling threatened. He could shoot someone else."

"I'll do my best to keep him from doing that."

"Don't want you to get hurt." Dave shook his head. "You can't talk with him if he's up on a cliff and you're in a boat."

"Maybe Pete has a megaphone. I know if Jesse shoots at the police they might shoot back. I don't want *him* to get hurt. I'll be all right. Jesse knows me." I sounded more confident than I felt.

"He's known me a lot longer than he's known you," said Dave, pointing to his heavily bandaged leg with a hand connected to an IV.

I grimaced. "I know."

Gram rejoined us, the roses now arranged in a large vase. She put them on the small bureau in the corner of Dave's room.

"Beautiful," said Dave. "Thank you."

I didn't mention the roses were regifted.

"What can we do for you?" asked Gram. "You'll need clothes. Toiletries? Anything need doing at your house?"

Thank goodness for practical Gram.

"My keys are in the top drawer," said Dave, pointing at the bureau. "The doctors say I'll be here for a few days. But I'll need loose pants to wear home. Ones that will fit over bandages.

Pajamas? And could you check to make sure my windows are closed?" He gestured toward the window, where, outside, dark clouds were gathering. "It looks like rain." His words started to slur.

Gram picked up his keys. "We'll check your house, Dave. And get your pajamas. If you think of anything else, let one of us know."

"Thank you," he said, as Pete Lambert walked in.

"Morning, Dave," said Pete. "Sorry to see you laid up."

Dave nodded slightly.

"Angie's told us her version of what happened out on King's Island, but I'd like to ask you a few questions." He turned to Gram and me. "Privately, if you don't mind."

"Of course," I said, glancing at Dave. "I'll check back with you later, Dave. And Pete, call me when you're finished?"

"Will do," said Pete. Luckily, he didn't mention my going with him to the island. Gram wouldn't be happy about that, and I didn't feel like arguing with her. She'd find out after I got back.

Jesse didn't have many friends. He'd need one today.

And, after all, I wasn't going out to the island alone. I'd have police protection.

What could go wrong?

Chapter 24

"From low pursuits exalt my mind,
From every vice of every kind,
And may my conduct never tend,
To wound the feelings of a friend."
—From a sampler stitched by Eliza Ann
Frazier of Steubenville in Jefferson County,
Ohio, in 1824. Eliza Ann was ten years
old. She included three different alphabets,
numbers, corner designs in rococo stitch,
and a satin-stitch sawtooth border.

Gram believed me when I said I had several business calls to make. She dropped me at home and went on to check Dave's house. What kind of pajamas did he wear? Ones with botanical patterns? Skeletons? Plain-colored ones? I wasn't sure I was ready to know.

I poured another cup of coffee. I was crazy to even imagine Dave's pajamas.

Pete called within fifteen minutes. "Still want to come with me to the island, Angie?"

"You got permission?"

"Not exactly. But Joe Floyd is going with me. I promised you wouldn't get in our way, and he agreed you might be a help."

"Joe Floyd?"

"I don't think you know him. He's a good guy, been on marine patrol several years now. Joe enforces the conservation laws, which're important to Jesse, and he helps us out when there's a problem on an island. Plus, Jesse knows him. He's checked on Jesse in the past. Everyone who knows Jesse worries about him, especially in winter, or when there are strong nor'easters."

"When are you leaving?"

"I'm picking up paperwork at the station. Then I'll be heading to the wharf. Joe's already there. Make sure you bring a slicker. Weather's coming in."

In Maine, "weather" meant rain or snow. "See you in a few minutes, then."

My heaviest sweatshirt was still soaking in the bathtub. I quickly drained the water and resoaked it, hoping the rest of the bloodstains would come out in the second soak. Then I grabbed one of the sweatshirts I'd saved when I'd cleaned out Mama's things two months ago. Mama's taste was a little brighter than mine. Her sweatshirt was yellow, appliqued with red tulips. But sweatshirts lasted forever, and it was warm. No one on King's Island would care what I wore. I wasn't looking to make a fashion statement.

On my way out I grabbed my Glock. Mama's sweatshirt and my yellow slicker would cover my holster.

Maine laws had changed in the past month; I no longer had to wait six months to apply for a concealed carry permit. I wasn't sure how Pete or the marine patrol guy would feel about my carrying when I was with them. But as long as no one knew . . . I had no idea what Jesse would do when we got to King's Island. I wanted to be prepared.

I pulled into the wharf parking lot next to Pete's police cruiser.

The side of Joe's boat, which looked like a repurposed lobster boat, was labeled UNITED STATES MARINE PATROL in large white letters. Anyone within one hundred yards would be able to identify it.

Good. Jesse would know who we were.

Joe looked about fifty, and seemed calm and totally in control. "Welcome on board," he said, waving at us as he adjusted his boat's controls. "We're about set. Understand you know Jesse, Angie."

"I've met him several times," I said, only exaggerating a little.

Joe was taller than Pete. Or Patrick. Or anyone else I knew. His thick brown hair was wavy and streaked with gray. His eyes were shaded by sunglasses. How many years had he been with the marine patrol? His skin was that permanent tan that marked men and women who spent hours each day on the water.

"Heard Jesse got a little carried away with island security yesterday," Joe continued.

"He's pretty protective of his island. And the great cormorants," I said.

"Law's on his side when it comes to trespassing. And nesting grounds shouldn't be disturbed. But shooting someone . . ." Joe shook his head. "Jesse's got to take it easy. King's Island is about three miles out. On the border of my jurisdiction and the coast guard's. He could have called either of us if he needed help."

"He doesn't have a telephone," I pointed out.

"There is that," Joe agreed. "Tried to talk him into having a battery-powered shortwave, in case of emergency, but he's a little set in his ways."

A little.

"Angie, you said on the phone Jesse was unhappy about something," said Pete. "Might as well tell us now, before we head out. Hard to hear without yelling when the engine's going."

"Gerry Bentley wants to buy King's Island," I said.

"Bentley? The guy with the yacht moored outside the harbor?" Joe frowned.

"Right. He has friends in town, and he wants Jesse to sell."

"Does he know about the seabirds' nesting grounds?" asked Joe.

"I don't know. But he does know Jesse owns

King's Island with his cousin, Simon Lockhart. He flew Simon in from Chicago Wednesday. I suspect Bentley thinks he can buy Simon, and Simon can convince Jesse to sell."

Joe shook his head. "That Bentley fellow must not know Jesse."

"I don't think they've ever met," I agreed. "Jed Fitch went out to the island and talked to Jesse earlier this week. Jesse told him he wouldn't sell." Jesse hadn't shot him, either.

"That's our Solitary," said Joe, sending Pete an affirming glance. "Money doesn't mean much to Jesse."

"But it's upsetting him," I added. "I think that's why he shot Dave Percy by mistake yesterday. He's especially nervous about people coming to his island."

"He's never liked anyone stopping in," said Joe. "Unfortunately, we're about to give him more company."

"We stop in to check on him every once in a while anyway. A welfare check. But he's never shot anyone before, either," Pete pointed out.

Joe shrugged. "Figured it was a matter of time. Jesse's got issues."

"Let's get on with it," said Pete. "Wish we could talk with him out on the island, where he's comfortable, but my boss insists we bring him in for questioning." He looked over at the dark clouds moving north, over Haven Harbor

Light. "Looks as though rain's coming in fast."

"Jesse won't be happy about coming with us," I agreed. "We could suggest he visit Dave in the hospital when he's in the Harbor. He doesn't know whether Dave lived or died. I thought he might row in himself this morning to find out."

"Haven't seen him around," said Joe. " 'Course I don't see him every time he comes into town, but usually someone mentions him to me. He was here a couple of days in a row earlier this week. That was unusual. I suspect he's staying to the island for now. Especially if he thinks he could lose his home."

"Bentley wants to buy it. Not steal it, buy it from him," Pete pointed out.

"I suspect Jesse would quibble with that wording," Joe said. "Let's get out there and see how he's doing. Explain the lay of the land. He won't be happy. But maybe he's calmed down since yesterday and won't pull out his bow and arrows."

We headed out of Haven Harbor.

The marine patrol boat was a twenty-six footer equipped with a lot of electronics. It was a lot bigger and had a much more powerful engine than the *Sweet Life.*

As we headed out of the harbor I pulled the hood of my slicker up. I should have tied my hair back; despite the hood, it blew into my face. Mama's sweatshirt helped block the winds. My slicker and the open cabin of the boat protected most of me, but the sharp rain and spray blew onto the deck and into my face.

This trip would be shorter than the one Dave and I took yesterday. Today I couldn't concentrate on the scenery.

Joe sped up as we passed the harbor buoy.

By the time we'd get to King's Island we'd be soaked. I kept reminding myself coming with the men had been my idea. I was only with them because I'd convinced Pete I might be able to help. Joe'd been polite, but I suspected my presence didn't fit within his regulations.

Rain trickled down my back and legs. My sneakers slipped on the wet deck.

The sea that had sparkled yesterday was now dark and menacing. We cut into the swells, pounding forward through whitecaps and foam. Few other boats were out and fewer birds. Not a day for a pleasure ride.

Joe expertly navigated around King's Island and headed toward the small cove where Dave had landed the *Sweet Life*. I scanned the shoreline, looking for Jesse.

Yesterday he'd been hidden in the trees. I hadn't seen him until he'd shot at us.

Today I couldn't see him, or any of the great cormorants, through the rain.

Had he seen us?

Pete secured a ladder and threw it over the side.

"Where was Jesse yesterday, when you got here?"

"Up on that cliff." I pointed. "He came down to the beach from there."

Both men looked up, following where I'd pointed. The ledges bordered the edge of sparse woods above us. Those ledges had been a part of King's Island, protecting the land from the sea around it, since before my Scots ancestors immigrated to Maine three centuries ago.

"If he's there now, he's well hidden," said Joe. "When I come out here I use the horn. Let him know I'm coming. He recognizes the boat. Not thrilled to see me, but he knows it's my job, and I try not to stop by during nesting season unless there's a storm warning I need to pass on. Coast guard keeps an eye on him, too, but he gets on better with me. Didn't use the horn today. Most of the birds are out of the nests, but officially it's still nesting season. Jesse's right not to want any loud noises that might disturb them. Or get Jesse more upset than he already is."

"In this rain, he's probably in his shelter," said Pete, scanning the tree line. "I suggest we pay him a call."

I climbed over the side. I hadn't done that in years. The basics came back pretty fast, but it would have been easier if the rain hadn't blurred my vision and made the ladder slippery.

I kept watching the woods above us, and the edges of the beach. I was shaking. The last time I'd been here Jesse had shot at Dave and me.

Pete took the rope and tied it around a large tree near the high tide mark.

"This way," said Joe, stepping over unsteady rocks and around crevices. We followed him up the hill. My feet slurped in my water-filled sneakers. The narrow path was muddy between rocks and barely visible. If Joe hadn't led the way, I wouldn't have found it. Once we were above the jagged granite ledges we had to step over exposed pine roots and through high, thin grasses.

Before we headed inland I turned around.

The view was spectacular, even in the rain. Maine waters were littered with islands. But most islands were low, deforested granite ledges, or nubbles—immense piles of stones submerged in high tides and winter storms.

King's Island rose high above the tides and still boasted trees, although many were skeletal.

During colonial days families pastured their sheep and cows and goats on islands near land, like the Three Sisters in Haven Harbor. The sea provided a natural boundary for livestock and didn't require cutting trees for fences.

During the American Revolution British ships took advantage of this tradition and stole most of the district's livestock and small boats. Since vegetables and grains didn't grow easily on the ends of the rocky peninsulas where people lived, and losing their boats meant losing their access both to fish and other communities, those years were hungry ones for many Mainers.

Had anyone lived on King's Island in those days? The island was too far from shore to have been used for livestock. But fishermen had often set up camps on islands like this, near where fish ran each year.

On the mainland Queen Anne's lace and goldenrod colored fields yellow and white. Here there were only rough yellowed grasses. We dodged dripping branches of low scrub bushes, but there were too many. If any part of me had still been dry when we left the beach, it was now soaked. I brushed the rain off my face, focusing on pushing my way after the two men along the rough path. At least we could see where we were going. How did Jesse manage at night?

He must know the island so well he didn't need light. Or he followed the ways of early settlers and slept when it was dark. On winter days Maine had fourteen hours of night.

Joe turned and headed into the woods, where whatever invisible path he was following was at least easier to walk. Winter ice and winds had left trees bent and naked, some on the ground. Jesse'd cleared the path here; broken tree limbs had been moved away. Little vegetation was below the trees.

No one spoke. How far into King's Island was Jesse's home?

Joe slowed his pace and turned to Pete and me. "Jesse lives just ahead. Strange. Either he hasn't heard us, or he's somewhere else on the island. Even in winter he shows up to meet me on the path."

Both men had their guns out, held quietly at their sides. I left mine concealed. We had more than enough firepower.

"Jesse doesn't have a gun," I said, hoping what Jesse'd told me was true. "He only uses his bow for protection."

"That bow almost killed Dave Percy yesterday," Pete said quietly. "Jesse could be hiding anywhere. He knows every inch of King's Island."

I glanced around. Compared to the coastal rocks and low bushes, the area we were in now was exposed. If Jesse were nearby, we should be able to see him.

And he could see us.

Joe kept walking. About twenty feet farther he pointed at a low pile of dead branches and driftwood covered with lighter branches, grasses, and pine needles.

"His place," he said.

"That's Jesse's home?" I blurted. I'd imagined he'd built a small log cabin or shack out here.

"He's done an amazing job with it," said Joe. "Someone must have lived here, or had a fishing camp, years ago. Early nineteenth century, or even before, King's Island must have been someone's wood lot. Nothing's left now but their cellar hole lined with sea stones. It's almost deep enough to stand in. Jesse added uprights from dead trees and a couple of aluminum poles, covered them with a four-season tent, and then covered the tent with the branches you see. He has two other tents for supplies and dry wood."

"Jesse!" Joe called out. "Jesse, it's Joe. Pete Lambert, from the Haven Harbor Police Department, is here with me. Your friend Angie Curtis is, too. We want to talk to you about Dave Percy."

"He's all right," I shouted. "Jesse, Dave's okay. He's in the hospital, but he'll be fine."

The only answer was the sound of the sea and the rain.

Where was Jesse?

"Jesse!" Joe called again. No one answered. Joe moved a weathered plank on Jesse's construction to the side and uncovered an opening to the house. "Want to see, Angie? I don't think he's home."

"I'll keep watch," Pete said.

I bent over and followed Joe down four granite steps leading to what had once been a cellar. Despite the darkness, I could see a low, rough pallet in the small room, the sort early settlers had used, filling muslin or wool bags with pine needles. This one was covered by two sleeping bags. Bags holding canned goods and water lined one wall. Jesse's bow and a small stack of arrows stood next to them.

Wherever he was, he didn't have his weapons.

"There's no light inside," I commented.

Joe looked around. "Jesse says he's like the animals. He hibernates in winter. Days are shorter then, and he sleeps a lot, so he doesn't need much food or light. He has a propane stove and flashlights. When it's warm and light enough to keep the door open, or sit in a sheltered spot on the island, he reads." Joe pointed at a small collection of books I hadn't noticed, propped on pieces of driftwood in a shadowy corner.

"He must be cold."

"He says he gets used to it. But few folks could live like this nowadays."

No wonder the coast guard checked on Jesse. I couldn't believe he survived with only a propane stove in the winter. My house was roofed and clapboarded and had a furnace and three fireplaces, and I remembered cold winds blowing through when I was a child.

"He's not here, for sure," confirmed Joe. "Let's get out of here."

I'd reached the top of the steps, with Joe close behind me, when Pete yelled, "Found him!"

Chapter 25

"May I with innocence and peace
My tranquil moments spend
And when the toils of life shall cease
With calmness meet my end."
> —Sampler stitched by Phoebe Doan, age
> thirteen, in 1834 in Clinton County, Ohio.
> She also stitched a large building, perhaps
> her school, four sheep, and a man with a dog.

Jesse was lying on the ground about twenty feet from his shelter, in back of a yellow tent that stood eerily glistening in the wet, dark pine woods.

"He's gone," said Pete, bending over the body. "Nothing we can do for him now."

"What happened?"

"I don't know. I suppose he could have slipped and fallen. But I don't see any rocks or branches here he could have hit his head on."

Shaken, I approached where Jesse was lying. I'd never seen Mama's body. She'd died too many years ago. But this was the second time in two months I'd seen the body of someone I knew. Both times the shock took me right back to Mama.

"Don't come closer," Pete cautioned. "Until we

know what happened we shouldn't disturb the scene."

"He was alive yesterday, about this time. He was fine," I said quietly.

"With all the rain it's hard to tell, but I'm guessing he bled a lot. Head injuries do that. And this one was in the front of his head, on his forehead," said Joe.

"If he'd slipped on pine needles or leaves wouldn't he have fallen forward? He wouldn't be lying on his back now," I said, looking at Jesse's body.

Pete stood. "I hate leaving the guy here, but looks to me as though the place should be checked by the crime scene guys from Augusta."

Joe nodded. "I agree. We need to get someone out here from the medical examiner's office, too."

"You mean we should leave him here?" I asked. "Alone? In the rain?"

"No. I'll stay. Make sure no one—or no animal or bird—disturbs the scene. Joe, you take Angie back to Haven Harbor and call for assistance. Let Ethan Trask know, too. In case."

In case Jesse'd been murdered. I shuddered. How could this have happened?

"Maybe he wasn't killed. Maybe it was an accident," I ventured. "If anyone else was here on the island, wouldn't Jesse have had his bow with him?"

"I don't know. What if he knew whoever was here? What if he didn't hear them coming?" Joe looked baffled. "I have no idea what happened."

The rain was lighter now. I looked up, hoping to see a little blue sky. Instead, I saw a pair of great cormorants sitting on a high branch of one of the skeletal pine trees, their wings outstretched. Dark sentinels.

Did they know their protector was gone? What could they have seen?

Unfortunately, whatever they knew would remain a secret.

Joe and I followed the path, now trampled by our footsteps, back to the beach at the small cove and headed back to Haven Harbor.

I'd been worried about confronting Jesse.

Now I was worried about telling Dave his friend was dead.

"Dead? Jesse's dead?" Dave's skin was pale, but he was sitting in his hospital bed. "That's impossible! He was fine yesterday. How? When?"

I shook my head. "They've called in the medical examiner and crime scene technicians to figure out what happened."

Dave caught on immediately. "Pete Lambert thinks someone killed Jesse? Who would want to do that? Jesse was one of the good ones. He wanted to live in peace with nature, with his birds." His eyes filled with tears. "He saw so many of his friends die in the Middle East. All he wanted was to be left alone. To make a small, positive difference in the world."

I handed Dave a box of tissues.

"He was my best friend." Dave kept shaking his head. "I can't believe it. You're sure it was Jesse?"

"I saw him," I said quietly.

"He'd found his place, his purpose. All he wanted was to protect his birds. Why would anyone want to kill him?"

"Someone wanted to buy his island," I pointed out.

"That might explain why Jesse freaked out and attacked me. But why would anyone kill him?"

"Maybe someone thought if Jesse was gone it would be easier to buy King's Island."

"Angie, get real. I can't believe a rich guy from California would sail out to King's Island on his yacht and knock Jesse on the head just so he could buy the place. Maine has thousands of islands. I never figured why Bentley wanted that particular island anyway. The only thing King's Island was good for was the cormorants." Dave winced. His leg must have been bothering him. "And Jesse. The island was good for Jesse." He rang for a nurse. "Sorry. Could I have more pain medication?"

The nurse looked at his tearful face and then at

me. "A little something to relax you, too? Your body won't heal if you don't rest."

"Whatever," said Dave, waving the nurse away.

"At least we won't have to worry about Jesse's losing the island now," I said.

"That's supposed to make me feel better? Jesse may be gone, but the great cormorants are still there. Jesse would want us to take care of them. Protect them, the way he did."

The birds would be affected by Jesse's death. But what could Dave or I do about them? Dave couldn't even leave the hospital right now.

"The birds will have to take care of themselves," I said, perhaps too hastily.

Dave winced again. Where was that nurse with a painkiller?

"We can't let that Bentley person buy the island. We owe that to Jesse. And to the cormorants."

"Let's talk when you're feeling better," I said, as the nurse returned with a long needle. I turned away so Dave could have privacy.

"I have a telephone. Even when I'm in here I can talk with people. We have to move fast. That Simon was supposed to arrive yesterday."

He'd been here since Wednesday night. But knowing that wouldn't help Dave feel better. "I see Gram brought your pajamas." They were folded in a neat pile next to the roses I'd brought that morning. "Is there anything else I can do for you?"

"When I saw you and Charlotte this morning I wasn't thinking straight. I forgot something important," Dave said. "So, yes. There is one more thing you can do for me. You can check on the kittens."

Chapter 26

"From the most remote ages, the employment of the Needle has formed a source of recreation, of remunerative work, and no less of economy, the useful occupation of time and charity, amongst all classes of women in all parts of the world."

—From *The Dictionary of Needlework: An Encyclopaedia of Artistic, Plain, and Fancy Needlework* by Sophia Frances Anne Caulfield and Blanche C. Saward, London, 1882.

"The kittens?" I repeated blankly. "What kittens?"

"The three in my barn," Dave said. "They were born there, about six weeks ago. The mother cat disappeared. Must've gotten run over or something. I've been feeding her babies. Three are still alive. Or were before we headed out to King's Island."

Kittens? I like cats as much as the next person, but I was more worried about whether Jesse'd been murdered. And about the cormorants. And about how fast Dave was healing.

But those were complicated questions. How complicated could kittens be? "Don't worry. I'll take care of the kittens for you," I assured Dave. "I'll go right now. You rest."

I hoped they'd survived. Dave didn't need any more bad news now. I didn't know much about kittens, but Dave had been away from home over twenty-four hours now.

Twenty-four hours in which he'd been shot and Jesse had died.

Faced with a problem I knew nothing about, I did what I usually did.

I called Gram. She knew more about cats and kittens, among other things, than I did.

"Why didn't he tell us about those kittens this morning?" she said. "And don't bother to tell me you didn't go to that island. Jed Fitch stopped in this morning looking for Tom. He told me you'd gone out with Pete and the marine patrol."

Was nothing in Haven Harbor a secret?

"Are you and Tom thinking of buying real estate?"

"Don't change the subject. Jed was here to tell Tom that Carole was going to have another treatment tomorrow. He was sad and frustrated. They'd thought she was doing better. He wanted Tom to stop in to see her, and said they wouldn't be able to be greeters this Sunday after all."

Right. Jed's wife, Carole, had cancer.

Gram sounded thoughtful. "I suspect they're having money troubles again, too. He asked me if I'd heard of anyone needing work done on their house, or stacking wood for winter. Jed's getting a little old to do handyman chores, but not much real estate is turning over in Haven Harbor these days."

"I'll have to call him about my snow plowing," I said. "And those window panes that need replacing."

"Good," said Gram. "But you haven't explained what you were doing with the marine patrol."

"I know what you said yesterday. But I really thought I could make a difference when Pete talked with Jesse."

"You know how dangerous that was."

"Relax, Gram. Remember, I didn't go alone. I went with Pete and Joe. And now I'm back, and I'm fine." Then I decided I had to tell her. "Jesse's dead."

For a moment she was silent. "I'll meet you at Dave's house and we'll see how those kittens are doing. And you can tell me about Jesse."

I parked outside Dave's house and walked around to his backyard. I'd sat on his patio several times in the past months, and I'd seen his fenced-in poison garden. I'd never paid attention to his barn. Most older houses in town had them. Not the enormous barns farmers needed, but smaller barns, or carriage houses, which once held two or three horses, their hay, tack, and a wagon or two. Today, people used them as garages or workshops and storage areas.

The warped sliding door on Dave's barn was ajar. No doubt that was how the feral mother had gotten in.

I pushed it open.

It didn't take long to find the kittens. They weren't newborns, but they were tiny. Three babies nestled together on a nest of soft blankets and towels in a cut-down refrigerator carton. Weak, but alive.

"Thank goodness," said Gram, joining me. "Dave was taking good care of them. He must even have bottle-fed them for a while." She pointed at several bottles on a shelf next to a box of powdered milk labeled FOR KITTENS.

"Will we need to bottle-feed them, too?" I asked. I couldn't take my eyes off those tiny creatures. When had I last seen a kitten that small?

Then I remembered. I'd been about five. I'd been playing in a neighbor's yard and found an injured kitten. She'd been gray, I remembered. And one of her legs was crooked and bloody. I'd picked her up carefully and carried her home, both the kitten and me crying the whole way. On my way a neighbor boy had stopped me. "That's the kitten Eric Dowling dropped out of the tree. He wanted to see if she'd land on her feet." He peered at her. "She didn't. Guess cats don't really have nine lives."

I'd run the rest of the way home, depositing the poor injured kitten in Gram's lap.

Despite Gram's ministrations, the kitten had died an hour later. I'd cried and buried her in our backyard, by the old pump house. I hadn't thought of that kitten in years. But I'd never liked the name Eric.

"The kittens are eating on their own now," Gram was saying. "See?" She pointed at several overturned Frisbees filled with food. "Dave's mixed up the special milk and left it for them."

"Plus plain water," I noted. "And that's a litter pan?" I pointed at a low baking pan filled with litter. The area around it was also liberally strewn with litter.

"I wonder if they need anything solid?" Gram said. "I've never taken care of kittens so small."

The little white kitten with black patches on her face and butt was fast asleep, curled next to her mirror image: a black kitten with large patches of white, and the third, a black kitten with only a few white hairs. That one looked up at me, but didn't purr or meow. She squeaked.

"Funny noise," I said. I reached down and picked her up. She weighed a little over a pound and had big yellow eyes.

"What would be best for these babies?" Gram asked. "We can't leave them here. We don't know how long Dave's going to be in the hospital, and they need watching. A dog or fox or owl could get in here and they wouldn't have a chance. And I suspect they'll need regular feeding." She refilled the water dish from the garden hose Dave had looped neatly and hung on the wall. "We can't be running over here every four or five hours."

"Would Juno take care of them?" I asked. I'd heard of older cats "adopting" kittens.

"I wouldn't count on it," said Gram drily. "Although a kitten would wake up my old lady." She stood. "Plus, they've lived out in the world. My guess is they all have fleas. I don't want Juno to get them, too. Or my house."

I held the black kitten away from my chest, where she'd been trying to snuggle.

"All right," said Gram. "We could probably each manage one. They're little enough so they could stay in a large box with blankets and food and a litter tray. I'd put mine in a room where Juno can't go right now. I'll take the little white one, and you have the black one. Ruth might take the third one."

"Me? Take a kitten?" I asked. "I don't have time for a kitten!" I looked at the little bundle of fluff who was kneading my chest. "She's so tiny."

"Cats are pretty independent," said Gram. "And they're Dave's cats. It may only be a few days before he'll be out and about and ready to take them back. You have one of those smart-phones. Check to see what these babies need. This morning I saw empty cartons in Dave's back hall. Call Ruth, too, to see if she'd like a kitten."

Gram strode resolutely toward Dave's back door.

Reluctantly I put down the kitten I'd been holding and pulled out my phone.

I'd just finished looking at a site about care of orphaned kittens when my phone rang. I answered it without thinking. "Dave? They're fine. Don't worry about them."

"I'm not Dave," said Patrick.

"Sorry! I was expecting a call," I said.

"Clearly," said Patrick.

"And I'm in the middle of a situation," I continued, hoping to change the subject. "A kitten situation."

"Kittens?" asked Patrick. "You have kittens?"

"I seem to," I said. "Or, my friend Dave Percy does. He was caring for three orphaned kittens in his barn. He asked Gram and me to take care of them while he's in the hospital. When you called I was looking up what to do with them."

"How old are they?" asked Patrick.

"Old enough to drink and use a low litter pan," I said. "I think Dave said six weeks old.

The Web site I looked at said abandoned kittens should be checked by a vet."

"Sounds like the right thing," Patrick agreed. "Is there a vet in town?"

"Gram will know. She has a cat," I said.

"Kittens are wonderful," said Patrick. "Are you going to take them all?"

"Gram's thinking we should find separate homes for them. They'll need a lot of attention."

"So you'll take one."

"And Gram will take one."

"And the third kitten?"

"I haven't called anyone yet. I'm hoping Ruth Hopkins will take it."

"I'll volunteer," said Patrick.

"You will? To take a kitten?" I asked.

"And I'll pay for all of them to be checked out by a vet. He or she'll make sure they're healthy, and check for fleas and worms and such before they move inside anyone's house."

"You really want a kitten?"

"I'd love one. I've always liked cats. And I could use company."

"When Dave gets out of the hospital he may want them all back," I warned Patrick.

"Temporary company, then," said Patrick.

Gram came back, carrying a box for the powdered milk and the Frisbee feeders and a smaller box for the kittens. "Gram, this is Patrick. He said he'd pay for a vet visit for all the kittens, and he'll take one."

"Tell him we accept his offer," said Gram. "Gratefully."

"Did you hear that?" I asked. "Thank you! I'll see you later, with your kitten."

"Ah . . . and could you pick up any supplies the vet says I'll need?" asked Patrick. "Litter pan, special food, toys, whatever."

"I'll need those things, too," I said. "Kitten caravan on the move."

Chapter 27

"When this you see
Remember me
And bare me in your mind
Let all the world say
What they will
Speak of me as you find."

—Charity Trimble, born in the year
1789, stitched this verse on her
sampler when she was eighteen.
Charity was one of nine children. She
and her family had emigrated from
Virginia to Pennsylvania, and then to
Ohio. In 1811 Charity married. She and
her husband had seven children, two of
whom died as infants, and lived in Ross
County, Ohio, the rest of their lives.

"Your friend Patrick is very kind," said Gram.

We put Dave's kitten supplies in a large carton in the back of Gram's car and then put all the kittens in a liquor carton.

"They're big enough to be scared by the car, or to jump around and scare me," said Gram. "So close the top loosely. We don't have far to go." Gram drove, and I put the carton of crying kittens on my lap.

I filled Gram in on Jesse on the way to the vet's office.

"I agree with Dave. We have to save that nesting ground," she said as she pulled into the parking lot of an animal hospital just outside downtown. "I've already talked to Anna and Ruth today. Jesse may be gone, but Dave's right. We can't let that island be sold to anyone who's going to build. The Audubon Society will help, too."

"But first we have to take care of the kittens," I put in.

The vet checked over each of our small charges, made sure they weren't dehydrated, and advised us what to feed them. "No cow's milk. Kitten formula, mixed with spring water. No chemicals. Mix in a little canned kitten food," she suggested. "These babies are pretty healthy. Your friend did a good job with them. Shall I have my assistant give them baths to make sure they don't take their fleas home with them?"

Gram and I gratefully agreed. The whole procedure didn't take long.

We were now the foster parents of three weary kittens.

"I'm going to keep Snowy in Tom's and my bedroom," Gram decided. "I'll keep the door closed until I know how Juno's going to react. She won't be happy about being closed out, but she'll cope."

The vet had said to keep each kitten in one room equipped with a litter pan and food and water until they were used to their new quarters. "Snowy?" I said. "You've already named one? You know they're Dave's kittens, right?"

"Every living thing should have a name," she said. "Where will you keep yours?"

"In the living room, I guess," I said. "The vet said we needed to keep them company, and I'm downstairs more than up. The kitchen would be good, but I can't close it off."

"And what's your kitten's name?" she asked.

The vet's name had been Beatrix. "Beatrix is a queen, right?" I asked.

"Netherlands," agreed Gram.

"Juno's the queen of your household," I said. "Beatrix will be the queen of mine. At least for as long as Dave needs me to keep her." I peeked into the carton. "I may call her Trixi, though. She's pretty little to be a queen. She's still a princess."

Gram patted my knee.

We picked up supplies for the kittens and Gram dropped Beatrix and me and the Unnamed One at my house. Trixi promptly inspected one section of the living-room floor and then fell asleep in the kitten bed I hadn't been able to resist buying.

Then the Unnamed One and I headed for Patrick's house.

Chapter 28

"O May I Always Ready Stand
With my Lamp Burning in My Hand
May In Sight of Heaven Rejoice
When Err I Hear the Bridegroom's Voice."
—Stitched in 1757 Boston by Prudence
Clark above a picture of Adam and Eve and
several animals standing below an apple tree.

Patrick peeked into the carton holding his kitten. "She's beautiful! It is a she, right?"

"A she," I confirmed. "Gram took her brother. Let me get you her supplies."

By the time I got back with the box of food and litter, the Unnamed One was purring on Patrick's chest. It was clearly a love match.

"You know this may be temporary? Dave may only be in the hospital a few days."

"I know," said Patrick, burying his nose in the kitten's fur. "What's her name?"

"That's up to you," I said. He was stroking her gently, and she was clearly responding. She didn't care that his hands were red and swollen. Maybe Patrick did need a kitten.

"Black cats with white patches on their chests are called tuxedo cats," he said. He put his hand on her head and said solemnly, "I christen you Bette."

"Bette?"

"After Bette Midler. She used to wear tuxedos in her act."

"I added a book on kitten care to your supplies. I got one for me, too. The vet suggested Bette should be kept in one room until she gets used to the space."

"I think she'll like my studio," he said. "She can look out through the glass walls, even though she's so little. And when it gets cooler, the floor will be heated."

When it got cooler? I had a feeling Dave would have trouble retrieving this kitten.

"What are the other two kittens like?"

"Mine's almost all black. Just a couple of white hairs on her chest. Gram's is white, with a little black."

"I'm glad you chose Bette for me. She's perfect." The object of his affection sat comfortably in his lap. "How's Dave? He's the biology teacher who does needlepoint with you, right?"

"Right," I confirmed. "Good guy. Ex-navy." I hesitated to tell Patrick, but better he heard it from me than someone else. "He had surgery yesterday afternoon. He'll be all right, but healing takes time."

"An accident?"

Patrick was probably the only one in town who hadn't already heard. "What your uncle Gerry heard was right. Dave was shot with an arrow while we were out on King's Island," I said.

Patrick frowned. "King's Island. Isn't that the place Uncle Gerry wants to buy from some weird hermit guy?"

"The weird hermit guy's name was Jesse Lockhart. He and Dave were close friends."

"And you were with him? Thank goodness you weren't hurt."

"I'm fine," I said. "And Dave will recover. But Jesse's dead."

"Did Dave shoot him?" Patrick looked at me closely. He knew I carried. "Did you?"

"Neither of us. He was fine when Dave and I left the island yesterday. This morning Pete Lambert and one of the marine patrol guys and I went out to King's Island to talk to him. We found his body."

"This morning?" said Patrick. "All that's happened since we had dinner Tuesday night?"

Patrick sat back. "Simon—the guy who's staying with Mom now—he's this Jesse's cousin, right?"

"I think so."

"Did Jesse have any other family?"

"Not that I know of."

"So Simon's Jesse's next of kin," said Patrick. "Have the police told him about his cousin?"

"I don't even know whether they know Simon's in town," I said.

"They should. Yesterday Simon went to the town hall to get copies of the deed to King's Island and the police department to see if they had any records about Jesse." Patrick hesitated. "Records of any arrests, or crazy behavior, you know."

"No. I don't."

"Uncle Gerry went with him. So did Jed Fitch. I think it was Jed's idea. You know Jed, right? The Realtor."

"I know Jed. What was his idea?"

"Your friend Jesse lived by himself on a remote island, in an unsafe habitation." Patrick hesitated. "They were looking for evidence he was incompetent."

"Incompetent!"

"So Simon could be named his guardian and make decisions about his cousin's life. And the future of the island."

I paced back and forth in front of the window.

Bette watched me, moving her head back and forth as if trying to figure out what I was doing.

I turned to Patrick. "Jesse wasn't crazy or incompetent. He'd decided to live his life a little differently from the way other people did. There's no law against that."

"But he shot Dave Percy."

"By mistake. He was worried about your uncle trying to buy the island, and he was confused about who was in our boat."

"You could have been shot, too."

"But I wasn't. And Jesse was really upset when he realized what he'd done." I hesitated. "We never really got a chance to talk with him."

"What did you want to talk to him about?"

"We wanted to warn him that your uncle Gerry was bringing Simon to town to try to convince him to sell King's Island."

"But there shouldn't be a problem with Simon's selling it now, right?"

"Jesse would have fought to keep it from being sold because of the birds. Now other people want to take on his cause."

Patrick looked confused. "Birds? What birds?"

"Jesse ensured King's Island was a refuge—a safe nesting place—for great cormorants. They're a threatened species."

"I didn't know that."

"The Audubon folks do. If there's anything they can do to protect the cormorants, they will." I hoped they would, anyway. Katie and Anna were working on that. Gram had gotten involved. And Dave said he'd do anything to protect the island.

"Cormorants. They're the big black birds who stand with their wings spread?"

"Right."

"I've tried to paint them. They're almost surrealistic. Like out of the past. They're endangered?"

"Not the double-crested cormorants, but the

great cormorants. Not endangered. Threatened. That's the step before 'endangered.' People haven't treated them well. In the eighteenth and nineteenth centuries people used cormorant feathers to make capes and decorate hats, like they did with puffin feathers. Very different attitude from medieval times when some people believed cormorants were symbols of Christ because when their wings were out they looked like crosses."

"You know a lot about them." He sat quietly, watching me pace and gesture.

"Jesse and Dave told me some things. I googled the rest."

"And this Jesse—he was protecting them?"

"King's Island's an official seabird nesting site. No one's supposed to be there between June first and August thirty-first. He posted signs and kept people away. The birds must have been used to him."

"So if Uncle Gerry buys the island and puts up a house and a dock and a heliport the cormorants will leave."

"Right."

"Does he know about the birds?"

"I don't know. I'll bet Jed Fitch didn't tell him. Even Simon may not know. Jesse said he hadn't seen his cousin in years."

Would Patrick talk to his Uncle Gerry about the island? Would he warn his uncle that even though Jesse was dead, other people wanted to keep King's Island for the birds?

Bette was purring so loud I could hear her across the room. Patrick was gently petting her, and she'd curled up in his lap.

"I should go and check on Trixi," I said, heading for the door.

"Trixi?"

"Bette's sister," I explained over my shoulder. "My kitten."

Chapter 29

"This life is like a morning Flower
Cut Down & Withered in an hour."
—Thirteen-year-old Hannah Smith
Merseilles of Bridgeton, New Jersey,
stitched this verse in French knot, eyelet,
stem, satin, tent and cross-stich in 1812.
She included three alphabets, a strawberry
border, and two baskets of flowers.

Trixi was fine. If you don't count the times she missed the low "litter tray" I'd put in the corner (at least she'd come close) and the bag of unfinished needlepoint projects and yarns she'd pulled out of my stitching bag.

Luckily, she was still a baby. She'd stopped pulling the wool out after one skein and was now sound asleep on top of it, ignoring her cozy cat bed.

No purrs for me.

I refilled her food-and-kitten-milk dish.

Sharing my home with another living creature felt good.

Dusk was falling. I was looking forward to a quiet evening.

I hadn't eaten since breakfast. Instead, I'd made two visits to the hospital, helped find

Jesse's body on an island, and rescued three kittens.

Gram would have reminded me I was twenty-seven and should have lots of energy.

But right now I felt too tired to cook. I glanced at the bottle of Soave chilling in the refrigerator. If I had one sip of wine I'd fall asleep on my feet.

I heated a can of vegetable soup. Even diced, boiled, and salted, vegetables were good for you, right? I opened a box of chowder crackers to go with the soup.

Gram made delicious soups. I should ask about her turkey noodle soup, and her bean soup, and . . . I was too tired to remember what else she made.

Trixi was still sleeping soundly.

What if she woke during the night? What if she needed more food? What if she was lonely and missed her brother and sister?

A picture of that kitten buried in the backyard flashed through my head.

Trixi was so tiny. So vulnerable. How could I leave her alone?

I changed into my sleepshirt, curled up on the living-room couch, and pulled one of Gram's afghans over me.

Three hours later paws kneading my arm and a tail tickling my face woke me. Trixi must have decided I was her new mother. A few minutes later she bit me lightly and scurried to the end of the couch. I checked to make sure her personal bathroom and kitchen were clean and accessible, and went back to sleep.

I wasn't ready for morning when my phone started humming.

First I checked on Trixi, who seemed to have mastered the art of the litter box during the night. Then I checked the text. It was from Dave. **Feeling better. How are kittens? Have ideas re: birds. Called Anna. Talk?**

I groaned. Hospitals wake patients earlier than I was ready to cope.

Dave must have been feeling as lonely as the little black kitten now following me around the living room. I headed to the kitchen for coffee. Trixi stood at the door of the living room and squeaked.

I gave in immediately and let her follow me. The vet had said "one room for now," but how could I explain "tough love" to a kitten so small she could fit in my hand?

Coffee and one of Gram's blueberry muffins for me, and kitten milk for her. While my muffin was defrosting in the oven I added water to the vase of roses.

Gram was right. They were beautiful, but they didn't smell.

Fortified, I called Dave back. "Kittens are fine. Or at least mine is," I said.

"Yours?"

"Gram and I thought it would be easier if three different people fostered them."

"So, which one do you have?"

"The black one. Gram has the white one, and Patrick has the one he said was a tuxedo cat."

"Patrick?"

"Patrick West. He called when Gram and I were at your barn. He volunteered to pay for a vet to look them over and deflea them, and said he'd love to take care of one."

Dave was silent.

"We know they're your kittens," I said quickly. "We're watching them until you're home. How do you feel this morning?"

"Better, but doctors are still worried about possible infections. Jesse's arrow wasn't sterile, and neither was the fabric it pushed into my muscle."

I winced. "So you're still on antibiotics. Were you able to sleep?"

"It's impossible to sleep in a hospital. I'm used to living by myself, where it's quiet. People here walk the halls all night, and nurses come in to take your blood pressure. I can't sleep, and I'm bored. I don't even have a good book to read. And I'm getting further behind on my work. Yesterday I called my boss to let him know what happened. He's on board. But I should be organizing my classroom and finishing my lesson plans."

"Anything I can bring you?"

"A pad of paper and pencils would be a help. And a paperback. I need something to keep me amused besides CNN and daytime talk shows."

"You've got it. I'll be by a little later."

"Heard anything more about what happened to Jesse? I can blame hospital noise, but Jesse's death's the major reason I couldn't sleep last night. I still can't believe someone murdered him."

"Maybe no one did. Maybe he slipped and fell and hit his head. I haven't heard anything one way or the other. The medical examiner and crime guys take time."

"I want to help, and I'm stuck in here. It's driving me crazy."

"Your message said you'd talked with Anna."

"Thanks for reminding me. The meds that are supposed to help me relax sometimes empty my brain. Anna has ideas about the cormorants. She and Ruth are coming by later. Any chance you could come then too?"

"Will they let you have that many visitors?"

"I have a private room. And one of the nurses used to be a student of mine." I could almost see him smiling. "Nothing like a former student giving you a sponge bath to make you feel old and decrepit."

"When will Anna and Ruth be there?"

"About ten."

"Good. I'll see you then."

"You're sure the kittens are fine? I was worried I'd left them alone too long."

"The vet said they were in great shape. Trixi's nibbling my ankle right now."

"Trixi?"

"Living creatures should have names. I named her Beatrix, but that seemed a little formal for a kitten."

Dave laughed. "I suspect that kitten isn't either a feral barn cat or mine any longer. Beatrix, eh? See you at ten."

Chapter 30

"Fear and Love; God Above.
Roses will fade and tulips wither
But a virtuous mind will bloom forever."
                    —Stitched in 1824 by nine-year-old
                    Mary Morse, under the instruction
                    of Mrs. Amanda Pratt. Mary married
                    John Fisher in 1836 in Alstead, New
                    Hampshire. They had five children.

I put Trixi back into the living room while I scrounged for legal pads and pens and sharpened pencils for Dave. Then I carefully photographed the sampler Sarah'd completed. I could return it to her while I was downtown.

On the advice of the owner of The Book Nook (who knew Dave and wanted to hear all the details about his injury) I bought paperback copies of Paul Doiron's *The Poacher's Son* and Kate Flora's *And Grant You Peace*, two mysteries set in Maine. I was assured he'd love both.

Then I stopped to see Sarah.

"Thanks for getting the sampler back to me so quickly," she said, tucking it under the counter. "I hope Mrs. Owens will like it."

"She'll be thrilled! You did a great job," I

enthused. Then I updated her on Dave's condition and Jesse's death.

Her lips tightened. "Count me in if the needlepointers are doing anything to help save King's Island for the cormorants," she assured me. "I can't come to the meeting this morning, but I'd like to help. It's awful to think of that island being developed. 'High from the earth I heard a bird, He trod upon the trees, As he esteemed them trifles, And then he spied a breeze.' "

Knowing Sarah, I was willing to bet that was another Emily Dickinson quote. "I'll let you know what Anna and Ruth have in mind."

"Tell Dave I'll try to stop in to see him tonight after I close up shop."

"I think it's a good sign he's getting restless and bored." I held up the bag containing the anti-boredom supplies Dave had asked for. "I'm taking him two mysteries and paper so he can outline lesson plans, but I suspect he'd rather have company."

"What about flowers? Food?"

"Flowers and food are always good."

Sarah glanced at the computer screen on her desk. "You'd better get going. It's after nine thirty, and your meeting's at ten o'clock."

By the time I got to Dave's room Anna and Ruth were already settled in the two guest chairs. I put my package on Dave's windowsill between a spectacular arrangement of yellow and orange late summer flowers and a green plant. I pulled another chair in from the hallway.

"Beautiful flowers," I commented.

"They are," Dave agreed. "The plant's from the high school. But I'm not exactly sure why the flowers are here. Maybe they're a bribe."

"A bribe?" asked Ruth.

"They're from Patrick and Skye West," said Dave, turning to me. "The note with those flowers thanked me 'for Bette.' Would you happen to know what that meant?"

"Bette's what he named the kitten he's taking care of."

"I suspected that." Dave sighed. "Actually, I don't mind that you found the kittens new homes. I couldn't keep them in the barn much longer, and it wouldn't be safe for them near my poison garden. They'll be safer as inside cats."

"Patrick did get excited about his kitten," I said. "I think he's lonely."

"A lot of us live alone," Ruth put in. "But at my age I can't chase a kitten. All I'd need to mess up my life would be to trip over one of those little creatures and end up in the hospital like you, Dave." She looked over at him. "No offense meant."

"None taken," said Dave. "Given a choice, I wouldn't want to be here, either."

"I suspect Gram won't want to keep Snowy," I put in. "He could come back to live with you."

"So you're keeping the one you have, too?" Dave said, grinning.

"If it's okay with you," I admitted. "She's awfully cute. Although she did get into my wool bag last night."

"That's just the beginning, I assure you," said Anna. "I wouldn't have a cat in my house. In the barn, for mice, sure. But I don't want any cat tearing my upholstery or getting into our needlepoint or sewing supplies."

"Dave said you had an idea about the cormorants," I said, deciding we'd talked enough about kittens.

"I talked to the director of the Maine Audubon organization," said Anna. "She's willing to be interviewed, if we need her. They're pulling together a short video clip about the need for nesting grounds for endangered or threatened seabirds. I hope you don't mind, Angie, but I told her you had a contact at one of the Portland television stations."

"No problem," I said. "One of my high school friends works at Channel Seven. I'll give her a call. When will the clip be ready?"

"It's Saturday now," said Anna, checking her notes. "She promised it would be ready by Monday or Tuesday."

"I've been watching local news," Dave added.

"Channel Seven reported a body was found on an island off Haven Harbor. They didn't mention Jesse's name, or his cause of death."

"The police are probably notifying relatives first," said Ruth. "And they don't know his cause of death yet, do they?"

"I don't think so," I answered.

"I've known Jesse for about eight years, and the only living relative he ever mentioned to me was his cousin Simon," put in Dave.

"The cousin he owned the island with?" Anna checked.

"And who's staying with Skye West right now," I confirmed. "Gerry Bentley flew him in from Chicago a couple of days ago."

"How did the Wests get involved with this?" asked Ruth.

"Gerry Bentley is Patrick West's uncle," I said. "He was visiting the Wests when he saw King's Island. He asked Simon to come to Haven Harbor to convince Jesse to sign off on selling the island. Bentley paid for the ticket and asked Skye to host him."

"Does Simon know Jesse's dead?" Dave asked.

"I don't know. I told Patrick, though, so I wouldn't be surprised if he knew. But the police should officially notify him."

"If they even know he's in Maine," Anna added.

"Think that would be a secret for long?" Ruth asked. "They know."

I decided not to mention that Simon and Gerry Bentley had been asking questions at the police department the day Dave had been shot. The day Jesse probably died. Dave didn't need to know they'd been thinking about having Jesse declared incompetent. Now that he was dead, that wouldn't matter.

"I like the idea of statewide publicity to get people excited about saving the cormorants," said Dave. "I had an idea that fits with the film clip."

"Yes?" asked Ruth.

"Visitors to Maine are fascinated by wildlife here. Moose, lobsters, puffins . . . and cormorants. Lots of tourists are also conservationists. We could educate them about seabird nesting grounds; make them part of our campaign."

"How?" asked Anna.

"Earlier you said 'save the cormorants.' Why not put that phrase, and a picture of a cormorant, on T-shirts? Hats? Posters? Tote bags? We could needlepoint it on cushions. We could get 'Save the Cormorants' into almost every store in Maine. How would Gerry Bentley feel about people walking around wearing a slogan that meant, 'Build Your Dream House Somewhere Else?'"

"I love that!" I said. "I saw Sarah this morning. She wants to be part of anything we do. And she knows Ted Lawrence. Maybe she could get him to design a logo for us."

"Perfect!" said Ruth. "Ted might agree to do that. Ask Sarah to check with him."

"I will," I said, taking notes. "But can we get this campaign off the ground in time? Jesse's dead. Simon's in town. Won't Simon inherit the island now?"

"I convinced Jesse to see a lawyer when this all came up. He didn't tell me exactly what he'd done, but he did say he'd changed his will," said Dave.

"I wonder if his lawyer would talk with me," I thought out loud.

"Probably not. But he might talk to the police. Legal consultations are private. But Jesse's dead."

"In Maine it takes six months to get a will through probate," Ruth put in. "Nothing can happen to property until then."

"I'll call the Audubon director back and tell her our ideas," said Anna. "I think she'll love them. Even if the King's Island problem is solved"— she looked around—"one way or the other . . . preserving seabird nesting grounds is important. All the posters and T-shirts and cushions will still be important a year from now. They'll remind people about saving our wildlife."

"Okay," I said, standing. "I'll contact Sarah about Ted Lawrence, and call my friend Clem Walker at Channel Seven and let her know about the film clip."

"You know Pete Lambert pretty well," Dave added. "Make sure he knows Jesse changed his will. The lawyer he used was Aaron Irving."

I wrote that down. "Okay. I'm on board. And I'll let everyone know what happens."

"I'm excited," said Anna.

"And I'll finish my editing," said Ruth. "I have the feeling I'm going to be doing a lot of needlepoint in the near future!"

"One thing we haven't mentioned," said Dave, as the rest of us were preparing to leave. "I hate to mention it. But if Jesse didn't have an accident . . . our whole plan could be complicated. King's Island might be the center of a murder case."

Chapter 31

"It were kindest to ignore nineteenth century needlework, but in a book treating of English embroidery something must be said to bridge over the time when Needlecraft as an Art was dead. During the earlier part of the century taste was bad, during the middle it was beyond criticism, and from then to the time of the 'greenery-yallery' aesthetic revival, all and everything made by women's fingers ought to be buried, burnt, or otherwise destroyed."
—From *Chats on Old Lace and Needlework*
by Emily Leigh Lowes, London, 1908.

As I left the hospital I remembered Gram. She'd started the Mainely Needlepoint business, even if I was its director now. She was one of the first people to visit Dave at the hospital. She was concerned about the cormorants.

And she hadn't been included in the meeting.

Big mistake.

Before I called anyone on my to-do list, I headed for the rectory.

"Come to check on Snowy?" she asked. "And how's Beatrix?"

"She's Trixi now," I said. "And she was fine a couple of hours ago."

Gram smiled. "I like 'Trixi'."

"Maybe it should be 'tricks,'" I admitted. "She got into my wool last night."

"She's a kitten!" Gram pointed out. "Sounds as though she's fine. Snowy's being in the house is driving Juno crazy. She keeps sniffing and scratching at the bedroom door."

"I was at the hospital. Dave sounded as though he'd be okay with our keeping the kittens," I told her. "But I said I wasn't sure about yours."

Gram shook her head. "Next time I see Dave I'll tell him Snowy's all his. Much as he's a fun little boy, I'd forgotten how lively kittens were. I'm just fostering him. What about Patrick's kitten?"

"Last night it looked as though he was in love. He's named his kitten Bette, after Bette Midler."

"Sophisticated name," Gram said, smiling. "Glad he's happy. Patrick's had a hard time this summer. Could be Bette will help keep his mind off his problems."

I nodded. "Some of the needlepointers are planning a campaign with the Audubon folks, to keep King's Island uninhabited and safe for the cormorants."

I told her what people were planning.

"I'm in favor of protecting the cormorants," she said. "But be aware. I don't think everyone in town will be enthused about your idea. They'll say birds can use other islands for nesting, and if Gerry Bentley moves to town he'll bring with him money, jobs, and publicity that will help our local economy."

"They'd want the island turned into a home for a multimillionaire instead of a refuge?"

"I've heard talk." She hesitated. "From Tom, too. He likes birds as much as the next person. But he's on the Chamber of Commerce. Ed Campbell's president this year, and he's been pressing them to think of ways to bring new businesses to Haven Harbor. Jed Fitch made a convincing pitch about how good for the town's future it would be if Bentley built here. With Skye West already in town and the Bentleys, too, he felt that would attract Hollywood and Silicon Valley visitors. People with money to spend."

"Who's Ed Campbell?" I'd only been back in Haven Harbor since May. I didn't know everyone yet.

"He owns a car dealership out on Route One. And he's president of the Yacht Club."

"And he's against the cormorants?"

"You're making it sound so simple. It's complicated," said Gram. "I'm on the cormorants' side, but I wish we didn't have to choose between them and economic development. I'm hoping Bentley will find land he can build on more easily. Land that wouldn't interfere with nesting grounds."

"I can't believe the Chamber of Commerce

would support selling King's Island. And attracting more multimillionaires? That's happened in other towns along the coast. Mainers have been taxed out of homes their families owned for generations. Working waterfront has been turned into private waterfront. Lobstermen and fishermen don't have access to the waters they've always used. I'd hate to see that happening here in Haven Harbor."

Gram shook her head. "You're right. But it's true our town could use more jobs. And new people mean real estate sales and construction contracts, and businesses like Sarah's antiques shop and Ted Lawrence's gallery benefit when people furnish those homes. It could help Mainely Needlepoint, too, Angie. You're in business now. You have to face the realities of Maine commerce."

"I'm trying to put Mainely Needlepoint on-line; make its products accessible throughout the country, twelve months of the year."

"Which would be great, if it works. You could even hire more needlepointers. But not every business can expand using the Internet."

The problem was more complicated than I'd anticipated. "We need to let people know about the great cormorants. We need to stand up and say their environment is important. If we let seabirds—or any other part of what makes people want to move to the coast of Maine—die out, that won't be good for the economy, either. We can't make the issue as simple as 'birds versus commerce.'"

"You should be on the Chamber of Commerce, Angel. You've lived away, and you see the situation clearer than folks here who think of it as 'us versus them.'"

"Or in this case, us versus the cormorants," I said. "I could talk to Ed Campbell about the Chamber's position."

"You could try. Who knows? You might win him over."

"I'll talk to Jed Fitch, too," I said, pacing Gram's kitchen floor. "Maybe he could convince the Bentleys to consider other properties."

Juno jumped onto Gram's lap. "Those men are pretty determined. They've been in Haven Harbor for years. They're convinced they know what's best for the town."

"Which side are you on?"

"I love cormorants. But Tom's convinced the Bentleys should be able to buy King's Island. Do I have to choose between the Needlepointers and my husband?"

I shook my head. "I don't know. I hope not."

"Go home and check on your Trixi. Make sure she's all right and has enough food. I'll talk to Tom about your plans."

"I'm going to go ahead and talk to Ed Campbell and Jed Fitch. What harm could it do?"

"You might not end up the most popular person in town, Angie. You need to take it a little slow if you're planning to settle here." Gram's expression was serious. "Which I hope you do. But it won't help you, or Mainely Needlepoint, if you alienate people."

"I hope we're on the same side, Gram."

"I hope so, too, Angie. But life isn't always as simple as it seems. And small-town politics isn't pretty."

Chapter 32

"In youth improve your tender mind
Let virtue be with knowledge join'd
Pursue the paths of truth and love
And you'll arrive to bliss above."
—Stitched by six-year-old Sarah Kidder
Haskell in 1811, Boston, Massachusetts,
in satin and cross-stitch with a strawberry
border and three alphabets.

Trixi was fine. I refilled her food and water dishes, cleaned her litter pan, and sat her on my lap as I made phone calls.

Sarah was excited about the Save the Cormorants campaign. "I'll ask Ted about the logo tonight," she said. "I was going to visit Dave, but he'll understand if I don't see him until tomorrow."

I left a message with Pete telling him about Jesse's new will and who Jesse's lawyer was.

Then I called Patrick. "How's Bette doing?"

"Frisky and fine," he said. "Glad you called. I've been thinking about those cormorants. Maybe we could convince Uncle Gerry to buy another island. He happened to see that one, but he didn't know about the seabird nesting issue."

"If you could do that, it would be great," I

said. "The Audubon people are putting together a film clip on why protected nesting sites for endangered and threatened species are critical. And I just left a meeting with several Mainely Needlepointers who want to campaign to save the island for the birds."

"I said *we* might be able to convince Uncle Gerry," said Patrick. "I'll need your help. He won't understand why I've decided to become an environmentalist overnight, especially since he hasn't been doing much but talking about that island and going out to see it."

"He went to see it again?"

"He's been sleeping on his boat, so I don't know exactly when, but he's mentioned cruising around, trying to figure out the best place for the house he's planning."

"Does he know Jesse's dead?"

Patrick hesitated. "Now he does. Pete Lambert came to Aurora this morning to talk to Simon."

"How's Simon reacting?"

"Mom said he didn't seem grief-stricken. Uncle Gerry said Jesse's death should simplify the sale: Simon can sign off on the island himself. He doesn't have to convince Jesse to sell."

"I heard Jesse made out a new will earlier this week."

"Changing his beneficiary?"

"I don't know," I admitted. "I'm guessing so. He was upset about your uncle's trying to buy

King's Island. It would make sense if he'd left his half of the island to someone else, not to Simon."

"Uncle Gerry hasn't heard anything about that," Patrick said. "He said Jed Fitch told him now the purchase would be a done deal."

"Maybe it is," I said. "I don't know much about wills."

Ruth had said it took six months to probate. Didn't that mean the property couldn't be inherited by anyone for six months? I wasn't a lawyer. But I suspected Gerry Bentley had access to plenty of legal advice.

My phone vibrated. "Patrick, I have to go. I have another call coming in. If you hear anything more, let me know."

The caller ID read HAVEN HARBOR POLICE DEPARTMENT.

"Pete?"

"It's me. Since you've been involved in this since the beginning, I wanted to tell you we just got the report from the medical examiner. Jesse was murdered. He wasn't hit on the head once—he was hit four or five times. Probably with a stone. King's Island is covered with them, of course. And they'd be easy to dispose of."

"In the ocean."

"Exactly. So now we have a murder investigation. I've kept Ethan Trask informed along the way, but now he's officially assigned to the case. We'd like to interview you. Then we'll talk with Dave at the hospital. You two may have been the last two people to see Jesse, before the murderer."

Ethan, my old high school crush, was now a homicide detective with the Maine State Troopers. He'd worked on Mama's case, and on several other murders I'd gotten entangled with since I'd been back in Haven Harbor. A good man. But given his job, I hated having a reason to see him again.

"I'll come right over," I said, lifting Trixi off my lap and putting her on the floor.

"And don't tell anyone else about this yet," said Pete. "If whoever killed Jesse is still in town, we don't want to tip him—or her—off right away that we're investigating."

"Got it."

I felt guilty at leaving Trixi alone again. I added a little food to her dish (for a creature so small she didn't seem to have any trouble emptying it) and picked up my car keys.

I knew the way to the Haven Harbor Police Department all too well.

Pete and Ethan were both waiting for me.

"Sorry to have to ask you to come in," said Ethan. "I know you've already talked with Pete."

"I was with him when he and Joe found Jesse's body," I said quietly.

"I know. But I need you to tell us all you know about Jesse."

"I saw Jesse for the first time last Monday morning," I began. "He was rowing into the town wharf. Arvin Trask and your brother Rob were about to go out for the morning. They told me Jesse was called The Solitary. That he lived out on King's Island by himself."

"Before that you'd never seen him."

I shook my head. "No. I'll admit, I was curious about him, and I followed him. I saw him go into the post office. Later I went back to the post office to buy stamps. Pax told me the man I'd seen earlier's name was Jesse Lockhart. After that I went to see Dave Percy, and Jesse was coming out of Dave's house. He didn't stop, and we didn't talk."

"But you asked Dave about him," said Pete.

"I did. But all Dave would say was they were friends, and that Jesse preferred to live alone on the island."

"And when did you next see Jesse Lockhart?"

"Tuesday night. Ruth Hopkins and I were having dinner at Dave's house, and Jesse came in."

"Was he expected?"

"No. He was looking for Dave. He said Jed Fitch had been out on King's Island, telling him someone rich wanted to buy it."

"Jesse was upset about that?" Ethan checked his recorder.

"Angry. He'd told Jed he wouldn't sell."

"And?"

"After dinner Dave took Ruth home. Jesse was going to spend the night at Dave's, so I stayed to talk with him. He told me he and his cousin Simon owned the island, but Simon hadn't been there in years. He said he and Dave met in a veteran's hospital in Massachusetts, and he'd lived with Dave when he first came to Haven Harbor. One day he'd seen boys throwing stones at the cormorants on King's Island and decided to live there. To protect them." I paused. "He felt violated that Jed had come to the island uninvited and told him he'd have to sell."

"That's what he said? He'd 'have to sell'?" asked Pete.

"Not in those words," I corrected myself. "But yes, that's how I think he felt. Then Dave came back and suggested Jesse see a lawyer. I don't know what they talked about after that. I went home."

"And when did you see him next?"

"Thursday. I'd heard from Patrick West that his uncle Gerry—Gerry Bentley—had paid for Jesse's cousin Simon to come to Maine. I was worried Jesse would be pressured to sell. He hadn't looked as though he'd react well to that, so I told Dave. Dave suggested we go out to King's Island and warn Jesse that his cousin was coming." I looked from one of the men to the other. "Jesse doesn't—didn't—have a telephone.

The only way to get in touch with him was to go to the island."

"Dave was Jesse's friend. But you'd just met him. Why did you go, too?"

"I'd been the one who'd heard about Simon's flying in. And on Tuesday night I'd gotten Jesse to talk a little."

Pete nodded. "So?"

"Dave borrowed his neighbor's boat, the *Sweet Life*, and we went out there. We were bringing the boat into shore when Jesse shot two arrows toward us. One missed the boat. One hit Dave." I looked at the two men. "You both know that."

"But we need to make sure we haven't missed anything along the way," said Pete. "Ethan hadn't heard the story directly from you."

I continued. "Jesse came down to the shore immediately. He was contrite when he saw Dave was bleeding. He said he'd been confused. Since Jed Fitch had been there, he'd been afraid of someone else coming to the island to disrupt his life, and his birds. He'd panicked when he'd seen two people in the boat."

"Did you tell him about his cousin?"

"We did. Then I had to get Dave back to Haven Harbor, get him medical attention."

"And did you see Jesse after that?" Pete asked.

"Not until I went out to the island again Friday with you and Joe. And you found his body." I could still see Jesse's pale body lying awkwardly

216

on the ground, soaked with rain. I shuddered, remembering.

Ethan was taking notes. "You said you'd heard from Patrick West that Simon Lockhart was coming to town. How did you happen to be talking with Patrick?"

"Last Monday I stopped in to welcome Patrick and his mother back to Haven Harbor. Gerry Bentley and his wife were there. Patrick introduced us. Bentley is Patrick's uncle."

"You didn't know Bentley's connection to King's Island then."

"Not for sure. Reverend Tom had said someone rich was interested in local real estate. When I was at the Wests' I figured it must be the Bentleys. But I didn't know they were thinking about buying King's Island. And I hadn't met Jesse then."

Pete didn't look at me. He looked at his notes. "So you heard about the possible sale of King's Island from Reverend Tom, who'd heard about it from Jed Fitch."

"At the Chamber of Commerce meeting. Yes."

"And from Jesse himself."

"Yes."

"And from Gerry Bentley himself."

"Not from Bentley directly," I corrected. "Patrick West told me."

"Who else knew about this possible deal?"

"My grandmother. Ed Campbell, and whoever

else was at the Chamber of Commerce meeting with Tom and Jed Fitch. Everyone at the Wests' house. Dave Percy, of course. Ruth Hopkins—she was at Dave's when Jesse joined us for dinner."

"No one else?"

"Not that I know of."

"You've been involved in murder investigations before, Angie," said Ethan. He didn't need to remind me. "You know we have to check out every possibility. Jesse Lockhart lived out on that island for a little over two years without making any trouble for anyone but the coast guard and marine patrol."

"So I've heard."

"As far as we know he didn't have contact with anyone in town except for those guys, Dave Percy, and Pax Henry at the post office."

"He might have known other people. He told me he had to discourage people from coming to the island during nesting season," I said. "He'd posted signs, but people ignored them. He said that was why he had the bow and arrows: to discourage guests."

"Not even a gun, like a normal guy," Ethan said, almost to himself.

"Dave told me Jesse'd had a tough time while he was serving in the army. Jesse himself told me he hated guns. He didn't even like sharp noises or fireworks. And gunshots would disturb the great cormorants."

Pete looked at Ethan. "Sounds like PTSD."

"Possible. My wife says some of the soldiers she's serving with in Afghanistan make her nervous; they're paranoid or defensive. Shoot before checking."

"But Jesse felt bad about shooting Dave," I put in. "And he didn't have his bow with him when we found him Friday morning."

"Did the medical examiner figure out when Jesse was killed?" I asked. "Dave and I left him late Thursday morning."

Ethan and Pete looked at each other. "No harm in telling you," said Ethan. "You're in the clear. Jesse was killed between three o'clock and nine o'clock Thursday. After you left the island."

"The crime scene guys took the bow back with them to Augusta to check for fingerprints. Someone could have taken the bow from him and put it back in his house so it'd look as though he didn't have a weapon," added Pete.

I frowned. "That doesn't make sense. If he'd had a weapon, then killing him might be self-defense."

"It could be," Pete agreed. "But most killers don't think through their defense at the time of the crime. Especially if it's a crime of the moment. Jesse wasn't killed with a weapon brought to the island. Premeditation seems off the table. It's a puzzle. Can you think of anything else that would help us figure out who killed him?"

I shook my head. Then I remembered. "I left you a message this morning. Dave suggested to Jesse he see a lawyer. He made out a new will on Wednesday before he went back to the island."

"A will that would . . . ?" asked Ethan.

"I don't know. He was afraid Simon would want to sell King's Island. I'm guessing he didn't leave his half of the island to his cousin."

"But you don't know?"

"Not for sure," I said. "But the lawyer Dave suggested to him was Aaron Irving. You're the police. You could find out. From what Patrick told me, Gerry Bentley was willing to pay a lot of money for King's Island. And Reverend Tom told me there were people in town who wanted the Bentleys to move here; they'd bring jobs and cash into Haven Harbor. I suspect Jesse was killed because Gerry Bentley wanted to buy King's Island."

Chapter 33

"How blest the maid whom circling years improve
Her god the object of her purest love
Whose youthful hours successive on they glide
The book the needle and the pen divide."
—Twelve-year-old Melancia Bowker from Fitzwilliam, New Hampshire, stitched this on linen in 1817. The verse and two alphabets and a pastoral scene of a girl holding flowers next to a basket of flowers are surrounded by an elaborate floral border. Melancia studied at the Ipswich Female Seminary with Mary Lyon (the founder of Mount Holyoke) and taught before her marriage. Her husband died three months after their wedding, Melancia returned to teaching, and then married again. Unusually for the period, all five of her children graduated from college.

I'd been told not to spread the word, but I had to tell someone. Who did I trust most? I had no doubt. "I just talked to Pete and Ethan at the police station. Jesse was murdered."

Through the line I could hear Gram take in a deep breath. "Have they talked to Dave yet?"

"They're on their way to the hospital to see him now."

"How are you doing?"

"Not too well," I admitted. "I keep thinking it's my fault. I shouldn't have moved home from Arizona. Every time I turn around someone seems to get killed."

"Rubbish! Bad things happen everywhere. They happened in Arizona, right?"

"But that was a big city. I didn't know all the people involved."

"What are you going to do now?"

"I'm not sure. I'd like to talk with Jed Fitch and Ed Campbell. Tonight I'll go back to the hospital to see Dave. Sarah was going, but she's going to talk to Ted Lawrence about Save the Cormorants instead. And Dave has the police there now."

"Good thought, Angel. Dave'll need a friend after the police leave. I was thinking of making cookies. Why don't you come over and help? You asked me for my maple raisin oatmeal cookie recipe a couple of weeks ago. We'll double it, and you can take a batch to Dave. They cook up quickly."

It took me a fraction of a second to agree.

Trixi was making herself at home checking out the furniture near the floor in the living room and testing her claws on the wallpaper in the corner. Whoops. Hadn't thought I'd have to redecorate for her.

I gently discouraged her from scraping off the wallpaper, so instead she climbed the drapes and made herself comfortable on the shelf Gram had installed for Juno to watch the bird feeder. "That's a good place for you," I told her. "But I'd really rather you didn't use the drapes as a highway." She seemed unimpressed by my suggestion. The male cardinal eating his supper on the feeder was much more interesting. He was bigger than she was for now, but wouldn't be for long.

"You're going to be an inside cat," I informed her. "Jesse was trying to protect the great cormorants. The least I can do is make sure our bird feeders are secure. And that you're away from the street, and fishers, and foxes." And poison gardens, I added to myself.

Gram had her mixer out and ingredients on her kitchen table by the time I arrived. "How's Snowy?" I asked.

"A little lonely in the bedroom," she said. "Why don't you go and say hello?"

I walked past Juno, who was carefully overseeing what was happening in the kitchen, and opened the bedroom door. Gram and Reverend Tom's bedroom. I felt like an intruder now that Gram was sharing a bedroom with her husband. My own bedroom suddenly seemed very empty.

I felt soft fur on my ankle and looked down. Snowy rubbed himself on me and then gave me a little bite. "Do you smell your sister on me?" I asked him. He streaked across the room and hid under the bed. "Your sister's friendlier," I told him.

I headed back to the kitchen. "He's cute, but a little shy," I said.

"I think Juno's yowls intimidate him," agreed Gram.

"Dave will probably take him back when he gets home," I said. "I feel a little guilty that Patrick and I each adopted one of his kittens."

"Don't feel bad. I don't think Dave was planning to keep all three anyway. After he gets out of the hospital I'll take Snowy over. He'll be company for Dave and Juno will have her peace restored. Now—get me the maple syrup out of the refrigerator. We'll want to heat it so it flows and measures easily before we add it to the dough."

I watched Gram and copied her recipe as she creamed butter and sugar and then added dry ingredients. "That's all?" I asked. "They've always been one of my favorites of your cookies. When I'd get home from school in the afternoon I'd smell baking and know all was well." I didn't mention how empty our house had seemed after Mama'd disappeared. No matter how many cookies Gram baked, it hadn't made up for Mama's not being there.

"Now it's your turn to bring comfort to people.

Nothing says love like oatmeal and raisins and maple. Here. You fill one cookie sheet. I'll do the other," Gram instructed.

The smell of baking cookies soon filled the room. "We're making a lot," I commented, as we filled the fifth and sixth baking sheets.

"You'll take some to Dave and keep some yourself." She looked at me sideways. "You could take a plate to your friend Patrick, too, and check on his kitten. And maybe find out what was happening with Jesse's cousin. You said he was staying at Aurora."

"Very sneaky, Gram," I grinned. "Not a bad idea."

"Cookies are never a bad idea. Who said the way to a man's heart was through his stomach?"

"I don't know. Probably you," I said, moving our first two sheets of cooled cookies into a tin box for Gram and Reverend Tom, and chewing on one myself.

"Plenty here for everyone. First rule of life: There can never be too many cookies."

"Did I hear the word 'cookies'?" Reverend Tom walked into the kitchen. His hand went straight to the cookie box. "Yum! Charlotte, what was my life like without your cooking?"

"Less caloric," she answered, and patted him on the rear as she went to take another cookie sheet from the oven. "These aren't all for us. Angie's taking some with her."

"Heard Jesse Lockhart was murdered," he said, as he snuck another two cookies off the rack.

"How did you know?" I said, getting out paper plates for the cookies I was taking with me. "Pete and Ethan were trying to keep it quiet for at least a few hours."

"I was making visits at the hospital and ran into them. Pretty clear why they were going to talk with Dave Percy."

"Jesse was his friend."

"Some friend, who'd shoot you," Tom commented. "But at least he's not a suspect. They can be pretty sure where he's been for the last couple of days."

"Wonder who did kill Jesse?" Gram asked. "All he wanted was to be left alone with those birds. No reason for anyone to want to hurt him."

"Pete and Ethan will figure it out," I said, more confidently than I felt.

"Guess we'll have a new neighbor soon, then," continued Tom.

"Who?" said Gram, turning toward him.

"Gerry Bentley. Now he'll be able to buy King's Island."

Chapter 34

"Now in the cold grave is Marian sleeping
Unfinished the work her fingers began
While we finish her task amidst sorry and
   weeping
We'll think of the frailty of short lived man."
     —Fourteen-year-old Marian Childs of
Shelburne, Massachusetts, began this sampler
     in 1820, but died before she was able to
     finish it. Family legends say the sampler
     was finished after her death, and birds
     and a cross were added then. Marian lived
     longer than any other child in her family.

I packed more than my share of the cookies (after all, I was dividing mine with Patrick and Dave) and left Gram and Tom planning to go to dinner with several other couples.

Couples.

Would I ever be a part of one of those?

Gram seemed so happy. And most couples I knew seemed at least comfortable and content. How did they find each other? How did they know "this is the one"? I'd helped solve several mysteries in my life, but I didn't have a clue about that one.

"I brought cookies," I said, as I knocked on the door of Dave's hospital room.

He looked paler than he had that morning. "Cookies? I thought you didn't cook."

"Gram and I made them together. But now I have the recipe, including her secret ingredients." I put the plate on Dave's wheeling table. "If you don't feel up to eating them, you could share with the nurses and doctors."

He picked one up. "No way. My cookies. You said."

"Are you nine years old?"

"I was thinking six," he said, grinning as he finished his first cookie and took a second. "Glad you stopped in. Talking to the law was exhausting. Maybe cookies will revive me."

"I won't stay long," I assured him. "I wanted to make sure you'd survived talking with Pete and Ethan."

"Talking? More like being grilled," Dave said, lying back on his pillows. "I told them everything I've ever known about Jesse Lockhart. But I wasn't able to help them with their most important question: 'Who killed him?' "

"Do you have any suspicions?"

Dave shook his head. "Not one. I'm still furious about it, too. How could anyone kill him? Jesse was the most peaceful person I've ever known. Ethan kept asking me whether he had any enemies. Enemies? He lived by himself on an island. Most people in town either didn't know him, or called him The Solitary because they didn't know his name. Who'd want to hurt someone like that?"

"He wasn't like other people. That might have made some people uncomfortable."

"Granted. He didn't go out of his way to make friends. But he never bothered anyone, either. The only people who were aggravated at him were the coast guard and marine patrol guys who felt they had to check on him in the winter. Being a nuisance isn't grounds for murder."

"But he had the bow and arrows to protect himself."

"To protect his privacy," Dave quickly corrected me. "His island. His cormorants. Once in a while he shot an arrow high to convince trespassers they should find another island to picnic or camp. But I'm the only one he ever hit." Dave rubbed his leg gently. "And I was his friend."

"Luckily for you, you were in the hospital when Jesse was killed."

"That's what Ethan pointed out. I would have been their number one suspect otherwise."

"When we were out on the island another boat was nearby, circling the island."

Dave shook his head. "I wasn't looking at other boats. As you'll remember, I had a few other things on my mind."

"I'm pretty sure I saw a boat, maybe a lobster boat, with several people on board."

"Could be. Ocean's full of boats. No reason one or a dozen wouldn't be near King's Island."

"But Jesse's killer must have gone to the island by boat."

"True. I haven't heard of anyone swimming that far," Dave said drily. "And no one's installed a helipad yet. But if the boat you saw looked like a lobster boat, it probably was a lobster boat. Several fishermen have traps out in that area, especially in winter."

"It's not winter yet."

"Angie, forget it. There aren't any cameras out on King's Island, and no one out for a day's boating, whether for work or pleasure, has to sign in and out."

"They do radio to other boats."

"Some do," agreed Dave. "Commercial fishermen do. When they need to. But most of the boats around Haven Harbor in August aren't commercial. If you want to think about who might have killed Jesse, think about the island itself. Who wanted him off it?"

"Gerry Bentley, of course. But would a multimillionaire go out to King's Island and bash in Jesse's head?"

Dave winced at my description. "Probably not. But who else would have benefited if Jesse sold the island?"

"His cousin Simon would get a share of the price of the island, or the whole thing if Jesse were dead. Simon arrived late Wednesday. He was in town when Jesse was killed."

"True. But he would have needed to get a boat." Dave sank back on his pillows. "My head's throbbing again. Go home, Angie. You look more tired than I feel. Pete and Ethan are looking into it all, and I'm sure they'll question Simon. Under the circumstances, they'll question anyone who knew Jesse, or who's connected to Gerry Bentley."

"I hope so."

Dave's voice was getting lower. "Sorry, Angie, but they have me on all sorts of meds. I need to sleep now. Thanks for coming. And for the cookies. Thank Charlotte, too. I'm lucky. I'm not like Jesse. I have a lot of wonderful friends here in Haven Harbor."

"Rest well, Dave."

Dave was right. He had a lot of friends here in Haven Harbor. He'd made a new life for himself here after his naval career, much as I was trying to make a new life for myself now.

I'd given myself six months to test the waters here. It was August. I'd been here almost four months.

Soon, according to the schedule I'd set for myself, I'd have to decide whether I stayed here permanently, or would leave.

Go back to Arizona?

My job as assistant to a private investigator

had kept me busy. But I hadn't wanted to do that forever. Friends? I'd known people there, sure. But no one I was even keeping in touch with. No one I counted as a friend.

On the other hand—none of those people had ever shot me.

I shook my head as I set out to see Patrick.

Relationships were complicated.

Chapter 35

"Then O Divine benevolence be nigh
& teach me how to live and how to die."
—From sampler worked by Wealthy
Griswold, age nine, in 1804. Wealthy was
born in Windsor, Connecticut, the eighth of
nine children. Her mother died when she
was three years old. Her sampler featured
a crowned lion, a rosebud border, and a
shepherdess looking over her flock. Most
of the figures are in cross-stitch, but the
background is in vertical long-stitches.

Patrick answered his door holding Bette. "Look, Bette! We have company!"

I couldn't help smiling. Patrick and Bette were bonded already.

"I brought cookies," I said, holding them out. "For you. Afraid I didn't bring any cat toys."

"You're welcome no matter," said Patrick, gesturing that I should come in.

I put the cookies on the coffee table. "Looks as though Bette is feeling at home," I said. The floor was littered with cat toys. "And she's not confined to the studio anymore."

"She seems to like it in here," said Patrick.

"She likes company. And her toys are mostly in here now."

He smiled sheepishly as he looked around his living room. "Mom stopped at a pet store yesterday and went a little crazy. Bette doesn't seem to mind, though."

Bette was ignoring all the felt mice and plastic balls and happily chasing a plastic bottle cap that skidded across the floor when she batted it.

"Those cookies look delicious!" he said. "Oatmeal?"

"Maple raisin oatmeal. My grandmother's recipe," I said as he bit into one.

"When did you find time to bake cookies?"

I shrugged. "Gram and I made them over at her house," I admitted. "I thought you'd like some."

"Right on target," he said, taking another one. "I do cook. Or, I used to, before the fire." Patrick looked away, as though remembering. "But I've never baked. Tasting these, I think I need to learn how. How's your friend Dave? The one who was shot?"

"Healing. He'll be in the hospital a few more days," I said. "The doctors want to make sure no infections set in." I hesitated. "Have you heard? Jesse Lockhart was murdered."

Patrick's hand moved from the cookie he was about to take and fell into his lap. "What? That hermit who lived out on King's Island?"

"Yes. The man who was protecting the great cormorants."

"Do the police know who killed him?"

I shook my head. "They interviewed me, and Dave, today. Maybe they talked with other people."

"The sergeant from the Haven Harbor Police Department who was here yesterday told Simon Lockhart his cousin was dead. He didn't say his cousin'd been murdered," Patrick said, sitting back on the couch.

"They got the medical examiner's report today."

"Are you and your Needlepointers still going to campaign to save the cormorants?" he asked. "I've thought about that. I did some research, and I'm with you. I know Uncle Gerry's the one who wants to buy the island. I told him about how building on the island would be bad for the birds."

"And?"

Patrick didn't look straight at me. "He listened, but said he was sure the birds could move somewhere else. That his wife liked that island, and with her expecting in a couple of months, he doesn't want her upset about anything."

"The cormorants would be the ones really upset," I said. "There are islands all over the Gulf of Maine and Down East that the Bentleys could buy. Not even counting all the estates overlooking the ocean out on peninsulas. Only a few islands are suitable for cormorants."

"He doesn't see it that way. He did say he'd mention the environmental aspects to his Realtor, though. The issue isn't completely closed."

"What does Simon say?"

"Uncle Gerry said he took Simon to see a lawyer when he first got here. Since then Simon's been driving around, revisiting places he knew when he was young. He'd planned to talk with Jesse, of course, but I don't think he had before he heard about Jesse's death." Patrick looked at me and shook his head slightly. "He hasn't decided what to do with the island."

Sounded to me as though Simon Lockhart was milking his hosts and hostess for a Maine vacation. "What did he see the lawyer about?"

"Don't know. Didn't ask."

"I'd like to meet him."

"I'm going to see him later tonight." Patrick glanced at his watch. "In fact, I have to get over to the house now. Uncle Gerry and June have other plans, so Mom's taking Simon and me to Camden for dinner. We're meeting an old friend of hers there." He looked down at his hands. "She thinks it's time I tried eating in public."

"Her friend who owns a shipbuilding company?"

"Right. You met him earlier this summer. I forgot that."

"You could mention to Simon that I'd like to talk with him. You could say I knew his cousin."

"Sure. Be glad to." Patrick got up. "I'll see you tomorrow, then, if he finds space on his busy schedule."

I suspected Simon's busy schedule was a myth.

"My schedule's flexible," I confirmed. "Although I do have to see a couple of people."

I was hoping to see Jed Fitch and Ed Campbell. Sunday was already sounding like a busy day.

"Could we have dinner again tomorrow night? Your cookies are delicious, but I don't think they'll sustain me for more than twenty-four hours."

We'd had dinner together only four days ago, but so much had happened since then. "I'd like that. I could fill you in on what we plan to do to help save the cormorants."

"Great," he said, moving toward the door. "Six o'clock? I've noticed people eat earlier here than they do out on the Coast." He looked at me. "The other coast."

"Six o'clock will be fine," I agreed. "Shall I bring something?"

"Your own charming self. And your appetite."

As Patrick walked toward Aurora, I got into my car. The aroma of oatmeal cookies there was tempting.

I was ravenous, and the only food purchase I'd made since my quick trip to the grocery Wednesday was cat food.

I headed toward a pizza place on Route One.

Who'd killed Jesse? Someone with motive. Opportunity. Means.

Means were simple. Rocks were all over King's Island.

Motive? I made a mental list of everyone who'd benefit from Jesse's death. Of course, depending on what Jesse had changed in his will, my assumptions might be wrong. But only a few people knew he'd changed the will at all.

Okay. Gerry Bentley and his wife. They'd get to purchase the island they wanted.

Simon Lockhart. He'd be paid. No doubt paid well.

They were the obvious people. Who else? Who wasn't obvious?

Jed Fitch, Gerry Bentley's Realtor. He'd make money if King's Island sold.

Gram'd said the Chamber of Commerce members were excited about the possibility of someone that wealthy moving to town. But I couldn't see the members of the Chamber of Commerce forming a posse and going out to King's Island to kill Jesse.

Or would they?

My meeting with Ed Campbell tomorrow could be interesting.

I ordered takeout. Vegetarian (I should eat more vegetables) with pepperoni.

The owner gave me a strange look, but said it would be ready in twenty minutes.

I sat at the bar, ordered a Sam Adams, and filled a corner of my stomach with spicy bar mix. I could still drive after one beer.

Who'd killed Jesse? My brain was a fuddle. A confusion of cormorants and kittens and cookies.

I was pretty sure of the people who might have wanted to kill Jesse. Means were simple. But opportunity? Who'd gone to King's Island last Thursday afternoon or evening?

I had no idea.

Did the police?

Chapter 36

"Jesus permit thy gracious name to stand
As the first efforts of an infants hand
And while her fingers o'er this canvass move
Engage her tender heart to seek thy love.
With thy dear children let her share a part
And write thy name thyself upon her heart."
—Caroline Vaughan's sampler, completed
October 28, 1818, when she was ten years
old, was "worked at Mary Walden's School."
Caroline included three alphabets, a basket
of flowers, a house, barn, trees, fence,
birdhouse, and several birds on her sampler.

That night I slept in my own bed instead of on the living-room couch. I shouldn't have.

During the night Trixi managed to turn her cat bed upside down, pull wool stitches out of one of my favorite of Gram's needlepoint cushions on the couch, and, worst of all, make me feel guilty for having left her alone.

I refilled her dishes while coffee was perking and resigned myself to sleeping on the couch until she was bigger. In the meantime, to apologize for my absence, I spent fifteen minutes playing "find the catnip mouse." The game didn't challenge her. Every time I hid the gray wool mouse she brought it back to me in triumph.

Where were Patrick and Bette sleeping these nights? Was my kitten the only crazy one? I gave her a gentle cuddle and listened to her purr.

Being a "fur parent" was addicting.

While Trixi circled my ankles I drank two cups of coffee and checked my messages.

I hadn't heard from Pete about Jesse's lawyer. Either he hadn't checked my suggestion, or the lawyer hadn't told him anything. Of course, I admitted, Pete might have decided not to tell me what he'd found out.

He and Ethan were investigating.

I was just a friend of the victim. And the cormorants.

I sent Clem an e-mail to alert her (and her producers at Channel Seven) about the cormorants possibly losing their nesting ground. I figured she'd be intrigued when I added that the body they hadn't identified on the news a couple of days ago was a hermit who'd lived on King's Island and protected the birds, software billionaire Gerry Bentley wanted to buy the island, and the Maine Audubon Society was preparing a short film clip in response.

That should give her enough possible leads to entrance her producer.

Then I realized it was Sunday.

Church.

When I'd been growing up, Gram had insisted I go to Sunday school and church every week. Mama always found an excuse why she couldn't go. Usually it was that she'd had to work a late Saturday night shift. Sometimes it also involved the amount she'd had to drink after her shift. By the time I was six or seven I knew Haven Harbor restaurants didn't stay open until two or three in the morning.

Gram always said we should pray for Mama. We'd prayed harder after she'd disappeared. It hadn't brought her home, but it had felt as though we were letting God—and maybe Mama—know we cared. That we needed her home. That we loved her.

But by high school, like Mama, I'd found excuses not to go to church. Some of my excuses were the same ones she'd used. Like mother, like daughter, people in town said.

But now I was back. Grown-up. Gram's husband was the minister. True, I hadn't made it to services every week this summer, but most Sundays I'd sat next to Gram in a conspicuous front pew, or, if the choir was singing and she was in the loft, sat self-consciously alone.

This week I certainly had things to pray about.

I scrambled to find a decent outfit that wouldn't embarrass Gram and made it through the wide pine doors of the Congregational Church with a minute or two to spare.

As I sank into the pew next to her, Gram handed me a hymnal turned to the opening hymn and patted my knee.

Tom's sermon was about unexpected tragedies, accepting that they were the will of God.

I glanced around the church. Carole Fitch's dealing with breast cancer was unexpected and she and her husband, Jed, and their two sons were having to deal with it. Patrick, who wasn't in church, had tried to save his mother from a fire and now had burn scars that would last the rest of his life. Dave was still in the hospital with his own pain, which would heal, and with the pain of losing a close friend.

All unexpected events that required acceptance.

But what about Jesse's death? Was murder the will of God?

I couldn't accept that. Murder was the cruelty of one human being to another.

How could anyone accept that?

After the service I headed to the reception hall where the Ladies' Guild had put out coffee and tea and homemade cookies and muffins. Breakfast for some, a snack for others. I took a bite of a cranberry nut muffin. I almost never turned down home-cooked food.

"Good morning, Angie." I turned, and Ethan Trask was standing next to me. Yesterday he'd been questioning me at the police station. Now he was on his own time. Next to him stood a beautiful dark-eyed child holding a sugar cookie as big as her hand. "This is my daughter, Emmie," said Ethan. "I don't think you've met her."

"I haven't," I said, smiling. I'd never met Ethan's wife. But Emmie didn't get her skin tone or eyes or hair from her dad. Ethan's wife must be African-American.

Emmie was the center of Ethan's life, especially since her mother was serving in the National Guard in Afghanistan. Weren't they pulling those troops back? Maybe she'd be home soon.

"Is that a good cookie?" I asked Emmie.

She nodded seriously. "I like chocolate. No chocolate cookies today."

"How old are you, Emmie?"

She held the cookie, whose crumbs now covered her mouth and the front of her classic pink smocked dress, with one hand, and held up her other sticky hand with three fingers raised.

"Three! Very grown-up," I said.

"How old are you?" she asked.

"Twenty-seven," I said.

She considered that for a minute. "That's old. Like Mommy."

Ethan smiled. "Mommy will be home soon, won't she, Emmie?"

"We see Mommy on the computer."

"Skype," Ethan said, explaining. "It helps a lot.

We don't want Emmie to forget her mom. And it makes Laura's deployment easier if she's able to see Emmie, even if it's on a screen."

"Being separated must be hard for all three of you."

"It is. But I didn't want to talk about me this morning. I wanted to thank you for answering all our questions yesterday. Pete and I were a little tough on you. Pete wants to be a homicide detective, and I let him help with local investigations. But I think this one means more to him, because he knew Jesse, and he was the one who found Jesse's body."

"Have you found out anything more about what happened?"

Ethan shook his head. "We still have a lot of people to talk with. If you have any more ideas, you'll let us know?"

"Of course," I agreed.

"Daddy, I need another cookie," said Emmie, brushing the crumbs off her dress and managing to get many of them stuck in the rows of smocking.

"Okay. Let's take care of that. And then Uncle Rob is going to take you home," he said.

Rob Trask waved from across the room. He was Ethan's younger brother, who'd chosen a more conventional Maine life: He hoped one day to have his own lobster boat.

"How are Rob's wedding plans coming?" I

asked. Rob and Mary Clough were going to be married in October.

Ethan shook his head. "They've put off the wedding for now. Mary's decided to finish high school."

"That's great," I said. "She and Rob are so young! They have lots of time ahead of them."

"I agree," said Ethan. "And she's going to keep her home, at least for now. You remember that needlepoint she found?"

"Of course."

"The Museum of Fine Arts in Boston told her they didn't know what it would sell for at auction—no other needlepoint like that has come on the market for years. Mary decided she didn't care. She's going to have it framed and keep it."

"She can always change her mind," I said.

"Of course. But she was making a lot of major decisions all at once. Now she's postponing some. And that's fine." Ethan looked down at Emmie, who was impatiently pulling on his pant leg, pointing at the table covered with plates of cookies. "Family is what's important. Family today, and family in the past. And the future, of course."

"I think a member of your family wants another cookie."

"One more," Ethan said, not quite sternly. "After that you're going home with Uncle Rob. Daddy needs to work. I'll see you later, Angie.

Keep in touch if you hear anything." He looked at me quizzically. "You seem to have a knack for that."

He was right. Since I'd been back in Haven Harbor, I'd been able to help with several investigations.

I had no desire to become a member of the police force. But when it came to friends and family being treated unfairly, or worse, I'd do whatever I could to find the guilty party. Then I'd turn the details over to the police.

Remembering people I wanted to talk to, I looked around. Jed Fitch and his wife must have left. Standing and talking with people might be hard for someone undergoing chemotherapy.

Gram was standing in back of the food table, helping keep the home-baked goods moving. She saw me coming and waved. When I got close to the table covered with goodies she leaned over. "You asked about Ed Campbell. He and his wife are over there." She nodded toward a generously sized man in a pale blue jacket standing next to a woman with short brown hair. "Go introduce yourself."

"Thanks."

The couple she'd indicated were sipping coffee and talking to each other. I interrupted, putting my hand out to shake Ed's. "Good morning. I'm Angie Curtis, Charlotte's granddaughter. I don't believe we've met."

Ed glanced at his wife and shook my hand. "No, I don't think so. I heard Charlotte's granddaughter was back in town, though. Nice to meet you. This is my wife, Diane."

Diane smiled.

"Reverend Tom told me you own a car dealership, and you're president of the Haven Harbor Chamber of Commerce," I continued, before I lost my nerve. Introducing myself to strangers wasn't my strong suit, although I seemed to be doing a lot of it recently.

"That's right. You're in the market for a car? Pickup?" he asked, looking more interested.

"No, not now. I just bought one," I admitted. Ed's attention wandered toward the food table. "But you might have heard, Charlotte's turned over management of her Mainely Needlepoint business to me. I'm interested in expanding the business. I was wondering if I should join the Chamber of Commerce."

"Of course, of course," he agreed. "Membership's open to everyone in town who owns a business or is head of an organization. We're all working toward the same goals: making Haven Harbor more attractive to businesses and tourists, so we have more jobs here in town."

"I'm curious as to how you do that," I said. I wanted to ask him what he'd been doing Thursday afternoon and early evening, when Jesse died, but that would have been too obvious.

"In the past week we had a meeting of the whole Chamber," he said. "And committee meetings on several days after that. This time of year we don't schedule as many meetings as in winter months because everyone's busy keeping their businesses going. Most meetings are in the evening. Sometimes I meet with a smaller group—like only people with businesses on Route One, or those here in town. Or I work with those who make their living from the sea."

"Sounds as though you stay busy."

"Too busy, so far as I'm concerned." His wife spoke up. "I hardly see the man between his business and that Chamber. The only reason we're in church together this morning is because he wanted to talk to other church members."

"Now, dear, you know that's not entirely true," Ed said, patting her arm. "I'm as religious as the next guy. But mixing a little religion with a little business? Nothing wrong with that, is there, Ms. Curtis?"

"Thank you for inviting me to join the Chamber," I said. "I think I may. I'm trying to think of different ways to attract new customers for our products, here in Haven Harbor, in other parts of Maine, and, through e-commerce, throughout the country."

"That's ambitious of you," he said.

I had his attention again.

"If I'm able to do that, of course, I'd be adding

employees to Mainely Needlepoint," I rattled on. "But first I'm looking for new customers. People who're influential. People I could use as references both in person, in our brochures, and on the Web site I'm developing."

"I remember hearing you did some work for Skye West earlier this summer. She's a good contact to have."

"And she's been generous with her praise," I agreed. She'd also been generous with her money. Her payments had enabled me to buy my little car. "I'm hoping she'll have other friends or relatives who might be interested in our services, too." Patrick had mentioned he'd like needlepoint cushions, right?

"You may have heard," said Ed confidentially, "but we may have another rich resident soon. Gerry Bentley's looking at property in town."

"That's funny." I frowned. "I'd heard he was looking for island property."

"You *have* heard," said Ed. "Yes—he's looking at building on King's Island. Taking a deserted piece of land and turning it into a *House Beautiful* retreat for his family. Of course, he's in the early stages of negotiation now, but once he starts building, you might want to connect with him, or with his wife, about doing work for them."

"That's an excellent idea," I agreed. "Thanks for suggesting it! Are you sure he'll be moving to Haven Harbor?"

"Can't be positive until all the papers are signed, of course. But I'm assured the deal will go through. And, between you and me, with both the Wests and the Bentleys in town we're bound to get other influential buyers and visitors. I see Haven Harbor as the next Southwest Harbor."

Southwest Harbor? "You mean, residents like the Rockefellers and Martha Stewart? And other celebrities?" I wasn't sure who lived in Southwest Harbor, but I knew whoever they were, they had money.

"Exactly," Ed beamed. "Good for every business in town."

I hesitated, as though in confusion. "But didn't I hear that island Gerry Bentley's interested in is a nesting refuge for great cormorants?"

"Those cormorants aren't endangered. No birds should stand in the way of progress. Besides"— Ed leaned toward me—"no matter what all those bird lovers say, we already have plenty of double-crested cormorants around. Great cormorants aren't essential to the coast of Maine. They nest in Canada, too. Let the Canadians worry about them." He shook his head. "America first. Don't you agree?"

"Thank you, Mr. Campbell. I appreciate all you've said," I answered. "I'll think about joining the Chamber."

"You do that, Angie. I'd be happy to sponsor

you. We need bright young women like you determining the future of Haven Harbor."

A future in which rich people counted far more than great cormorants.

Gram had been right. Ed Campbell was on Gerry Bentley's side.

Chapter 37

"Look well to what you take in hand,
For learning is better than house or land;
When land is gone and money is spent
Then learning is most excellent."
　　　　—Verse stitched on a sampler by Maggie
　　　　　　Tolliver, heroine in *The Mill on the
　　　　Floss by George Eliot [Mary Ann Evans]
　　　　　　(1819–1880), published in 1860.

Now I was able to put a face on the president of the local Chamber of Commerce. Did Ed Campbell want Gerry Bentley to buy King's Island and build a vacation home there? Yes.

But would he have killed Jesse Lockhart?

I couldn't see that.

On the other hand, I knew from experience that killers couldn't be identified by their looks or their words.

I also wanted to talk with Jed Fitch. Carole needed to rest. I'd met both of them earlier in the summer; he'd been Skye West's Realtor when she bought Aurora. According to Patrick, she'd been the one to recommend Jed as a Realtor to Gerry Bentley. Whether in small towns or big cities, a lot of business was based on relationships.

Patrick had said he'd try to find a way for me

to meet with Simon, but I wanted to hear Jed's story first.

After I checked on Trixi I headed downtown to see if Jed was at his realty office. I'd been meaning to talk to him about a home maintenance issue anyway.

In August real estate offices were open seven days a week—as were most businesses. Strike while the tourists were hot, so to speak.

Correction. Seven days a week, but not before one o'clock Sunday afternoon. I read the sign on Jed's office door twice and decided to stop in to see Sarah instead of standing in the street for half an hour looking as impatient as I felt.

The little nineteenth-century brass doorbell she'd installed jingled softly. "Afternoon, Angie! I was going to call you today. How's Dave?"

"Better, I think," I assured her. "I saw him late yesterday. He's disturbed about Jesse's murder, of course. I visited him after Pete and Ethan questioned him."

"And he's probably still in pain," Sarah added. "I'll try to get over to the hospital after I close up today. I called once yesterday afternoon, but he didn't answer. Maybe he was having tests."

Or he was being examined by the police. "How was your evening? Did you get a chance to ask Ted Lawrence if he'd help our Save the Cormorants campaign?"

"He agreed!" she said. "He's a dear. A little

lonely. I like him, and I think he likes having me around. I told him you'd want something simple—more symbolic than realistic—something we could embroider, or have printed on tote bags or T-shirts. He promised to have sketches to show me today."

"Perfect!" I said. I wanted to ask her more, but I knew Sarah well enough to know she'd tell me more when she was ready, not before. "When you've seen his drawings, why don't you and I meet with the rest of the Needlepointers and talk about next steps?"

"Can do," Sarah said. "So—what else is new in your life?"

"I have a housemate," I shared, smiling.

"Who? When? Man or woman? Tell all!" asked Sarah.

"Kitten."

"Ooh, I have to visit!" said Sarah. "Can we have the meeting at your house? When did you adopt a kitten? How old is he—or she?"

"She," I said firmly. "Her name is Beatrix, but I'm calling her Trixi. Dave had been taking care of her and her brother and sister. Now that he's in the hospital, they needed new homes."

"So who else was lucky enough to get one?"

"Gram has one, but she plans to return hers to Dave when he gets home. And Patrick has the third."

"Patrick?"

"I happened to mention them to him. I think he's lonely living there at the carriage house. He can't drive yet. Anyway, he's smitten. He named his kitten Bette because she's a tuxedo cat."

"Cool." Sarah straightened papers on her counter. "I didn't know you and Patrick were close."

"You suggested I drop in to welcome him back to Haven Harbor," I reminded her. "He invited me to have dinner. We're friends."

"Friends?" she said.

"Friends," I said, firmly. "You said you weren't interested in him. And you're spending a lot of time with Ted Lawrence."

"Not the same thing at all." Sarah looked at me as though I'd suggested she was dating a ghost.

"Then what is it?"

She turned away and put the papers she'd been sorting on a shelf in back of her register. "Ted's a friend. Just a friend."

"And Patrick's my friend," I repeated. "Nothing more. I think I have him swayed to our side in the cormorant situation, too. He even talked to Gerry Bentley—his uncle Gerry—about it."

"And?"

"Unfortunately, Uncle Gerry was more interested in buying King's Island than in the cormorants."

"I'll call you when Ted finishes his cormorant sketches," said Sarah. "And I do want to meet your Trixi. My old cat's a dear, but kittens are so much fun! I'd be tempted to adopt one myself, but I don't think Ruggles would want to share his space." She glanced at the staircase leading to her apartment, as though Ruggles could overhear her.

"I'm going over to talk with Jed Fitch," I said. "I'd like to find out more about what's happening with the sale of King's Island."

"Jesse was murdered. I'm not surprised you're checking into it," said Sarah.

"You helped me with a couple of investigations earlier this summer," I pointed out.

"True. But it's not something I do on a regular basis. You used to be a private investigator. Asking questions is part of who you are."

"An assistant to a private investigator," I corrected. "I'm checking into this because Jesse was Dave's friend. And because I care about what happens to those cormorants."

"I care about birds, too, Angie. But I care about people more. I suspect you do, too."

Chapter 38

"We sew, sew, prick our fingers, dull our sight,
Producing what? A pair of slippers, sir,
To put on when you're weary—or a stool
To stumble over and vex you . . . 'curse that
    stool!'
Or else at best, a cushion, where you lean
And sleep, and dream of something we are not
But would be for your sake. Alas, alas!
This hurts most, this—that, after all, we are
    paid
The worth of our work, perhaps."
    —Elizabeth Barrett Browning (1806–
        1861) from *Aurora Leigh* (1856).

The windows of the real estate storefront were covered with pictures of Haven Harbor houses and lots for sale.

I slowed down to read the listings. I was a new homeowner, but I had no idea how much my house was worth. The week before she and Tom were married Gram had transferred the title of our family home to me. She'd explained about real estate taxes and home insurance, and about home heating oil in winter and basic maintenance.

She'd also suggested I call Jed Fitch about plowing the driveway in winter.

It was August. I hadn't done that yet.

But it gave me a reason to talk with him. The last time I'd done that was when Skye West had asked me to do some investigating for her. She'd known Jed years ago, when they'd both been in high school.

In Haven Harbor that wasn't unusual. Most people in town had known one another for decades. Maybe even generations. Known their challenges and their successes, their relationships and their secrets.

Growing up in town I'd overheard gossip, but hadn't paid much attention to it. My world was focused on me, on my classmates, and on Mama and Gram.

What other grown-ups were doing wasn't interesting to me. All I'd wanted was to survive— and get out of Maine.

Now, ten years later, I had a lot to catch up with.

Information Gram, who'd lived in town all her life, took for granted.

I pushed open the glass door to the office.

"Angie Curtis!" said Jed, who was sitting at one of the front desks. "Good to see you. I'm on the Chamber of Commerce with your—what should I call him? Your step-grandfather. He talks about you all the time."

He did? "Good to see you, too, Jed," I said, sitting in one of the two green-leather chairs opposite his desk.

"Heard you own the old Curtis home now," he said. "Big old house for a young single lady like yourself. Lots of maintenance, too. If you ever want to sell it, get something smaller, you know where I am."

"I do," I agreed. "That maintenance is one reason I'm here today. Gram said you've been plowing our drive for years. Can I count on your doing that this coming winter?"

Jed made a note in a worn black notebook on the side of his desk. "Can do, Angie. I'll make sure your house is on my list."

"And two windows on the second floor are cracked."

"My schedule's full right now, but by early September I could get to those for you." He hesitated a moment. "Unless life interferes, of course."

"Gram told me your wife is ill. I'm sorry."

Jed's salesperson demeanor changed. "Thank you, Angie. Kind of you to think of her. Carole's having a hard time right now. Having chemo in Portland once a week. Aggressive treatment, they call it."

"That must be hard on both of you."

"Harder on Carole, of course. But yeah." He leaned toward me. "Watching her's the hardest thing. Watching the medical bills climb isn't easy, either." He looked past me, out the window. "Carole and me, we've always been healthy. Never had any big medical problems until—wham!—now we do."

"That must be hard."

"Don't want Carole to worry, of course. She has enough problems, dealing with the side effects of the chemo and thinking what will happen if the chemo doesn't work. But driving her back and forth to Portland every Friday means I'm not here, or showing houses to potential buyers, or even doing the repairs folks hire me to do. Our income is going down, as her bills go up."

"Rough." How did families cope with illnesses like that?

"It is. The chemo takes a while, so some days I can race back to Haven Harbor to show a house or get paperwork done while she's having a treatment, but of course it's at least an hour each way." He straightened up. "But you didn't come here to hear my problems. Was it just about the plowing? Because that's not a problem. I'll make sure your drive is clear within an hour or two after the snow stops. Been doing it for Charlotte for years. Your place is on my usual snowplow route. And I'll get your windows fixed before temperatures drop. Don't you worry."

"I won't," I assured him. "But I did want to ask you about something else. My friend Patrick West told me you're working with his uncle, who'd like to buy in the area."

"That's true. Forgotten you were such a friend of the Wests," said Jed. "Skye was kind enough to refer her brother-in-law to me."

I leaned over and said quietly, confidentially, "I hadn't planned to sell my home. But you know it. Do you think it'd be the sort of place he'd be looking for?"

Jed shook his head. "Sorry, Angie. If you do decide to sell I'll do my best for you. But this guy wants to build his own place, to his own specs. Has his eye on an island—can you believe? Islands aren't an easy sell, even when they're close to shore. People from away think island living is romantic. They don't think about boating to town for groceries, or needing propane for electricity, or getting fresh water . . . or even about the isolation, unless you're living on an island like Islesboro or Monhegan or Swan or Peaks, where there's a year-round population. The island Gerry Bentley's set on is three miles out and unpopulated." Jed looked out the window for a moment before he turned back to me. "I think we can get it for him. But if the deal falls through, that will be the end of it far's I can tell. He's made it clear he isn't interested in anything in town."

I ignored his comment about King's Island being unpopulated. After all, as of right now, it was. Except for the great cormorants, of course. "You think he'll get this island?"

"I do. And if so, it'll be a good sale for me. But in the meantime there are a few complications. No property sale is simple, but this one's more involved than most."

I tried to look as though I was concentrating. Should have taken acting lessons during the short time I was at Arizona State. "You're not talking about King's Island, are you? That bird sanctuary where a strange hermit died this week?"

"That's the one," Jed agreed. "You keep your ears open, Angie!"

"I know the Wests."

"Of course, of course. Yes—that's the place. Seemed like an easy deal: Offer some guy who has nothing a decent price for an island. He can go somewhere and buy a little house, raise chickens, whatever. But then he goes and dies on us."

Maybe Jed hadn't heard Jesse'd been murdered.

"Rough on your sale, I assume. Having to probate the will and all that takes time."

"Right you are, Angie. A couple of lawyers are checking it out now. Don't know what will happen." He leaned toward me. "But between us, I think money will tell. And if it does, my six percent will go a long way toward taking care of Carole and keeping our boys in college."

I stood. "Good luck. To you, and to Carole."

"And keep me in mind if you ever do decide to sell, Angie," Jed said, standing. "And, if not, I'll see you in September about those windows, and then after the first Haven Harbor snowfall."

Chapter 39

"Blessed is he that considereth the poor. Psalm 41"

—Needlework sampler stitched in 1824 by Eliza Baynard at the "Valley Town Mission School, Cherokee Nation," (now Cherokee County, North Carolina). Eliza was a Cherokee student at the school. This simple sampler was given to one of the school's patrons, who lived in Baltimore, Maryland.

Didn't sound to me as though Jed knew a lot about what was happening, although he was counting on selling King's Island. Or he didn't tell me all the details. He had said the sale "had complications."

If Jed needed money for medical bills, of course he'd do whatever he could to facilitate the sale—and earn his percentage.

Before I headed home I walked to the town wharf. Happily, someone had cleaned Dave's blood off the *Sweet Life*. I'd hoped to do that myself, but as Jed had put it, life interfered.

Tourists nibbling saltwater taffy or licking Round Top Ice Cream cones were walking along Water Street, carrying bags from Haven Harbor stores. I hoped some of them contained Mainely

Needlepoint cushions. Maine T-shirts and sweat-shirts were big sales items in Haven Harbor, along with lobster and starfish jewelry, books of Down East recipes, stuffed toy red lobsters (did they ever think that red lobsters were dead?) to take home to children or grandchildren, and perhaps a small painting or print of a moose or lobster boat. For Sarah's sake, I hoped a few of those bags also included antiques.

Haven Harbor's sky was a clear pale blue, with only a few cumulous clouds. The rippling sea below was gray. The tide was coming in; all the boats anchored in the harbor faced the mainland.

Once as a child I'd heard someone from away say, "Mainers always park their boats facing the same direction."

Before I'd had a chance to comment, Mama'd clapped her hand over my mouth. "They don't know," she'd explained. "They don't understand. They don't know what we know."

It was the first time I'd understood that growing up in a harbor town meant I'd absorbed a lot about tides and storms and boats and fishing . . . facts that were a part of my life. Facts that were fascinating to those for whom they were new phenomena.

Everywhere in the world people grew up with special knowledge. I'd built fairy houses in the woods and collected periwinkle and slipper shells on the beaches. I knew which gulls congregated near people and which didn't. I knew sailboats had the right of way. I knew buoys were different colors and why, and I could read their messages to boaters.

I'd taken for granted the smell of tidal flats at low tide and why old sneakers shouldn't be discarded. (They should be saved to wear when swimming, so you didn't cut your feet on rocks or barnacles or broken sea urchin shells.)

I'd known why cormorants stretched out their wings, and herons walked carefully in shallow waters.

Someone had once told me those things. Or maybe I'd absorbed them, like sunflowers absorbed sunlight. They were part of my world.

I ignored the feel of my vibrating phone and walked over to Pocket Cove Beach, between the wharves and Haven Harbor Light.

Not surprisingly, the beach was strewn with brightly colored blankets and towels. Mothers held toddlers' hands as they braved the cold ocean water. Older children ran in and out of the low surf, screaming and giggling with delight as waves lapped their legs and bodies. A group of teenagers had strung a net across one corner of the beach and were playing volleyball. An old couple sat in matching red beach chairs, holding hands.

August.

I was enjoying the warmth of the sun on my

head and arms, and feeling thankful for the normalcy of Haven Harbor, when a picture of Jesse's body, lying cold and alone on the wet ground on King's Island, flashed into my head.

Not everyone was enjoying this Maine day.

I turned and headed for home. I hadn't seen Dave today. Had he heard when he'd be released from the hospital?

I checked my phone. Patrick had left me a message. Simon's here for afternoon. We're having a lobster bake. Come? Five o'clock.

I texted back: I'll be there.

Patrick hadn't forgotten I wanted to talk with Simon. Good.

A cloud covered the sun for a few moments. I could feel the difference in temperature on my shoulders and arms. The afternoon was disappearing. But I'd have time to stop and see Dave before I went to Aurora.

A lobster bake? Catered, I assumed. The Wests might have money, but they didn't have a beach. You couldn't have an authentic Maine lobster bake without a beach.

I hadn't been to a bake since high school, when friends had gathered on Pocket Cove Beach. In those days a lobster bake hadn't been a novelty. In fact, I'd avoided a number of them.

I'd had enough lobster and corn and clams working the steamer on the wharf for summer folks. Once in February I'd pulled a sweatshirt from the bottom of a pile in my room and refused to wear it. It still smelled of lobster.

But that was over ten years ago. Ten years since everything I'd owned—from my hair to my underwear—had smelled of lobster.

I was ready for a lobster bake.

Was Trixi a little young to eat lobster? I'd save the meat from a couple of legs for her.

I smiled as I headed up the hill.

I wasn't sure I'd accomplished anything so far today. But I felt more relaxed than I had in days. Probably Pete and Ethan had already figured out who'd killed Jesse. Dave was healing. I hoped Gerry Bentley had decided to buy a house near Seattle, or Portland—the other Portland.

The cloud moved, and the sun returned.

What could go wrong at a lobster bake?

Chapter 40

"This needle work of mine doth tell
When I was young I learned well,
Though by my Elders I was taught,
Not to spend my time for naught."
        —Verse on eleven-year-old Sally Wales
    Turner's sampler, 1810, in the Leominster
    area of Massachusetts. Sally stitched a large
        house, an orchard, and an asymmetrical
    border on her unusual oval-shaped sampler.

Trixi was curled on the blanket I'd left for her in the cat bed. But she'd pulled the blanket out and arranged it to her satisfaction on the floor. She looked tiny and vulnerable, and meowed piteously when I reached down to gently stroke her.

"I'm sorry, little lady. But I have to go out again. I'm sorry you don't have your brother and sister to play with." I looked around and found a bottle cap. She immediately claimed it as her own, chasing it on the bare floor outside the large rug that covered most of the living-room floor.

I changed her water. That made me feel a little less guilty.

"I won't be gone long," I promised, hoping my words wouldn't make a liar of me. "I have to visit Dave at the hospital and tell him how you're doing."

She looked up at me, doubtfully.

I suspected she'd rather have me stay home.

I glanced in the mirror over the hall sideboard on my way out.

Whoa.

I'd changed into jeans and a T-shirt after church, but since then I'd been walking all over town, and the wind had blown my hair into an arrangement I couldn't call artful.

I was supposed to be going to an event. Not that one dressed up for a lobster bake. Lobsters were notoriously messy—and that didn't count the butter on the corn or the clam broth.

But I should look as though I cared.

I changed my jeans, put on a long-sleeved T-shirt, and took a sweater, in case the evening chilled off. It was August, after all. After looking in a mirror I changed my grungy (but comfortable) sneakers for sandals, and put on dangly sea-glass earrings.

Not exactly ready to greet the queen, I grimaced as I combed windblown snarls out of my hair and added lipstick. But better.

Did I have anything to take to Dave in the hospital? I snapped a couple of pictures of Trixi with my phone. "See, lady? I'm going to show Dave how well you're doing here."

She looked unimpressed.

I drove to the hospital.

Dave was sitting up—in a chair!

"You're better, I see."

"Not ready to run any marathons. And still on painkillers. But I've graduated from injections to pills, and the nurses have me walking a little." He looked me over. "You look nice today. Different."

Was that a compliment or a put-down? "Thank you. So—no infection?"

"No infection," he agreed. "Thank goodness."

"So when can you go home?"

"The doctors say I'm not ready for climbing stairs," Dave said. "But if I keep my leg elevated for a few hours and sit instead of stand in my classes, I should be okay to be at school the first week in September."

"That's great!"

"Luckily, my bio lab is on the first floor. My doctors weren't enthused, but since it's my left leg they've said I can even drive back and forth to school by then. They're getting me a temporary handicap sign so I can park close to the entrance for a while. The principal's even agreed to hire an aide to work with me for the first couple of weeks to help with handing out papers, rounding up stray students, and setting up the classroom."

"What about grocery shopping? And the stairs in your house?" I asked.

"I haven't figured it all out yet," he admitted.

"For now, I'm planning to sleep on the convertible couch in the living room."

"I could move some of your clothes downstairs for you," I volunteered. "And get you some groceries."

"That would be great," he said.

"But," I added, "I'm not going to go near that poison garden of yours!"

"No problem. Growing season's almost over anyway."

"Here, let me show you how one of your little girls is doing." I showed him the pictures of Trixi on my phone. "See? She can climb the drapes. And she moved her blanket to her favorite corner and smooshed it up to make a soft nest."

"You sound like a new parent," Dave said, shaking his head. "Yes, she's very cute. And thank you for showing me the pictures. I'm not at all worried about her, I assure you."

Had I gone a little overboard?

"So with a little help from my friends, to quote someone famous, I should be all right. But I keep thinking about Jesse. He had such a rough life, and he'd worked so hard to find a place where he was comfortable. And someone killed him. For what? It doesn't make sense."

"I've been talking to people around town, and I haven't come up with any serious suspects. I'm going to meet his cousin tonight, though. Maybe he'll say something to give me an idea."

"You're going to meet Simon?" Dave asked.

"Over at Aurora," I confirmed. I didn't think it was necessary to mention that Patrick had invited me.

"So he's still around." Dave hesitated. "Do you know if he's planned a funeral for Jesse?"

I hadn't even thought about a funeral. "I don't know if the medical examiner has released his body yet."

"I'd like to be at the funeral," Dave said. "If you get a chance, would you tell Simon I'd like to say a few words at the service?"

"I will," I promised. "I'll let you know what he says. In the meantime, have you heard anything new about the Save the Cormorants plan?"

"Sarah called. Her friend Ted has designed a couple of logos. She's going to bring them by tonight for me to see. And Ruth called twice to see how I am. The Audubon people are monitoring this whole situation. They'd like the island to be an official refuge for seabirds. That makes sense to me, too. That's what Jesse would want. But since he only owned half the island, the decision will rest with Simon."

"I'll try to find out how he feels," I promised. "And I'll check back with you tomorrow. You'll still be here?"

"Another day or two," Dave said. "It seems forever, but I've only been here since Thursday afternoon. Three days. The doctor says I'll be able to get out Tuesday."

"Make up a shopping list," I said. "You'll be tired when you get home. Write down what you'd like and I'll take care of it before you're released."

Several of us should also make casseroles or cakes or whatever so Dave wouldn't have to cook at all during his first week at home. Maybe Gram could call on the culinary resources of the Ladies' Guild. Something else for *my* to-do list.

I waved good-bye and was happy to see Dave pick up one of the mysteries I'd brought him. No hospitalization was fun. Under Dave's circumstances it was nightmarish. At least he would be going home Tuesday.

I wished Jesse had known that.

He never knew his friend was going to be all right.

Chapter 41

"Knowledge and virtue both combined
Like flower and fruit in youthful mind
Yield charms of brighter lustre far
Then wealth can boast or beauty wear
Virtue and wit with science joind
Reform the manner please the mind
And when with industry they meet
The whole character is complete."
—Sampler completed by Susan Jane Hazen
    (1826–1901) from Hartford, Vermont.
    Susan completed her sampler in cotton
    and silk on linen in 1837, when she was
eleven. She included a picture of Dartmouth
    Hall, in Hanover, New Hampshire, with
    its distinctive cupola. Several members of
    her family attended Dartmouth College.

As I'd suspected, a catering truck (TRADITIONAL MAINE LOBSTER BAKES—YOUR CHOICE OF LOCATION!) was in the driveway at Aurora.

I was deciding whether to knock on the door or go around to the back of the mansion when Patrick waved from the direction of his house.

"Glad you're here!" he called. "Everyone's out back in the field."

276

I waited for him. "Sounds like fun. Did your mom invite many people?"

"Simon and you and Uncle Gerry and his wife," Patrick answered. "Oh, and I think Jed Fitch and his wife—Carole?"

"I know them."

"I've never been to an actual lobster bake," Patrick confided. "I assume you're an expert."

"Not an expert," I cautioned him. "I've been to a fair number, but none since I got back to Haven Harbor last spring. Most of the ones I used to go to were on Pocket Cove Beach."

"The caterer told Mom bakes were usually on beaches. But too many people know her. In June, that was all right, since not many tourists were around. But in August? She decided we'd have the caterers put up their equipment here, where we can have privacy."

Being a famous movie star had its downside.

"I'm sure it'll be fine," I said. "What's important is the food, and the seaweed."

"The seaweed? People eat seaweed?" Patrick asked seriously.

"People do eat seaweed," I assured him. "It's a Maine crop. But not at a lobster bake. Seaweed is critical to the bake process. All the food at the bake—lobsters, clams, onions, potatoes, corn, and eggs—is steamed under rockweed or kelp."

"Eggs? I didn't know people ate eggs at a lobster bake."

I tried to keep from laughing. This must be one of those things Mainers knew that people from away didn't. It wouldn't be fair to laugh.

"Several raw eggs are always put under the layers of seaweed, with the rest of the food. The eggs are timers: When they're hard-boiled, the rest of the food is ready."

"So people don't eat the eggs," he said.

"It depends. There's no rule against it, and wasting food isn't good. But sometimes several eggs have to be broken and tested before the rest of the food's declared done. There's no rule for how long a lobster bake takes. It depends on the amount of food, and the type of wood, and how dry the wood is, how much seaweed is used— even on the air temperature and the winds."

The caterers were digging a deep hole for the fire. Sand on a beach wouldn't catch fire. Grasses in a field might.

"Right you are," said a young woman leaning back on her shovel. "The way we set up our bakes, the food takes about thirty minutes to cook. But if there's wind, or more food than usual, it can take twice that time."

"Fascinating," said Patrick. "And anyone could do this?"

"Anyone can, and often does," she assured him. "But hiring us ensures it'll be done well and safely. And you don't have to gather driftwood and seaweed. We bring it all to you and do the work." She smiled. "Plus, we bring haddock chowder to start with, and whoopie pies for dessert. Why don't you go over to the bar and get a drink? We'll serve the chowder in about half an hour, after we get the fire going."

"Good plan," said Patrick. "Thank you!" His hand lightly on my back headed me over toward where picnic tables and chairs were arranged overlooking the harbor and a young man was standing behind a table covered with a red-and-white tablecloth and a selection of glasses and bottles.

"What would you like to drink? May I suggest a cocktail now, and champagne when the lobster is served?" he said. "We also recommend the Sweetgrass Winery's cranberry gin. A local product. And such a lovely color." He held up a bottle to demonstrate.

"I'll try the gin," I said. "I've never had that."

"Make it two," added Patrick. "This evening is a Maine experience."

The young man poured our cranberry gin into martini glasses. I held mine up to the light. "You're right. It's a beautiful color."

"And tastes remarkable," Patrick agreed, sipping his. "When I'm painting again I think I'll have to try a wash of this color over a gray-blue sky. Like a sunrise."

We walked slowly toward those already seated. Skye waved, and I waved back. I recognized

Gerry Bentley walking slowly down the hill toward the Harbor. A tall, thin man wearing slacks and an oxford shirt was with him. Definitely not a Mainer. He must be Jesse's cousin, Simon Lockhart.

Jed and Carole Fitch were sitting together on matching lounge chairs, while Uncle Gerry's pregnant wife was surrounded by pillows on another. Mrs. Bentley and Carole were holding glasses of orange juice; the others were holding cocktails. I took a sip of my cranberry gin. Delicious. And, I could tell immediately, potent.

"Good to see you again so soon," said Jed, standing. "You've met my wife, Carole."

"I have," I agreed, nodding at her. "Earlier this summer. Please, sit down."

Jed sat, but to my surprise, Carole stood. "I haven't talked with you in a while, Angie. And the food won't be ready for a while. Would you mind taking a little walk with me? I'd like to stretch, and it's a glorious day."

"Of course," I agreed. Why had Carole chosen me to be her walking companion? Her husband was right next to her. "The weather is spectacular. August is one of my favorite months in Maine."

Patrick seemed surprised, but took Carole's place on the chair and turned to Jed. "I've been meaning to talk with you. I heard you can arrange for plowing and roof raking in the winter."

I smiled to myself. Yes, Jed could arrange

for such things. He did them himself. The real estate business in Maine was quiet during winter months.

"I'd like to walk around the house," Carole Fitch was saying. "I haven't seen it since it's been fixed up."

I followed her, glancing back to see if anyone was paying attention. No one was.

She walked toward the house.

Carole had been plump when I'd seen her in June. Now she was thinner, her large dark eyes were deeper in her face, and her short hair was thinner than it had been only two months ago. She seemed almost lost inside her long, loose dress.

Gram and Jed had both told me Carole had cancer. What was the etiquette for such things?

"I've heard you're having health problems," I said.

"Cancer," she answered, without hesitating. "Breast cancer. Stage four."

"That must be difficult," I said, hoping I didn't sound too maudlin.

"It sucks," she answered, with a small smile. "That's about it. Plus, what's worse, is Jed's taking time off to take care of me, and the boys are both in college. Without his income, they may have to drop out. This summer George is working down at the lobsterman's co-op."

The job I'd had as a teenager. Not easy.

"And Linc, our older boy, is sterning for any lobsterman who needs a backup." Another rough job with an undependable income. "Neither of them can earn enough to pay for their college. It's impossibly expensive today."

I'd taken a couple of classes at Arizona State, but I wasn't an expert on colleges. Or college tuition. But college was important to Carole. "That's rough."

"Not rough. Impossible. I never went to college, and Jed and I agreed years ago we'd find the money to send our boys if they wanted to go. They're bright, both of them. They deserve to go. And now they may have to drop out. And it's all my fault." Her voice shook, but was determined. "I hope you never have to go through anything like this, Angie. Cancer doesn't just kill one person. It tears families apart."

"Jed told me you're having chemo. I've heard of people going into remission, or getting rid of cancer totally. You can't give up hope!"

"Remission happens. But not often with the cancer I have." Carole stared at Aurora. "Skye's done such a beautiful job of restoration, hasn't she? Aurora almost looks the way it did back in the late sixties and early seventies, when Jed and I and Skye were all young and full of dreams."

I hadn't been around then, but I'd seen pictures. "It looks beautiful."

"She had the money to do it. What must it be like not to worry about how much things cost?"

"For most of us spending money the way she does would be a fantasy," I agreed. Like wanting a lobster bake and having it catered in your backyard.

Carole turned toward me and touched my arm. "You understand, Angie. I hoped you would. We both grew up in Haven Harbor. We know how hard people work to get by."

"Most have two or three jobs," I agreed.

"Jed's been doing odd jobs for people for years, in addition to selling property, but it's not enough. Not now, with the boys needing more money, and my medical bills. When I heard you were coming tonight—Patrick mentioned it to Jed—I felt it was meant. I have to ask a favor of you."

"What do you need, Carole?" My mind raced through possibilities. I didn't have any money to help them out. Carole and her family needed more than needlepoint right now. Maybe she wanted me to help with food? Or rides to Portland? I could do those things.

"It's this King's Island real estate deal." Carole had stopped walking and was looking directly at me. "If the deal goes through, Jed's percentage of the sale will be enough to keep us solvent for months, even with my medical bills. The boys won't have to leave college, or take out bigger loans."

"It's an important deal for him."

"Very important. At first it seemed simple: Offer that Solitary fellow enough money, which Gerry Bentley was prepared to do, and he'd sell. When he refused, Bentley flew in his cousin, Simon—you saw him over there in his fancy clothes, waiting for his lobster dinner and champagne. He and Gerry Bentley even dreamed up a plan to have that hermit declared incompetent, so Simon, as his only relative, would get control, and could sell the island." She shook her head. "Money talks. Jed wasn't happy about what they were planning, but in the end he'd get his percentage. All would be fine. We'd get some financial relief."

"But then Jesse—his name was Jesse—died."

"Yes. At first that seemed to answer all our problems. Simon would inherit. It was simple. But now it's gotten complicated."

"Gotten complicated?" I asked. Now? The whole situation had always seemed complicated to me.

"Seems that man who lived on the island changed his will at the last minute. Seems he was obsessed with some birds who nest there."

"The great cormorants," I put in.

"Right. He wanted to leave the island to those Audubon people. But he didn't have enough money to leave a trust to care for it, which they needed. So he left his part of the island to the biology teacher over at Haven Harbor High."

"Dave Percy? Jesse left his part of King's Island to Dave Percy?" Why hadn't Dave told me he was inheriting Jesse's part of King's Island?

"Right. That's his name. Percy. So Gerry and Jed and Simon figured Percy would sell. But before anyone could even talk to him, he and some other people—most of them, Angie, people who work for you—started a campaign to keep the island from being sold. They want to create a bird sanctuary out there. Simon won't be able to sell his part of the island unless this Dave Percy agrees."

I didn't know what to say. Carole was more up-to-date than I was.

"They're your friends, Angie. You're their boss. Please, please, get those environmental nuts to back off. Birds can live anywhere. Jed and I need Dave Percy to talk with Simon and agree to sell King's Island."

Chapter 42

"As I hope to be forever blest
May I be industrious pious &
Meek & benevolent virtuous wise
Dutiful to my Parents."
> —Stitched in 1808 by Polly Wyatt of
> Newbury, Vermont, when Polly was
> fifteen years old. Polly's sampler was
> bordered with an unusual combination
> of vines, geometric designs, and flowers.
> She was the oldest of nine children.

"Promise me you'll help, Angie? Get your friends to stop campaigning for those birds? Dave Percy can use the money from the island's sale to buy another island for them. But this is Jed's and my only chance. Jed's already talked to the Bentleys about other real estate. That island is the only one they're interested in." Carole was begging.

"I'm sorry. I didn't know Jesse left his share of King's Island to Dave. This is all new. I do know about the Save the Cormorants campaign and, yes, several of the Mainely Needlepointers are involved. So is Ted Lawrence. And they've been in touch with the Maine Audubon folks. I've been so busy during the past few days, I haven't been as involved as perhaps I should be. But I have to say, I've been out to King's Island, and it is a perfect place for the cormorants. I can't understand why the Bentleys want to develop it."

"So you won't help?" Carole's voice was bitter. "I didn't ask you to do anything complicated. Just something that will save my family."

"Carole, I'd be happy to drive you to chemo treatments if that would free Jed to work. Gram could arrange for the Ladies' Guild at the church to provide meals for your family, so you and Jed won't have to worry about those. But I can't stop the Save the Cormorants campaign." I took a deep breath. "And I don't want to. I believe in that cause."

Carole's face reddened. She was furious. For a moment I thought she was going to throw her orange juice in my face. Instead, she stumbled toward me, dropping her glass. I grabbed her and put my arm around her waist to hold her up.

"I don't know what else to do," she said softly, crumpling in my arms. "I'm sorry, Angie. It isn't your fault. It's mine."

"It's not your fault you're sick," I assured her. Together, we slowly headed back to where the others were waiting. When we were almost there Jed saw Carole leaning on me and lumbered toward us to help.

"What is it, dear? What happened?"

"I was a little faint," she said, smiling at him as though nothing were wrong and our conversation had never happened. "Angie was kind enough to help me. I need my pain pills."

Jed put his arm around Carole from the other side, and the two of us almost carried her the rest of the way and helped her down onto her lounge chair.

She took a pill bottle out of her purse.

"Should I take you home?" Jed asked solicitously.

"No, no," said Carole. "I need to rest a little and let the pills work. I'll be fine here. When the food is ready I'll be able to eat a little." She smiled at Jed. "You know I can always eat lobster."

Patrick came over as I stood awkwardly next to Carole, not sure of what I should do next. "Are you all right?"

"I'm fine," I said, picking up on Carole's cue. "She was a bit dizzy. We walked too far. I'll get the glass she dropped. You don't want anyone stepping on it, or a lawnmower running over it."

"I'll come with you," he said.

We were out of earshot of the rest when I said, "Did you know Jesse Lockhart left his share of the island to Dave Percy?"

Patrick frowned. "Your friend who's in the hospital? The one who saved Bette and the other kittens?"

"That's the one," I said. "He didn't tell me."

Patrick shook his head. "I'd heard Jesse might have changed his will. Simon went to the police department to ask them about it. But I hadn't heard what was in the will."

I stopped and looked around for Carole's glass. It had rolled into a tall clump of goldenrod. "Carole said Gerry and Jed and Simon were planning to talk to Dave, and try to buy his share of the island."

Patrick shook his head. "I have no idea. I didn't know. But I haven't been at the big house a lot. I'm trying to live by myself. And I've been taking care of Bette for the last couple of days. I haven't been paying a lot of attention to this island mess."

Mugs of chowder had been served by the time we got back to the others. Everyone except Carole and Jed were sitting at the wide redwood table, where trays of food and stacks of napkins were arranged. The bartender was holding a magnum of champagne, and full crystal flutes were already at our places.

Jed had taken his food and Carole's over to her chair, where he was cracking the claws of her lobster for her. I sat across from Patrick, between Mrs. Bentley and Simon.

Uncle Gerry stood and toasted, "To Maine, and all its glories!" which I assumed encompassed islands and lobsters, and Skye. The table was quiet as we focused on bowls of haddock chowder, and then on platters of lobsters, clams, mussels, corn, onions, and potatoes the caterers set in the middle of the table. (A small bowl of hard-boiled eggs was there, too.) The lobsters, clams, and mussels were getting the most attention, although I noticed Mrs. Bentley was eating a piece of chicken instead.

"You don't like lobster?" I asked, sucking the meat out of one of my lobster's legs. I remembered to put several legs in a napkin to take home to Trixi.

"Allergic to shellfish," she explained. "The caterers cooked a piece of chicken separately for me. It's delicious. And I can eat the chowder, and the corn and onion and potato."

"When is your baby due?"

"In a little over a month now," she confided. "I'm going to have a little girl! The nursery is beautiful. I had my decorator paint the walls pale pink, with white lambs playing in a green field. The lampshades and rug match, too."

"It sounds lovely," I said, minding my manners. I figured if you were expecting you bought a crib and a changing table and friends gave you baby clothes at a shower. Maybe you painted a room. The Bentleys' daughter-to-be had a decorator do her room? A different world than the one I knew.

"You must be excited," I said, stating the obvious. "Will you be heading home soon, so you can be near your doctor?"

"This trip has taken longer than we'd planned," she admitted. She glanced over at her husband, who was deep in a discussion with Skye. "I'd feel better if I were at home. Gerry's made arrangements to leave our boat with a friend of Skye's we met in Camden the other day. His shipyard has space to winter it over. I don't want to take our baby on any expeditions, at least until spring. Gerry likes me to be with him when he travels, so I'm not sure how long I can manage that. Having a nanny will help."

Of course a nanny would help. "Your first child?"

"Yes. It's been a long wait. We've been married almost three years now!"

I glanced at Uncle Gerry. He was at least twenty-five years older than his bride. "I'm happy for you." I meant it.

"Do you have any children?" she asked.

I almost choked on my clam broth. "No. I'm not married."

She shrugged. "It's the twenty-first century. You don't have to be married to have children."

"True," I admitted. I should know. Mama had never married. And that had been way back in the twentieth century. "But no. No children."

"Soon?" she suggested. "You don't want to be as old as I am before you try to get pregnant."

"How old are you?" I blurted.

Her voice dropped. "Thirty. Almost thirty-one."

Four years older than I was. I felt as though I'd aged a decade or two in the last two minutes.

"I've heard you and your husband want to live on King's Island," I said casually.

Her voice stayed low. "Not really. We already have three homes. That's plenty for me, especially since we can travel to other places whenever we want to. With a little one it'll be more complicated, even with help. But I like Skye and Patrick, and it would be convenient to have a place near them. Gerry always has to have a project to keep himself busy. Right now he has this idea about living on the rustic coast of Maine, so I'm supporting him. It's his money, his choice." She patted her bulging abdomen. "Who knows? Our little princess may love the outdoors."

Mrs. Bentley wasn't the one pushing the purchase of King's Island.

"You don't mind that the cormorants will have to find new nesting grounds?"

"I'd never heard of cormorants until we arrived in Maine. Strange black birds." She shuddered. "They make me nervous. The way they look— with their wings all spread out—they're menacing. As though they're threatening other birds. Or even people."

I tried not to smile. "I don't think they threaten anything but fish," I said. "But I grew up here. They're part of the Maine seacoast. I'd hate to see them lose their nesting grounds."

"They can find other nesting grounds as far

as I'm concerned," she said, selecting an ear of corn. "Once Gerry has construction going on out there, I don't think those birds are going to feel welcome."

That was the truth.

Carole and Jed joined the rest of us at the table.

"Feeling better?" asked Skye. "Is there anything we can get for you, Carole?"

"No, I'm fine," she said. "Weary. I had a treatment Friday. The first couple of days afterward are the hardest." She put several clams on her plate, opened one, and dunked it in her mug of broth.

"How long will you be staying in Maine, Simon?" asked Jed.

Simon had been talking with Patrick. He turned around. "All the papers are signed. I need to get back to Chicago. I'm planning to fly home Tuesday."

All the papers? What papers?

He looked around. "I've had a wonderful time with all of you, revisiting Maine. I loved this part of the coast when I was a boy, but I hadn't been back in years. Your hospitality has made my stay memorable."

"What about Jesse?" I blurted. "Are you arranging his funeral?"

Simon turned to me. "My cousin told me years ago, before he went in the army, that if he didn't make it back he wanted to be cremated and his ashes dumped in the ocean. He didn't want a service. I've left instructions here with the local police; they'll take care of it after his body is released. I see no reason to stay around for that."

"I'm sorry you didn't get to see him when you were here," I said. "He was a special person."

"I did see him," said Simon. "He was a pain in the . . . Anyway, I did see him. Not that it's any of your business. Who are you, anyway?"

"Simon, this is Angie Curtis. She's the head of a local needlepoint business. Jesse was a friend of hers," Patrick explained.

Simon looked at me again. "Sorry. I didn't know that. I've had a lot on my mind while I've been here."

"When did you see Jesse?" I asked. Everyone at the table was listening.

"Gerry took me out to King's Island Thursday afternoon, on his launch. Gerry wanted to see the interior of the island, and I wanted to see Jesse. He and I talked for about an hour. We did some reminiscing and talked about the future of our island. We didn't agree on what that would be, but we had a good talk."

The medical examiner had said Jesse died Thursday afternoon or early evening. "What time was that?"

"Early in the afternoon. *Before* he was murdered," Simon said. "In case your next question was whether I'd killed him." He looked around the table. "For the record, I did not kill my cousin. Jesse and I didn't agree on a lot of things, but he was family. He was alive when Gerry and I left King's Island."

"Why don't we have another round of champagne," said Gerry Bentley, breaking the silence. "Today we should be thinking about this beautiful state, and how lucky we are to be here. A toast to my wonderful wife," he said, raising his glass. "And to our daughter to come!"

I sipped my champagne and tried not to ask more questions. I certainly had a few.

A few minutes later Patrick put his hand on my arm. "Why don't we go and get the whoopie pies?" he asked, pulling me out of my seat.

I followed him, down the field. Not toward the dessert table. "What's happening?"

"Before you talked to Simon, he told me Jesse's new will is problematic. Jesse left his share of the island to Dave Percy, yes. But Uncle Gerry has lawyers questioning whether Jesse had the right to do that if he and Simon owned the island together. Because Jesse was insistent about making his will out quickly, his lawyer didn't check the deed to King's Island to see exactly how it was worded. Jesse might not have known he couldn't leave the property to Dave. It would automatically go to Simon."

I shook my head. "Too many details. I'm not a lawyer."

"Jesse and Simon inherited the island from their grandfather, whose will was made in Illinois. The lawyers need to go back and look at that will. Bottom line: I don't think anyone's going to be able to sell that property anytime soon."

"But what papers did Simon say he was signing?"

"In case this all gets settled and he's the full owner of King's Island, he's selling Uncle Gerry first refusal to purchase it. Since Maine doesn't permit distribution of property until six months after the owner's death, even if the island ends up as Simon's property, no one will be building on it until next spring, at the earliest."

"Which will give us time to campaign for the cormorants," I said.

"Yes," said Patrick. "If Jesse hadn't made out that new will it would be simple. Simon would automatically have inherited the property. But Uncle Gerry's lawyers are saying Dave could make a claim to Jesse's half of the island, since the ownership agreement isn't clear by Maine law."

I shook my head.

"If Jesse *could* leave his part of the island to Dave, Simon can't sell it. Bottom line, Angie: Dave's in the middle of a legal mess."

"What can we do? Dave didn't ask for any of this!"

"No. But he was Jesse's friend. And he wants to help those birds, right?"

"Right."

"The best we can do right now is to support Dave, and the cormorants. Save the Cormorants should continue. The worst that could happen would be King's Island would be sold, but other Maine birds would benefit from the publicity about the need for safe nesting areas for threatened and endangered seabirds, right?"

"I guess so." That wasn't what I wanted to tell Dave and the Mainely Needlepointers, who simply wanted to keep King's Island free of construction. "I can't believe Dave didn't tell me about Jesse's will."

"He never told you?"

I shook my head. "He didn't mention any of it to me. That's strange, since we've been talking about Jesse and the cormorants every day."

"I'm surprised, too."

I looked over the field at Haven Harbor. The sun was setting; the sky was streaked with orange and red and purple. "It's late. It's been a long day. I have a lot to think about. I'll go to see Dave first thing in the morning. He's hoping to be released from the hospital Tuesday."

"Would you like me to go with you?" Patrick asked.

I was tempted. "No. I think I have to do this myself. But I'd like you to meet Dave after he's settled at home. I think you'd like each other."

"Whatever you want done, Angie, you let me

know. I'm living here in Haven Harbor, too. I want to be a part of what's happening here."

"This legal mess isn't going to help Jed and Carole either, is it? That island won't be sold for months, at the earliest."

"It doesn't seem so," Patrick agreed. "But they must know that. Or at least Jed does. I don't know how much Carole is involved. With her illness, I don't think he's been telling her every detail."

Details she should know. She was already involved.

And she wasn't happy.

Chapter 43

"Remember time will shortly come
When we a strict account must give,
To God, the righteous Judge of all
How we upon this earth do live."

> —Sampler completed in 1824 by
> Mary Graves, age twenty-six, and
> Hannah Carpenter (perhaps her teacher)
> in Philadelphia. Their sampler is
> embroidered in silk on linen using cross,
> satin, and petit point stitches, and has
> a wide border of vines and flowers.

Bright sunshine woke me earlier than usual. Trixi was still sleeping as I slipped into the kitchen and brewed my morning coffee.

I had to see Dave. I wanted to confront him about Jesse's will. Why hadn't he told me he was Jesse's beneficiary?

On a more practical note, I also wanted to find out what groceries he'd like in his house when he got home tomorrow.

But before that I needed a break. I left my cell phone on the kitchen counter and headed to the harbor. Had it only been a week ago when I'd first seen The Solitary rowing into the harbor in the fog?

It seemed like a lifetime. Jesse's lifetime, for sure.

Today there was no fog. The tide was high, and the early sun, still glowing pink from the sunrise, was reflected in the water.

I waved at Arvin Fraser and Rob Trask, who'd been here last week. They were getting ready to go out and check their traps.

"Good morning!" I called to where Arvin's boat was moored.

"Morning, Angie!" Arvin called back.

"Heard you're working with my brother on another case," added Rob.

"Not exactly working together," I said, continuing down the ramp. Voices carried over water, and the world didn't need to know more than they did already. "But he did question me about Jesse Lockhart. Sad situation."

Rob nodded. "Mom and Dad kid him about it. They like seeing Emmie. But it's hard to know seeing their granddaughter means someone in town's been murdered. I didn't know Jesse. Recognized him, but that was about all. He didn't seem interested in getting to know other folks in town. But it's sad, all the same."

"Most folks hardly knew where King's Island was a week ago. Now everyone's talking about it, and about the cormorants. Some of us who lobster have even had people asking us to take 'em out to see the place." Arvin shook his head in amazement.

"But it's a murder scene!" I said.

"Folks are fascinated by the whole idea. A few tourists have asked for tours of where the guy's home was!"

"Some have asked to rent the boat for a couple of hours, so they could tour themselves around," Rob agreed.

"Curiosity seekers," said Arvin. "I ignore them. The *Little Lady*'s my living. I don't rent her out. I wouldn't even loan her to anyone I didn't know well."

"Has anyone asked to borrow her lately?" I asked.

"Jed Fitch. He and his son Linc borrowed it once or twice last week. Linc works for me once in a while. Knows what he's doing. I didn't see the harm."

My investigative antennas went up.

"When was that? That Jed borrowed the *Little Lady*?"

"When was that, Rob?" Arvin paused a moment. "Wait—I have it written in my log." He disappeared inside the open cabin briefly. "Here it is. Last Tuesday, and again Thursday. Both times in the afternoon." He looked at me. "You're curious because of Jesse Lockhart's death, right? But I don't think Jed and Linc borrowing the boat means anything. He does it pretty often. Takes

301

prospective buyers out to see properties from the water, or take pictures of waterfront houses and property. As long as he keeps my tank filled and doesn't want to use my *Lady* when I need to, it's no problem."

"Say—you guys know everything that happens here in the harbor. Any theories on what happened to Jesse?"

"Not one," said Arvin. "Honestly, no one paid him any mind until he shot Dave. Coming into the wharf with one of our teachers bleeding all over the boat from an arrow wound . . . that started people talking."

"I'll bet it did," I admitted. "I'm glad someone cleaned up the *Sweet Life*. I hated to leave it a mess, but I had to get Dave to the hospital."

"Those 'someones' would be us," Rob said, looking at Arvin. "We figured the guy who owns the *Sweet Life* wouldn't be happy about how it looked. I checked with my brother before we touched it. He took a look and said it would be okay to wash it down. So we did. Got tired of folks coming to the pier to look at it, or take pictures."

"Pictures?" I almost squeaked.

"Of the blood," said Arvin. "We've had more blood on board the *Little Lady* when we've been fishing and got dogfish instead of blues, but folks were fascinated by the *Sweet Life*."

"Thank you for cleaning it," I said.

"It wasn't just us," Rob added. "Linc helped, too. He was hanging around, and volunteered to help."

"Linc. That's Jed's son. The one you said worked with you."

"Right. He goes to college in Massachusetts. Hasn't been around much the past few years. Takes extra courses in the summer."

"He was in my high school class," said Arvin. "One of those kids who acted like he was better than the rest of us. Didn't want to work on the waterfront; wanted to get educated and make millions on Wall Street."

"But he's back this summer."

"His mom's sick. He's been working when someone needs an extra hand, and spending time with her."

"The Fitches only have a small sailboat," Rob added. "When his mom is well enough, Linc sometimes borrows someone else's boat after the day's work is done, and takes her out. He says she loves being out on the water."

"Yeah. He borrowed my boat once last week for that," said Arvin. "He may pretend to be high and mighty, but he knows how to handle the *Little Lady*. If my mom were sick like that, I'd want people to help out."

"Kind of you," I agreed.

"We have to get going," Arvin added. "Good day like this, we can pull almost all the traps.

Traps got to be pulled every couple of days, but with the market hot like it is most Augusts, the more bugs we bring in, the better."

"Understood. Don't want to delay you any longer. Have a good day!" I waved as they shoved off and headed toward the mouth of the harbor.

Jesse was gone, but work continued for those who pulled their living from the sea. Arvin and Rob, like many their ages, drank too much sometimes, but they were steady young men. Arvin had a wife and daughter, and Rob was engaged. As long as global warming didn't mess up Maine lobstering the way it had winter shrimping, they'd be permanent residents of Haven Harbor.

I finished my coffee and headed up the hill. The last time I'd been here this time of day I'd stopped at the patisserie and bought croissants for Dave's and my breakfasts.

Their pastries had to be a lot better than hospital food. I made a turn and bought two cinnamon rolls, still warm, with frosting seeping into their crevices.

Chapter 44

"Needlework as a national art is as dead as the proverbial door-nail; whether or not it ever regains its position as a craft is a matter of conjecture. Personally, I incline to the belief that it is absolutely extinct. The death-knell rang for all time when the sewing machine was invented."
—From *Chats on Old Lace and Needlework* by Emily Leigh Lowes, London, 1908.

Still in hospital? I texted Dave.

Breaking news! May be released this p.m., he answered.

C U soon, I replied. Trixi and I cuddled a bit, and I ate my cinnamon roll. She wanted to lick my fingers, but I beat her to it. Haven Harbor was lucky to have Henri and Nicole's real French patisserie. If I didn't curb my enthusiasm for their products I'd have to buy a new, wider wardrobe by the time leaves fell.

"Gram?" I said, remembering I hadn't called her last night. "Dave may be leaving the hospital today. I'm going shopping for him. Could you ask the Ladies' Guild to help out? It would be great if someone could deliver a meal to him every day for a week."

"Done," Gram agreed. "I'll make him something for tonight, and by tomorrow we'll have the wheels in motion. We do that for any parishioner right after they've left the hospital, especially if they've had a baby, or live alone, or have trouble getting around."

"Dave hasn't had a baby, for sure," I said, smiling at Gram's explanation of the Ladies' Guild. "But he'll have logistical challenges for a while. What about his kitten, do you think?"

"I'll talk to him about that this afternoon," she said. "I suspect he'd like to have Snowy back, but I want to make sure he can take care of a kitten. I can take the little guy over tomorrow if Dave wants him right away."

"Put me on the list to bring one dinner," I said. "I want to do my part." I hadn't a clue as to what I'd bring, but I'd find something.

I could hear the smile behind Gram's voice. "I'll let you know which day you're assigned, Angie. Thanks for volunteering. Wasn't Dave going to have a meeting with the group working on Save the Cormorants today or tomorrow?"

"I'm going over to see him. I'll find out what he wants to do."

I didn't mention the will to Gram. I wanted to talk to Dave first.

He was wearing one of the T-shirts Gram had brought for him, his legs covered with a blanket.

"Waiting for the doctor?" I asked as I walked in and handed him the patisserie bag.

"Yum," he said. "All I had for breakfast was orange juice and cold cereal." He tore off a piece of the cinnamon roll and popped it in his mouth.

"You have a lot of friends," I commented, pointing at the bulletin board across from his bed covered with "Get Well" cards.

"Students," he admitted. "Some names I didn't even recognize. Maybe this year's crop, hoping to get a head start on a good grade."

"So when can you get out of here?"

"Can't leave before I'm officially released. I've read both of those mysteries you bought me, and could recite the headlines of the news. I'm ready to get out. Word is, early this afternoon."

"Did you get your lesson plans done?"

"Enough. A lot of my notes are at home, in my study. I can finish at home. Still have ten days before school opens. How was your evening at Aurora? Did you meet Simon?"

"Yes." I had so many questions it was hard to know where to start. "He said there won't be a funeral for Jesse. That Jesse wanted to be cremated and his ashes put in the ocean."

Dave was silent. "I'm sorry. But that sounds like something Jesse would have said, although we never talked about it. I would have liked to have said good-bye."

I nodded.

"He was like my brother, Angie. We were very different people, but we'd shared some of the same experiences. Neither of us had family to go back to after we left the service, so we became each other's family."

"Dave, you suggested Jesse get a lawyer, right?"

"Aaron Irving. He went to Aaron's office that Wednesday morning after he'd spent the night at my place. If Jed was pushing the sale of the island Jesse should have had all the help he could."

"And he changed his will."

"I didn't tell him to do that. Aaron might have." Dave's shoulders dropped. "I hoped he'd change his will to take Simon out, and put the Audubon folks in. I figured it would show his intentions, if anyone questioned his ownership of the island. Or his competence." He waited a few seconds. "That competence thing had happened before, when he first got to the VA. He had brain injuries. He's been doing fine. But if someone wanted to make trouble for him, they might find those old records."

"Why didn't you tell me Jesse'd left his share of King's Island to you?" I blurted. "When I heard that last night I didn't know what to say. Here I was trying to find out what Simon was going to do, and I didn't even know what *you* were going to do! How could you put me in that position?

It was embarrassing not to know. I thought you were my friend!"

"I'm sorry, Angie. Really, I am. But I just found out yesterday. Jesse didn't tell me he'd done that. Ethan stopped in around lunchtime and dropped that bomb on me, along with another whole string of questions. Now I legally benefit from Jesse's death. Luckily for me, half the medical staff at Haven Harbor Hospital can testify I was unconscious and then in surgery during the period the medical examiner says Jesse was killed. Otherwise, I'd be the top suspect in his murder. I still don't know what the will is going to mean—what rights I have, and what rights Simon has. I tried to talk to Aaron yesterday, but he said he couldn't represent both Jesse and me. I have to find another lawyer as soon as I get home."

"You were the first one to say King's Island should be saved for the great cormorants."

"And that's what I believe. I haven't changed my mind, Angie. But I don't know what I can do, or when. There's that six-month rule in Maine; property can't be legally transferred until six months after someone dies. But Pete said Gerry Bentley and Simon were questioning the original deed to the island. The way it's written, neither Jesse nor Simon might legally be able to transfer ownership to someone other than each other. So I may not have any say in what happens to King's Island despite Jesse's revising his will."

"So—the Save the Cormorants group?"

"I've called everyone but you. We're meeting tomorrow morning at my house. I'm not calling off the campaign. I think we should continue the plan to let people know about Jesse's birds. He would have wanted that. I hope the island can be saved for them, but even if it can't, people will know more about the importance of the nesting grounds all along the coast of Maine. Not just for great cormorants. But for puffins and piping plovers and common eiders and great black-backed gulls . . ."

Dave was looking paler and more tired.

"You need to rest. We can't solve the problems of all endangered species in Maine this morning. Do you have someone to drive you home?"

"Reverend Tom volunteered for that duty. The doctor's going to call him when I'm officially free and released."

"Good. I'm going to go and get your groceries. Can you think of anything you'd especially like?"

"No Jell-O!" Dave said definitively. "Ice cream. Chocolate. I'm going to be taking pills for pain and have to keep something in my stomach, but I'm not hungry."

"You will be soon. What about yogurt?"

"That's healthy, right?" He didn't look enthused.

"Blueberry yogurt?"

"Better." He smiled. "I need the basics. Milk,

eggs, butter. I have oatmeal at home. And hamburger. That's easy to cook."

"Got it," I said, writing down what he'd asked for. "Plus ice cream, I promise. That should get you through a couple of days, until I make another grocery run." If he needed anything else after the Ladies' Guild filled his refrigerator.

"You're going to sleep on your couch downstairs?"

"That's the plan. I'm supposed to keep off steps for at least a week."

"Okay. I'll find clean sheets and get the couch set up for you. And I'll bring towels and toothpaste and stuff downstairs."

"I hate for you to do all that, Angie."

"I don't mind. And you can't do it, at least not right away." I pointed at the cards on the bulletin board. "Got to get you healed and ready to go back to school, right? And we needlepointers need to stick together."

"I wish we knew who killed Jesse," said Dave. "I keep thinking about it. Nothing makes sense. I'm hoping when I get home, and don't have to take all the pills they keep handing me here, the answer will come into focus."

"I hope so, too, Dave," I said. "But it's not simple. I'm not taking pain pills. And Jesse's death is still a mystery to me."

Chapter 45

"While on this glowing canvas stands
The labour of my youthful hands
It may remain when I am gone
For you my friends to look upon."
       —From sampler stitched in 1837 by Mary
       Caley in Chester County, Pennsylvania.
       Mary embroidered in silk and chenille on
       linen using cross, bullion knot, satin, and
       stem stitches. Her sampler lists her parents,
       brothers, and sisters, including her sister
       Ann, who had died, and whose name is
       embroidered on a black square. Mary also
       included a weeping willow tree, symbolic
       of death, in the landscape below her verse.

By the time Reverend Tom brought Dave home, at about two o'clock, I'd done all I could think of to make his house easy to live in while he was still in pain.

I had no doubt about the pain. His face showed it, as he walked in using crutches. The first thing he did was put a bottle of Vicodin on the side table next to the couch—now his bedside table.

"Thanks, Angie," he said, looking around.

"If you think of anything else I can help with, let me know."

Reverend Tom brought in the plant Dave had received in the hospital, and the flowers "Bette" had sent. My roses weren't fit for transport.

"Add them to the flowers on the mantel," said Dave. "Where I see there already are flowers."

"No one can have too many flowers," I said. "They're just from the floral department at the grocery, but they brighten up the place."

"They do. And you got food, too?"

"Ice cream, no Jell-O, and an assortment of other easy-to-prepare sandwich and breakfast foods," I said.

He'd sunk down on the bed.

"Don't worry about looking until you want something. I put the food I bought in the refrigerator or on your counter so you could find it easily." Dave was meticulous about keeping his home neat. He'd want to arrange everything his own way. "And Gram will be by in a couple of hours to bring you dinner. The Ladies' Guild at the church is supplying your dinners for at least the next week. Longer, if you need them. Gram'll talk to you about that. If there's something you can't eat, or don't like, tell her, and she'll pass the word along."

"That's not all necessary," said Dave. He winced in pain. "But I'll admit it's appreciated. I guess I'll have to attend church more often once I get myself more together. You and Charlotte are miracle workers." He stretched his leg out on the bed. "The doctor says I'll be able to drive after I'm off the pills, but that will be a few days. Up to a week, he said. I'm taking fewer now, but especially when I'm moving around, my leg really hurts. I have to admit: Jesse got me good."

"I'm going to let you rest," I said. "But call me if you need anything. Anything at all. I'm only a couple of blocks away. I put clean clothes on the dining-room table—but if I've forgotten something, let me know."

"I'm fine," he said. "Just relieved to be out of that hospital. I suspect I'm going to sleep a lot in the next few days. With all the bustling about, hospitals aren't the best place to rest. I'm exhausted."

"I'm leaving right now," I said. "Gram should be here about five o'clock with your dinner. And I think she's going to ask you whether you're ready for feline company."

"Kittens? I thought you'd already solved that problem."

"Kitten. Singular. Trixi and Bette have found homes," I assured him. "But the white kitten has been with Gram, and Juno, her older cat, isn't happy about that. So—you can decide. And you could say you'd like the kitten, but not for a few days."

"I really appreciate all of this."

"Remember to call if you need anything. I don't want to call and wake you when you're trying to rest," I said. "And for now, is it okay if I leave your front door closed but not locked? That way you won't have to get out of bed when Gram gets here."

"That's fine," Dave said, his voice a little lower. "I think I will take a nap now."

I headed home to check on Trixi. I hadn't been there to play with her for hours. Was I a bad cat parent? Probably. But she wasn't a perfect cat, I reminded myself, picking up pieces of tissue I found all over the living-room floor. We'd have to cope with each other.

After cleaning the mess, I called Gram.

"Gram? Dave's at home. I told him you'd be coming over tonight with his dinner. I left his front door unlocked."

"Thank you, dear. I'm going to take him my chicken noodle soup tonight, and I'll heat some French bread when I'm there."

"That sounds fine. He says he's tired. How's it going with finding people to bring him food for the next week?"

"Not a problem. In fact, I was surprised—I called Carole Fitch to see how she was, and she volunteered to take him a meal tomorrow."

"She's feeling better, then? I saw her over at the Wests' yesterday and she seemed a little weak."

"But she was out of her house. Good for her. She must be feeling better. I was wondering when we should put her family on the dinner list."

"Which day am I assigned?"

"I'm taking tonight, and Carole has tomorrow, so if it's okay, you can do the day after."

"No problem. If you think of anything else I can do for Dave after you see him later today, let me know, all right?"

"I will."

A busy day. But Dave was home, his dinners were (thanks to Gram) arranged. And I had a few hours off. What would I take on my night to bring food? Fried haddock, I decided. I'd finally mastered the art of panfrying using panko instead of cracker crumbs. And peas and potato salad. Easy.

I rolled an empty spool toward Trixi. She jumped on it and somersaulted over. I laughed at her, to her embarrassment. I hadn't laughed a lot recently.

I rolled the spool again, this time more gently.

Then my phone rang.

"Angie? Patrick. Thought you'd want to know. Simon's staying in Haven Harbor a few more days."

"I'd thought he went back to Chicago yesterday."

"He was planning to. But his lawyer looked over Jesse's will and the deed to the island. Their grandfather left it to them with the right of survivorship. That means they owned the island together, as they both said. But if one died, the island had to revert to the other party. It doesn't even have to go to probate. In other words . . ."

"In other words, Jesse couldn't leave his half of the island to Dave."

"That's what the lawyer said."

"That means—no safe nesting site for the cormorants."

"Unless someone tests the deed."

"What?"

"When I was at Mom's house this morning I overheard Jed and Uncle Gerry and Simon and this lawyer arguing. Jed Fitch said Simon had the right to sell the island, so he and Uncle Gerry should sign the contract he'd drawn up. At first Uncle Gerry and Simon seemed pleased. But this other guy—this lawyer—said not to get too excited. That Dave had the right to contest Jesse's will. That might not change the outcome, but it would delay any sale. Possibly for years."

"So—we need to tell Dave. He needs to get to his lawyer about that, fast, right?"

"That's the idea. Because Uncle Gerry is already hesitating about this whole deal. His wife is pushing him to fly back to California before the baby is born, and I heard him say he loves the island, but he doesn't want to be held up in court for years. He'll look for somewhere else to buy—maybe in Oregon. Mom said he was always welcome to stay at Aurora if he wanted to visit Maine."

"Wow. Great. Do they know you're calling me?"

"No way. They only know I was concerned about the birds. I wanted you to know as quickly as possible. I don't know your friend Dave. I didn't want to call him out of the blue."

"Of course," I agreed. "He's at home resting. But I'll let him know."

"Between you and me, I think if he even threatens to contest the will, Uncle Gerry will back off."

"Simon must be frustrated," I said.

"And you should have seen Jed Fitch! He kept saying something would work out, or he could find Uncle Gerry another island. A better island. That's when Uncle Gerry said he'd had it with islands. It had been fun to think about living out there, but he didn't think it would work."

"What a relief!"

"Don't call off the Save the Cormorants campaign, though. Not yet. Simon hadn't thought about that island in years, and now he thinks it's worth a lot of money. Jed was telling him they might find another buyer."

"I doubt it. Unless a conservation organization—the Island Institute, or the Audubon Society or the Nature Conservancy—could get someone to donate enough money to keep it open for the birds," I said. "Not many people are like your uncle Gerry and have the money to consider putting a home out there. You never saw where Jesse lived. It wasn't a place most people would find habitable."

"I hope I'm right," said Patrick.

"I do, too. And I'll let Dave know. I don't see any reason why he wouldn't contest the will. He wanted the island to be left the way Jesse wanted it."

I started to call Dave and then decided I'd wait until morning. He was exhausted. He needed to rest. And it was already the middle of the afternoon. He could call his lawyer in the morning. A few hours wouldn't make a difference.

At least, I hoped it wouldn't.

Chapter 46

"Where shall the child of sorrow find a place
  for calm repose?
Thou Father of the Fatherless, pity the
  orphan's woes.
What friend have I in heaven or earth, What
  friend to trust but thee.
My father's dead, My mother's dead, My
  God, remember me.
Thy gracious promise now fulfilled and bid
  my troubles cease
In thee the fatherless shall find both mercy
  grace and peace."
—Narcissa Lyman, born in 1813, stitched
this sampler on linsey-woolsey in 1827. The
poem had been published in 1826. Narcissa
and her brother, William, were orphaned
by the deaths of her parents in 1821 and
1822, and William died a few weeks after
she completed this sampler. She added his
name and date of death. Narcissa attended
school in Portland, Maine, and married a
Congregational minister in York in 1832.

Monday night I tried to read a book on the
history of needlepoint (Betty Ring's *Girlhood
Embroidery*) but I couldn't concentrate. I

kept thinking about Jesse. The legal issues surrounding King's Island might be complicated, but for the first time I felt as though there might be hope we could at least delay the sale of the island. By buying time, we'd also increase the possibility that one of the conservation groups—Audubon or another—would be able to raise enough money to buy the island and support it.

Not easy, but possible.

But who'd killed Jesse?

A few days before I'd made a mental list. Tonight I got out pad and pencil. I knew more than I had earlier. But did I know enough?

The key must be something that happened last Thursday afternoon.

Thursday morning Jesse had been nervous and worried. He'd mistakenly shot Dave. But he hadn't seemed incompetent—I hated that word—and he hadn't seemed crazy. Stubborn, yes. And concerned that he'd shot Dave. In fact, he was angrier when we left King's Island than he'd been before we'd gotten there. Angry at himself. He hadn't meant to shoot Dave.

Would he have tried to shoot someone else?

But when Joe and Pete and I found his body the next morning his bow and arrows weren't with him; they were safely stowed in his shelter.

Okay. Whoever killed him had been on King's Island between three and nine p.m. that Thursday.

Who'd been there? Why? Who'd had a motive to kill Jesse?

Simon Lockhart. He wanted to sell the island. He'd been out on King's Island Thursday afternoon, and he'd said he'd argued with Jesse. They didn't agree on selling the island. Simon had said Jesse was alive when he left the island. Had he lied? Possibly.

At the same time, Gerry Bentley was on the island. He'd given Simon a ride, and he'd been walking around by himself (Simon hadn't said anyone else had gone out with them) while Simon talked with Jesse.

Had he talked with Jesse alone? Not likely, since Simon was there and Simon had a connection with Jesse. Gerry and Simon both wanted the same thing: Jesse to agree to sell King's Island.

When Dave had been shot, I'd ended up covered with his blood. Jesse'd been killed by several sharp blows to his head. His murderer would have to have been close to him. Had Jesse fought back? I didn't remember seeing any defensive wounds on his hands, and Pete hadn't mentioned them. Wouldn't he have fought back? He was a strong man. And head wounds bled a lot. Anyone who'd killed Jesse by bashing in his head had to have blood on his hands, or face, and certainly on his clothing.

If Simon had been covered with blood when he

walked out of the woods to meet Gerry Bentley for their trip back to Haven Harbor, Bentley would have noticed.

So—who else would have been on that island?

Arvin and Rob said Jed Fitch borrowed the *Little Lady* Thursday afternoon, probably to take pictures for his real estate business. But was that what he'd done? His son Linc was with him. Maybe I should talk to Linc. Or ask Jed straight out whether he'd gone back to King's Island to try to convince Jesse to sell.

That made sense. Jed's wife was ill and his sons needed tuition money. He'd made it clear he'd really wanted that commission.

If he'd been covered with blood, would his son have kept quiet?

I didn't know Linc, but that seemed possible.

It all made sense. Jed was the killer.

Except . . . Jesse knew who Jed was. He'd told him not to come back to the island. Would he have welcomed him without a weapon a few days later?

Or had Jesse been so upset about shooting Dave he didn't trust himself not to hurt anyone else? Dave kept saying Jesse'd wanted peace, for himself and for his birds.

Ultimately, last Thursday afternoon he'd found peace. But not the kind he'd wanted.

Chapter 47

"And must this body die
This mortal frame decay
And must these active limbs of mine
Lie mouldering in the clay."
—Stitched by Elizabeth Cooke Crittenton,
age twelve, in 1818, in Wethersfield,
Connecticut. Elizabeth's sampler included
a garland border on the top, two houses
shaded by trees on a riverside, boats on the
river, and a hill on the far side of the river.

"I slept better last night, but my leg still throbs."

Dave's voice was in my "missed messages" Tuesday morning. He'd called a little after four in the morning.

"Thanks again for all the food in the kitchen. I just cooked a batch of ham and eggs. Best thing I'd had to eat in days, except for your grandmother's chicken soup last night. I'm going to take an extra Vicodin now, so I'll sleep in a little. Would you let the others—Anna, Charlotte, Ruth, and Sarah—know the Save the Cormorants meeting will be today at two? I could text everyone, but I need to sleep."

I could do that. I'd hoped Dave would be feeling better once he was home, but being by himself in that house wasn't a good idea. He was on Vicodin and cooking in the middle of the night?

It was eight fifteen. I'd call the cormorant team and then check with Dave to make sure he was all right this morning.

"I'm glad Dave is out of the hospital, but I can't get to a two o'clock meeting," said Sarah. "I want to share Ted Lawrence's cormorant designs with everyone, though. Could I drop them off with Dave before my shop opens this morning? I was about to go out for a walk anyway. Once in a while I like to get out into the world. Sitting inside all summer isn't my favorite part of having a shop."

"He wanted to sleep in this morning. Why don't you leave the sketches in his mailbox? I'm going over to see him later this morning and I'll check the mailbox before his regular mail is delivered."

"Thanks. Be sure to tell Dave I'm thinking about him, but I'm tied to my store this time of year."

"I'll tell him. But I'm sure he understands," I assured her.

Anna and Ruth agreed to be at the meeting.

So did Gram. "How was he last night when you took him dinner?" I asked Gram.

"Hungry," she answered. "He ate two bowls of chicken noodle soup and half a loaf of French bread. They must have starved him in the hospital."

"He doesn't like Jell-O."

"That explains why he was hungry." I could hear the smile in Gram's voice. "I'll see you at two o'clock. Dave's going to be tired for a while. We should keep the meeting short. Carole's going to bring him dinner tonight. Our meeting should be over before then."

"Agreed. I got a message from him this morning. He was cooking ham and eggs at four this morning."

"Still hungry?" Gram asked. "Or bored. Or both."

"He said he couldn't sleep because of the pain."

"Let's hope he's feeling better today."

"Are you going to bring Snowy this afternoon?"

"No. We decided to wait until Dave's a little more mobile. He's having difficulty getting around on those crutches, and he's afraid the kitten will get in trouble and he won't be able to rescue him."

"You don't mind keeping Snowy a few more days?"

"Not at all. I'll see you at two."

I took care of Trixi and scrambled an egg for my own breakfast.

I hadn't had any late-night inspirations about who might be Jesse's killer, although I wished I could talk with Jed's son Linc. He'd know whether or not his father had been on King's Island last Thursday.

But Linc was probably out working on one of the lobster boats now.

Had anyone questioned him?

I decided to ask Pete.

"Morning, Angie," he answered. "Heard Dave was out of the hospital."

"He is," I said. "I'm going to see him later this morning. I know you can't say a lot, but are you and Ethan any closer to figuring out who killed Jesse? Not knowing is driving me crazy—and it's not easy for Dave, either."

"We're still working on it," said Pete. "Not a lot of information. The crime scene didn't help at all because of the heavy rains last Friday."

"Have you or Ethan spoken with Linc Fitch?"

"Linc? No. Should we have?"

"Yesterday Arvin Fraser told me Jed and Linc borrowed the *Little Lady* Thursday afternoon. He assumed they did that to take pictures of real estate from the water. But Jed had already been to King's Island once last week. I wondered if he'd made another stop."

"Good point."

"Simon Lockhart told me he'd talked with Jesse Thursday afternoon. Gerry Bentley took him out to the island. But Simon insists Jesse was alive when they left."

"We questioned both Simon and Bentley, and

the crew of Bentley's yacht. Their story seems to fit when the crew saw them leave and return."

If either of them had been bloodstained, someone might have mentioned that to the police. I hoped.

"Jesse's will seems to be a problem," I added.

"A problem for Simon Lockhart, anyway," Pete agreed. "The lawyers will have to fight that one out. But Simon's leaving today, so I think the sale of the island is off the table for a while."

"Last night Patrick West told me Simon had changed his mind. He's going to stay in Maine a few more days."

"Maybe he wants to extend his vacation. There's nothing we're looking at him for."

"Dead end?"

"For now, that's the way it looks," said Pete. "Although I'll try to talk with Linc Fitch later today, on the chance he knows something. Thanks for the tip."

"Let me know?"

"If I can, Angie. But don't worry. We're doing what we can."

But were they doing enough?

Not as long as Jesse's killer was still free.

Chapter 48

"O may my Genius upwards rise,
Search Wisdoms, found where Knowledge
lies.
On wings sublime trace Heaven's abode,
And learn my Duty to my God."
—Elaborate sampler stitched in 1808
by Nancy Sibley, age ten, in Barrington,
Massachusetts. Nancy used silk on linen
with silk, chenille, and paint on appliqued
cotton for her three alphabets, numbers,
and an elaborate scene of a shepherdess
with her flock under trees by a riverside.
The wide appliqued black silk border was
done in metallic threads and painted paper.

"Dave? Good morning!"

"Angie." Dave's voice was slurred.

"Did I wake you?"

"I've been drowsy. I fell asleep." Dave's voice was beginning to sound more normal.

"I contacted all the people involved in the Save the Cormorants group," I continued. "Everyone but Sarah's set for this afternoon at two at your house. Sarah can't come because of the store, but she's going to drop Ted Lawrence's logo ideas at your house, in your mailbox, in the next hour."

"Good," said Dave. "Sorry I asked you to do that. I had an awful night. Sleeping on this old couch isn't comfortable, and my leg hurt, and I kept having nightmares about how Jesse died."

"I've had those dreams, too," I said. Dave had known Jesse much better than I had. But I'd seen Jesse's body. I was glad Dave hadn't been with us when we found it. "I talked with Pete this morning. They're still working the case."

"I wish they'd find whoever did it," said Dave. "I can't think about much else right now."

"I have to talk with you about Jesse's will before the meeting," I said. "Mind if I come over early? Say, one o'clock?"

"Why don't you come for lunch?" he asked. "Yesterday you brought a ton of food here, and Charlotte brought more than dinner last night. Plus, I'd like the company. I'll unlock the front door now. You and Charlotte were right. That's easier for me than getting up."

"I'll be there at one o'clock," I promised. "In the meantime, make sure you rest. Your afternoon's going to be busy."

"I'm looking forward to it. The meds make it hard to follow the story line in a book, and even though I'm drowsy I can't seem to sleep. I'm looking forward to having company and focusing on something positive. Maybe it'll take my mind off my leg."

"Anything I can bring?"

"I'm fine for now, Angie. Thanks for asking."

I spent the rest of the morning playing with Trixi and straightening out my living room. It had been the office of Mainely Needlepoint for months, but in the past week it had also become my bedroom and Trixi's playroom, bathroom, and kitchen. Kitty litter was in strange corners, books and papers had mysteriously fallen from my desk onto the floor, and the wastebasket had been overturned, its contents scattered over the floor.

I didn't remember Juno causing messes like that. But Juno was an adult cat. Trixi was exploring her world, which also happened to be mine.

About twelve thirty I'd done enough straightening and cleaning for the day. I headed for Dave's house.

Sarah had slipped a large envelope into his mailbox. I looked forward to seeing what Ted Lawrence had designed for a cormorant logo.

Dave's door was unlocked, as he'd promised.

"Dave?" I said as I went inside. "It's Angie."

Dave was sitting on his leather recliner, his injured leg propped on the footrest. He clicked his television set off. "Glad you're here. After we talked I napped for a while and since then I've been watching talk shows. I'm now up-to-date on weight-loss drugs, gluten intolerance, and the pros and cons of artificial eyelashes."

"Sounds fascinating. If I want to learn about any of those topics, I'll know who to check with. How's your leg?"

"Not great. But no worse. I took a pain pill about fifteen minutes ago. I'm hoping it'll kick in so I'll be okay for our lunch, and for the meeting."

I held up the large envelope I'd taken out of his mailbox. "These must be Ted Lawrence's sketches. I'm dying to see them. Do we have to wait for the meeting?"

"Open the envelope," he said, smiling. "Bring them over here so I can see them, too."

I'd never seen any of Ted's work, but his sketches were great. One was a great cormorant standing on its nest, a young bird's head visible below him. Another showed a cormorant in flight. "This one I love," I said, looking at the third. It was the simplest of the drawings, showing a great cormorant with his wings outstretched.

"Me too," Dave agreed. "And it would look great on a poster or T-shirt."

"And be easy to needlepoint," I added. "That's important. I think we have our design. Ted Lawrence gets the first cormorant pillow. He did a great job. Exactly what we need."

"Right now I could use a little lunch," Dave said. "Something light."

"I'll fix something for us."

He hesitated. "Thank you. I don't want to

use all my energy before anyone else gets here. And while we eat you can tell me what the will situation is."

"Anything special you want?" I asked, heading for his kitchen. "So far you've had noodle soup and ham and eggs and bread since you've been home."

"And an apple and banana earlier this morning," he added. "I don't want a lot. Tuna salad?"

"No problem. With onions? Olives? Pickles?"

"All three would be great."

It didn't take long to find a can opener and two plates in Dave's organized kitchen. The cans of tuna I'd brought yesterday were still sitting on the counter. "Lemonade?" I called to him, as I mixed the salad.

"Great," he answered.

"There's a lone brownie on a plate on the kitchen table," I added. "Want that, too?"

"I guess," he answered. "I don't remember seeing that this morning."

He hadn't been looking. Maybe Gram had brought it last night. She always added something sweet for dinners.

A few minutes later we were sitting in the living room, salads on our laps.

"Now. What did you want to tell me about Jesse's will? I haven't found a lawyer to talk to about it yet. I haven't felt up to it. I told you—I didn't know Jesse had put me in his will until

Ethan Trask told me on Sunday. And he said there were questions about it. Frankly, that will hasn't been my top priority."

"I think it needs to be," I said. "I talked with Patrick last night. Simon's been staying at Aurora, so Patrick's heard a lot about the will. The question seems to be whether Jesse could legally leave his share of the island to someone he chose—you—or whether the island would automatically revert to Simon."

Dave nodded. "I understand."

"Simon's already sold rights of first refusal to Bentley, in case the island is his." I hesitated. "Although Patrick thought all these complications were discouraging Gerry Bentley from wanting King's Island."

"I think that's good news," said Dave, hesitantly.

"Patrick suggested that if it looks as though the ruling on Jesse's will is going toward Simon, that you contest it. Quickly. Before anything else happens. That should delay everything. During that time the Save the Cormorants campaign can raise money toward setting up a trust fund to maintain the island. If it turns out you do own part of the island, you can donate your share to the Audubon people. If the campaign is successful enough, it could raise enough money to buy Simon's part of the island, too."

"That's what Jesse would have wanted," Dave

said slowly. He took a bite of his brownie. "Although I'm sure he didn't dream it would be this complicated. And there's no guarantee I'll end up with any part of the island, much less the whole thing."

"True. And it would be a hassle. But I think Jesse would have wanted you to do it."

"King's Island could be the Jesse Lockhart Sanctuary," said Dave. "I'd like that. I guess the first step is finding another lawyer."

"I don't have one to recommend," I said. "Maybe Ruth or Anna does."

"Good idea," said Dave. He leaned back in his chair. "I want all this to be over. It's horrible enough that Jesse's dead. But to lose King's Island for the cormorants, too? It's a nightmare."

Dave looked ashen. He needed to rest. "I'll wash up our dirty dishes. No one else will be here for ten or fifteen minutes. You rest."

"All right," he said, his voice fading. "Right now I don't feel too good."

"You relax until Ruth and Anna and Gram get here."

I'd almost finished the dish washing when I heard Dave choking.

Chapter 49

"May spotless innocence and truth
My every action guide
And guard my unexperienced [sic] youth
From arrogance and pride."
—Sampler stitched by Mary Greenman in
Providence, Rhode Island, in 1796. Mary's
words, and a man and woman, two trees, and
three dogs, in front of a house, are arranged
inside two columns, and the whole sampler
is surrounded by a border of flowers.

"Dave!"

He'd collapsed over the side of his chair and was vomiting violently. His skin was pale. And he looked scared.

I ran to the kitchen for a bowl, and to the bathroom for a damp cloth and towels. I did my best, but he was still throwing up when Gram walked in the front door.

"How long has he been vomiting?" she asked, immediately taking the bowl he'd been using and bringing back a clean one.

Dave tried to answer her, but couldn't talk.

"Six or seven minutes," I said.

"Call nine-one-one," Gram instructed calmly. "He may be having an allergic reaction to one of the drugs he's on. He needs to get back to the hospital."

Dave tried to say, "No." Then his head fell to the side.

He'd passed out.

Ruth and Anna arrived as I was talking to the dispatcher and Gram was trying to clear Dave's airways so he could breathe and wouldn't choke on his vomit.

"What can I do?" Anna asked after she'd helped Ruth to a chair.

"More clean towels," Gram said.

I raced upstairs to Dave's linen cabinet. I'd only brought two towels down the day before. Anna found rolls of paper towels in the kitchen and brought a bowl of clean, warm water.

Dave didn't know what was happening, but between all of us we got him (and his carpet) a little cleaned up by the time the emergency squad arrived.

"We're taking him to the hospital," said the young man I remembered from last week. "Mr. Percy needs to be seen by a doctor immediately. Do you have a sample of what he vomited?"

Luckily, I hadn't emptied the bowls. I handed one to him and the others on the squad put Dave on a stretcher and carried him to the ambulance.

"What happened?" asked Anna.

No one had a chance to answer before Pete Lambert and Ethan Trask burst into the room.

Chapter 50

"Tho' age must show life's best pursuits are
vain,
And few the pleasures to be here enjoyed,
Yet may this work a pleasing proof remain,
Of youth's gay period usefully employ'd."
—Stitched by Martha Newbold in
1818 in black silk on linen at the
Wilmington Boarding School in
Delaware. Young women in Maryland
and Delaware were not as likely to make
samplers as girls from the New England
states, and therefore samplers from those
areas are prized by collectors today.

"Where's Dave Percy?" Ethan asked, looking
around as though we'd hidden him under the
opened couch. "Is he all right?"

"The ambulance squad just took him to Haven
Harbor Hospital," I said. "He was vomiting and
then passed out."

Ethan looked at Pete. "Call the emergency
room and tell them."

Pete stepped outside and began talking on his
phone.

"What's happening?" I said.

"Dave's been poisoned," said Ethan.

Ruth gasped, and I took a step backward. "Why? How?"

"Will he be all right?" asked Gram.

"Did Dave eat any brownies in the past hour?" Ethan asked.

Anna and Ruth looked at each other in confusion.

"Yes," I said. "He and I had lunch together. He ate a brownie."

"Did you eat any of it?" asked Pete.

"No. There was only one," I said.

"Where did it come from?" asked Ethan.

"It was on a paper plate on Dave's kitchen table. I thought Gram had brought it with his dinner last night. I found it when I was making our lunch."

"I didn't bring any brownies last night," Gram said with assurance. "And I didn't see any brownies in the house when I was here."

Ethan turned to Pete. "She must have brought it over this morning."

"Who brought it over?" I asked. "What's happened?"

The men ignored me. "But then Dave would have known who'd given it to him. He wouldn't have thought Charlotte brought it."

"Dave slept most of the morning," I said. "He left the door unlocked. Anyone could have come and gone without his knowing it. But what happened?"

Finally Ethan turned to me. "We won't know for sure until we hear from the hospital. But this is the second poisoning today."

"Who else?" asked Gram.

"Carole Fitch," said Ethan. "She made the brownies, and added a lot of her pain and cancer meds. She was trying to kill Dave, and herself."

"She left a note," added Pete. "That's how we know."

Carole Fitch?

"How is Carole?" asked Gram.

"She's alive. Having her stomach pumped out at the hospital. She'll be all right. Luckily, Ethan and I got there in time. Angie'd suggested we talk to Linc, the Fitch's oldest boy. We found him at the boatyard. He seemed almost relieved to have someone ask him questions. Seems he took his mother out to King's Island last Thursday afternoon so she could try to convince Jesse Lockhart to sell the island. He said she was desperate. She knew she was dying, and she didn't want to leave her family with medical bills and college tuition unpaid. When Jesse refused to sell the island and told her he'd changed his will, she became furious."

"Carole Fitch killed Jesse?" asked Ruth. "Carole?"

"Her son Linc told us. He didn't see her do it,

but he saw the blood on her clothes, and the next day he heard Jesse was dead."

"After we talked to Linc we went to the Fitches' house, to confront Carole. We found her unconscious on the kitchen floor."

"She'd left a confession in what she planned to be a suicide note," said Ethan. "She wrote that without her medical bills there'd be money for her sons' tuition. She was taking Dave Percy with her, because now he owned part of the island. She wanted Simon to sell that island so her husband would make enough money to pay their bills. She wrote over and over that their financial situation was her fault. That if she hadn't been sick, they wouldn't have had any problems."

The room was silent.

"That's horrible," said Gram. "She felt guilty about having cancer?"

"She told me that when I saw her Sunday," I said. "But I never dreamed she'd kill anyone. Or herself."

"I can't imagine. She must have been crazy," said Anna. "She wasn't thinking straight. Maybe the meds she was on messed up her mind."

"I don't know about that," said Ethan. "But cancer or no cancer, if she survives she'll be arrested."

"And Dave?"

"I told the emergency room he'd eaten whatever Carole had," said Pete. "Plus whatever medications he was on for his injury. He's going to be feeling pretty awful for a day or two, but they said he should be all right."

Chapter 51

"When wealth to virtuous hands is given
It blefses like the dews of heavn
Like heaven it hears the orphan's cries
And wipes the tears from widows' eyes."
—Sampler worked by Sarah Kurtz, age nine,
        Georgetown, Washington, DC, in 1804.

Wednesday afternoon the hospital finally let me visit Dave.

I brought flowers and a tiny version of the Save the Cormorants logo that Sarah had stitched for him.

"I love it," he said. His voice was hoarse from tubes and medication, but his color was good. And, best of all, he was alive.

"I still can't believe it was Carole Fitch," I said. "She's in intensive care, but they say she'll survive."

"Unlike Jesse," Dave said. "No wonder he didn't have defensive wounds. He wouldn't have hit a woman. He might not even have defended himself from one."

"I have good news," I said. "Patrick West and Simon Lockhart came to my house last night. Neither of them had met you, but they knew we were friends, and I was involved with the Save the Cormorants campaign. Seems Simon was shaken when he heard what Carole had done to Jesse, to you, and to herself. He's decided he doesn't want anything more to do with King's Island. Once you're out of the hospital he'll even pay for a lawyer to do the paperwork, but he wants to make the island a bird sanctuary, in Jesse's memory."

Dave's eyes filled. "That's what we wanted, wasn't it?"

"Exactly. And Anna and Gram and Ruth and I talked to the Audubon people. We've decided— assuming you agree—to continue our plans for the Save the Cormorants campaign. All the money made will go toward maintaining King's Island, or other safe seabird nesting areas in Maine. Sarah's already working on the first pillows, and the Audubon people said they'd contact a local company about printing the logo on T-shirts, sweatshirts, tote bags, and hats. Ted Lawrence's cormorant is going to be all over Maine within six months."

"And Jesse won't be forgotten," said Dave softly. "His death will help ensure the future of the birds he loved. He would love that."

"So do I," I agreed, putting my hand on Dave's shoulder. "So do I."

Gram's Maple Raisin Oatmeal Cookies

1 stick + 6 tablespoons softened butter
¾ cup brown sugar
½ cup white sugar
2 eggs
1½ teaspoons vanilla
¼ cup pure maple syrup
1½ cups flour
1 teaspoon baking soda
1¼ teaspoons cinnamon
½ teaspoon salt
3 cups uncooked oatmeal
1½ cups raisins

Heat oven to 350 degrees.

Beat butter and sugars in electric mixer until creamy. Add eggs and vanilla and maple syrup and beat well. Combine flour, baking soda, cinnamon, and salt; add to creamed mixture and mix. Stir in oats and raisins.

Drop dough onto ungreased cookie sheets and bake until light brown (about 10 minutes, depending on your oven). Cool on cookie sheets for two to three minutes, then put on wire racks to cool. Store tightly covered.

Note: Cookies are soft and slightly sticky; best

to separate layers in cookie tin with waxed paper so cookies don't stick to each other.

Recipe makes about four dozen cookies and doubles well.

Acknowledgments

With thanks to . . .

My wonderful agent, John Talbot, and editor, John Scognamiglio, who made the Mainely Needlepoint series possible.

To my wonderful copyeditor, Gary Sunshine, who found my foolish errors and corrected them.

My husband, Bob Thomas, whose love and faith in me makes all things possible. And who cooks while I write!

My sister Nancy Cantwell, who this time around was my first reader under extraordinary circumstances.

The real Sarah Byrne, of Australia, who won a "character naming" at a Bouchercon auction, and Pax and Beatrix Henry, whose grandmother won "naming rights" at a benefit for the Wiscasset Library.

To Janet Buck, who generously shared her great-great-grandmother's sampler with me. I cited it at the beginning of chapter twenty-nine.

My fellow Maine Crime Writers (www.maine crimewriters.com), with whom I share a blog, a state, a profession, and, most of all, a friendship.

Henry Lyons, who keeps my Web site (www .leawait.com) up-to-date.

All my Facebook and Goodreads friends, who

read my books, write reviews, tell their friends, and whose enthusiasm keeps me writing, even on dark days. I invite all my readers to check my Web site (www.leawait.com) for questions for reading groups and links to free prequels for some of my books. And please, friend me on Facebook and Goodreads to keep up-to-date on my writing—and reading.

Books are produced in the United States using U.S.-based materials

Books are printed using a revolutionary new process called THINKtech™ that lowers energy usage by 70% and increases overall quality

Books are durable and flexible because of smythe-sewing

Paper is sourced using environmentally responsible foresting methods and the paper is acid-free

Center Point Large Print
600 Brooks Road / PO Box 1
Thorndike, ME 04986-0001 USA

(207) 568-3717

US & Canada:
1 800 929-9108
www.centerpointlargeprint.com